OUT FOR BLOOD

"There's one of them now!" a woman's harsh voice screamed.

"Huh?" Shadow looked around quickly, then froze as two things became clear: first, that a large crowd of angry-looking humans was rapidly approaching; and second, that they meant *her*.

Large hands gripped at her tunic.

"Kill her!" several voices roared.

"No, bleed her!" others argued.

"Whoa, wait a bit!" Shadow shouted. "At least take the time to rob me first." Wriggling one hand free, she ripped loose her belt pouch and flung it as hard as she could. The broken ties opened, spilling coins and gems across the ground.

Some of the shouts changed tone and a few of the hands released her; the others loosened in surprise.

Shadow pulled out two daggers and used them, slashing desperately at feet, shins, calves and thighs indiscriminately. A boot caught her squarely in the side of her head while another slammed into her belly.

But what frightened her more was the knife that came flashing down, missing her face by only a fingerbreadth . . .

PRAISE FOR *SHADOW:*

"A ROLLICKING GOOD ADVENTURE!"

—*Science Fiction Review*

Ace Books by Anne Logston

SHADOW
SHADOW HUNT
SHADOW DANCE

SHADOW DANCE

• DANCE •

Anne Logston

ACE BOOKS, NEW YORK

This book is an Ace original edition,
and has never been previously published.

SHADOW DANCE

An Ace Book / published by arrangement with
the author

PRINTING HISTORY
Ace edition / November 1992

ISBN: 0-441-75990-4

Ace Books are published by The Berkley Publishing Group,
200 Madison Avenue, New York, New York 10016.
The name "ACE" and the "A" logo
are trademarks belonging to Charter Communications, Inc.

PRINTED IN THE UNITED STATES OF AMERICA

10 9 8 7 6 5 4 3 2 1

For Paul,
whether he knows it
or not

ONE

The guards eyed Shadow with suspicion tinged with some surprise: first, that Shadow arrived openly at the palace at the *front* door; second, that she had two Guild members in tow, both carrying apparently heavy sacks; and third, that she came in style, dressed in rich green and amber silks as befitted an elvan Matriarch and Guildmistress of the Guild of Thieves, and riding in a hired carriage. This amazing occurrence so stunned them that the Palace Guard did not bother to question her, but admitted the party with wide eyes and muffled whispers.

Shadow stifled a chuckle, but her entrance was not to be utterly mysterious and dignified; rounding a corner, she collided squarely with Donya. Moreover, as the Heir was dressed in full regalia, including her surcoat and "official" armor, the collision proved almost as damaging to Shadow's nose as it was to her dignity.

"Ooof!" Shadow grunted, rubbing the offended feature. "More shame to me, if I can't hear you coming dressed in cnough metal to plate the Guildhouse floor."

"Shady!" Donya exclaimed, her expression flickering through surprise, pleasure, puzzlement, and finally concern. "What are you doing here? And dressed like that? Is something wrong?"

"No, something's right, and for once I wasn't even here specifically to see you." Shadow laughed. "Can't you tell, since I came in the front door? No, tag along, if you have time. This is a momentous occasion."

Donya frowned dubiously and glanced down the corridor, but she fell in beside Shadow as the group walked to the City Tax Collector's office. That small, plump official and his three assistants looked every bit as puzzled as Donya by this invasion, and Shadow amusedly imagined that their worried expressions were probably due to the presence of three thieves, including the Guildmistress, in the receiving room of the city treasury!

"There you are!" Shadow said with satisfaction as her two companions dropped the heavy bags onto the Collector's desk.

"Guildmistress?" the man asked confusedly, glancing from the bags to Shadow and back again.

Shadow grinned and pulled open the bags' ties, gesturing at the gold inside.

"Taxes," she said casually. "This should settle the Guild's back taxes up to today. The Guild's records were messier than a cesspit, but we finally muddled it out."

Donya's brow wrinkled.

"Shady, do you have any idea how long it's been since the Guild's paid its taxes?"

"Seven years." Shadow nodded. "Since Ganrom took the seat. Go on, count it," she told the Collector. "I want a receipt."

It took the Collector and all three assistants to count the coins and track down the appropriate records. Finally, sweating over the last dusty volume from the storage room, the Collector nodded.

"Paid to the last copper, Guildmistress," he said, smiling broadly and marking the books. "Chon, write up the Guild-mistress's receipt and I'll sign it."

"Well, I *am* impressed," Donya said, shaking her head. "Not to mention amazed. Where did the Guild come up with that much gold in the less than two years you've held the seat? I can imagine what the Guild treasury looked like when you took over."

"An empty room is what it looked like," Shadow grimaced. "If Bobrick's plan to destroy the Guild hadn't worked, lack of funds might've done it for him. Fortune alone knows what Ganrom did with all that money—the cost of those ridiculous separate tokens, plus the bribes from Bobrick, plus what was already there from Evanor's term—when not a copper went out to maintain that slimepit of a Guildhouse or the Guild's responsibilities."

"What did you end up doing about those tokens?" Donya asked curiously as Shadow pocketed the parchment receipt.

"Just a minute." Shadow turned to the two thieves who had accompanied her. "You can go on back," she said. "Take the carriage if you want. It's already paid for."

"Bought most of them back," Shadow sighed, following Donya down the corridor. "Replaced them with a typical copper token and paid the members back the difference in fees out of my own pocket. Then I melted the rest of those damned things down for silver and gold."

"That's not what I meant," Donya said. "I mean, what did you do about the token system?"

"Threw it into the chamber pot," Shadow said cheerfully. "How do you think we made all that money? I went through the Guild members one by one, interviews and tests, figured out who was good and who wasn't, who could handle responsibility and who couldn't. Lot of dead wood, I'm afraid, but who knows, maybe they'll learn given a century or two.

"Anyway," Shadow continued, "I set up a hierarchy *within* the Guild. The really good thieves—the few responsible ones with real potential—I put in charge of certain areas of the city. The Guild gets ten percent of anything they make from their area, and *they* get ten percent of anything other thieves make in their area, but they're also responsible for keeping control and passing news on up to me. They can assign smaller areas, too. So the money just moves up the chain to me, and the headaches move down the chain to them, and all I have to do is keep a tight hand on the few top people."

"Impressive," Donya admitted. "Rather like the City Guard, except for the money."

"Ha!" Shadow grinned. "Shows what you know about the

City Guard—you can take off the 'except for the money.' But
enough about me. You look like I interrupted you on your way
somewhere important.''

Donya grimaced. "I suppose you did," she said. "Actually
I was stalling. I'm going to Inner Heart to see Aspen. Want to
come along?''

"You're going to go riding through the Heartwood dressed
like *that*?" Shadow asked incredulously. "And you think *I'd*
want to?''

Donya shook her head, glancing around to make sure there
was nobody listening nearby.

"Mother got together with a few of her mage friends and
they created a Gate between here and a hut Aspen set up for the
purpose," she said. "After all the trouble we've had in town,
I suggested it would be a good idea to have a direct route to the
elves and vice versa. She and Father agreed, and they worked
it out with Aspen. We'll come out on the other side of Moon
Lake—a goodish walk, but Aspen didn't want such powerful
magic sitting in the middle of his village, and I can't blame
him.''

"I never heard about this Gate," Shadow accused.

"It was only set up a month or two ago," Donya shrugged.
"It's not a state secret or anything, but it's only to be used for
important matters, and with the Royal Family's permission or
Aspen's.''

"Maybe it'll make the elvan delegates a little happier about
attending council sessions," Shadow grinned.

"Nothing could do that, short of several kegs of wine,"
Donya retorted. "But what do you say? Will you come? I could
use some bolstering right now.''

"Bet on it," Shadow said, nodding. "I wouldn't miss trying
a Gate for anything less than a free bottle of Dragon's Blood.
But what are we going *for*? And why do you need bolstering?''

"Well, first of all, Aspen sent for me," Donya sighed,
motioning Shadow down a corridor she'd never seen before.
"He wants to consult with me about someone the patrols
apparently found trespassing in the Inner Zone. He apparently
didn't want to say too much via messenger, and he's one of

those elves who never leave the forest themselves, even with the Gate.''

"Well, that doesn't sound too terrible," Shadow shrugged. "But if that's first of all, what's second?"

Donya looked even more disgusted, if that were possible.

"I need to get Aspen's advice," she mumbled, "about finding a husband."

Shadow laughed. "That's good, Doe, and I'm going to Vikram's for a tumble."

Donya was silent.

Shadow glanced sideways at her, chuckled again, then glanced over again. "Fortune favor me, Doe, you aren't serious, are you?"

"I'm serious," Donya said glumly. "Mother and Father's advisers have been at them—and me—day and night for months, since Father's brother in Bryndwel died without an heir. There's no collateral line to the family now, no one to inherit but me and no one to take the throne after me. So it's important that I find a husband and produce an heir as soon as possible."

"What, just like that?" Shadow asked amazedly. "Go find a husband, just like you'd shop for a scarf at the market?"

Donya shrugged. "I'll have to find an elf who's responsible enough to be the High Lord of Allanmere," she said with a sigh. "And, of course, he's got to be fertile."

Shadow laughed again. "How do you plan on finding that out?" she chuckled. "That should be fun."

Donya stopped in the hallway and looked at Shadow quizzically. "There's got to be some way to know," she said.

"If there is, generations of elves haven't found it," Shadow grinned.

"Well, Mother and Father managed to have me and . . . have me," Donya said, a fleeting look of pain passing over her face.

"That's a little different," Shadow said, diplomatically postponing her curiosity. "I know I'm barren; most female elves know. When they ripen—every quarter century or so—they can feel it. Just to be safe, I imagine your father waited to be sure Celene was pregnant before they married."

"Actually they waited until just before I was born," Donya nodded. "But I can't do that! I mean, I can see that it's my duty to find an elf to marry. I can understand that. But surely it's too much to expect that I go around tumbling elvan fellows and then wait each time to see if I get pregnant! If I do that I'll be old and gray before I'm wed! Not that I'm so looking forward to the prospect, mind you, but the City Council can't wait."

"Well, you can't be the first female heir in a similar position," Shadow said practically. "If I were you I'd do it the elvan way."

"What do you mean?" Donya said uneasily.

"Well, you pick out the fellow you want," Shadow suggested. "After all, it's more important that he be a good husband and a good High Lord than that he be fertile! Then you go to the Heartwood and round up two dozen or so doughty fellows, including your fellow, of course, and have the greatest High Circle the forest's ever seen. Then when you're pregnant, you say it's your fellow's, of course. It's as likely his as anybody's, anyway."

"I can't do that," Donya protested. "I can't marry a man in good faith and then have a child that may be a bastard!"

"Elves don't have a concept of bastardy," Shadow shrugged. "Most of us are High Circle babies anyway. So your husband won't care, and the elves certainly won't care, and nobody else even needs to know."

"I don't know," Donya said doubtfully. "I'll ask Aspen what he thinks."

"Doe, are you *ever* going to tell me?" Shadow said after a pause.

Donya looked at her blankly.

"Tell you what?"

"Come on, Doe," Shadow said patiently. "I've been in Allanmere two years now. Plenty of time to hear the gossip and study the Compact. The Heir's supposed to have been fostered with the elves for at least ten years prior to inheritance. I *know* your worried City Council wouldn't have let the Heir wander the country as a common hire-sword for years, not when they knew Sharl would refuse to father another heir elsewhere and Celene would abdicate as soon as Sharl died. So how long are you going to keep up the awkward silences and the verbal feinting with your best friend?''

Donya halted again, but this time she didn't look at Shadow. When she finally turned to her friend, she looked haggard and—old, and Shadow was uncomfortably reminded of Donya's mortality.

"It's a long story," Donya said tiredly. "I do trust you, Shady. It's just that it's hard to talk about. But you deserve to know."

Shadow nodded and squeezed her friend's hand.

"After we went our separate ways," Donya said slowly, "I came home. Somehow the idea of traveling alone just seemed—I don't know, not as exciting. My brother—my twin brother, Danyel—was wild, though, for a journey to somewhere he'd never seen. He'd been fostered with the elves, you see, since he was very young, and except for coming to town to visit, he'd hardly left the forest in all those years. He was pledged to an elvan girl, too, and planned to marry her soon. She was already pregnant, so as soon as they were married, Mother and Father could step down anytime they liked.

"Mother and Father, of course, didn't want him to leave town," Donya continued. "He was the Heir, of course, and couldn't just go gallivanting around the countryside like his second-born sister. But Danyel convinced them to let him go for a short journey. He'd be safe with me, he said," Donya added bitterly. "And they believed him."

Donya was silent for a few steps.

"I'd already been south and east," she said at last. "Danyel wanted to go west. I didn't; there aren't many towns that way, lots of forest. That meant no inns and no regular supplies. But it was Danyel's first—and probably only—journey, so I gave in.

"The first and second weeks out we ran into packs of bandits," Donya continued. "Nothing we couldn't handle; Danyel was almost as good with a sword as I am, although he was smaller—favored Mother, you know. But the bandits worried me, and I wanted to turn back. Danyel talked me out of it. After the second week we were so far into the wilderness

that there weren't even any bandits. I thought that was
wonderful.'' She laughed bitterly.

"To put it simply,'' Donya said, "a week later we were
surprised in camp by a pack of skinshifters. Only four of them,
but that was enough. We managed to kill two and the other two
ran away, but I'd been clawed and Danyel had been clawed and
bitten, too. We could have both been infected with the shifter
sickness.

"After that there was no talk of turning back. We'd never
have made it home in time for treatment. But there was a town
on our map only a week away, and that might—just might—be
soon enough. But there was a monastery on the map, too. It
meant going out of our way, but it was a little closer. We
decided better to be safe.'' Donya sighed. "Three days later we
reached the monastery. We pleaded with them, but they said we
were tainted with the shifter curse and locked us out. We
hurried as fast as we could to reach the town, but by then there
was no hope. Two days out from the town Danyel caught the
shifter madness, and I—'' Donya drew a breath, then continued
stonily, "I killed him. I killed my brother.''

Shadow shivered in sympathy and patted Donya's arm.

"There was nothing else you could've done,'' she said
comfortingly. "There's no spell to cure the shifter curse once
it's caught. Danyel would've thanked you if he could.''

"I couldn't even bring him home,'' Donya continued, as if
Shadow hadn't spoken. "It was too far. So I buried him there
in the forest. He would've loved that, at least,'' she added. "He
always liked the forest better than the city anyway.''

Shadow could think of nothing to say, so she said nothing.

"So I came home,'' Donya said expressionlessly. "Danyel's
mate died in childbirth and her daughter with her. That's the
story, Shady, and I'll thank you if you never mention it to my
parents. It hurts them too much.''

"All right, Doe,'' Shadow said softly. "I promise.

"So let's see this Gate,'' she said, changing the subject. "At
least you picked a good night for this errand of yours.''

"Yes, tonight's some sort of festival in the Heartwood, isn't
it?'' Donya remembered, curiosity momentarily overcoming
her grief.

"Uh-huh; tonight's the Planting of the Seed," Shadow nodded. "A big celebration on the calendars of the worshippers of the Mother Forest. I'd have gone myself, but I felt a little awkward. Sometimes other elves look at me a little awry because I worship Fortune. But you've given me a good excuse to go, and a way to get there, so why not? Anyway, you probably couldn't pick a better night for husband-hunting. Good night to try them out, too," Shadow added slyly, hoping the festival would at least distract Donya. She wished she'd never asked for the story.

"Here's the room," Donya said, unlocking the door and ignoring Shadow's last statement.

The room Shadow saw had probably once been a storage room; Shadow could see the marks on the stone where shelving had been removed from three of the four walls. The fourth—

There was no fourth wall. Opposite the door was a shimmering silver curtain that extended from wall to wall, from ceiling to floor.

Shadow frowned uneasily. It was bigger than she'd expected, and impressive. It looked a little too much like the wizard Baloran's work for her comfort. Only the thought that Celene had supervised the Gate's creation kept her from backing out of using it.

Shadow wondered privately if Donya had gotten the idea of having the Gate from Baloran's arrangement; she doubted, however, that it would be wise to ask. Donya's treatment at Baloran's hands—her confinement to a body that would not obey her, helplessly forced to do anything Baloran told her—was to the proud warrior a humiliating memory that Shadow had learned it best not to invoke.

"Well," Donya sighed at last, "I guess we'd better go."

"You go first," Shadow said, eyeing the shimmering curtain dubiously.

"If it doesn't work and I'm sucked out into Berblek's Nine Hells in forty-two separate bits," Donya said practically, "how will you know from here?" She smiled brightly, stepped forward into the Gate, and vanished.

Shadow sighed irritably. When Donya was right, she was right. She shrugged and stepped forward.

There was no sensation but a momentary disorientation as she stepped from flagstones to earth, from a lighted room into a dim hut. She stumbled momentarily, and Donya's hand steadied her.

"I'll get the door," Donya said. "It's a magical lock, set to recognize only a few people. We didn't want the elves using the Gate just for fun."

Shadow grinned to herself. A magical lock might keep curious servants out of a stone-walled, windowless room in the palace, but it wouldn't keep a determined elf out of a flimsy hut in the woods. Still, no need to add to her friend's worries; any elf who used the Gate out of curiosity would likely simply step right back through rather than try to explain their way out of the palace!

Moon Lake was as beautiful as always. Shadow grimaced; the beauty of Inner Heart always evoked ambiguous reactions in her. Part of her sighed pleasurably, relaxing in the feeling of *home*; part of her winced in regret that somehow she never completely belonged here, that the forest had never been quite large enough to contain her restless spirit.

"It'll be beautiful from here tonight," Shadow told Donya. "They'll have lighted lanterns to shine across the lake. Going to stay for the whole three nights, or just tonight? I'll have to use your Gate to get back if you stay; they aren't expecting me to be gone from the Guild, and Aubry might panic."

"Just tonight," Donya said regretfully. "I have to meet with the City Council tomorrow. It's too bad; I love elvan festivals. I almost wish I *had* been fostered here."

"Would have done you good," Shadow grinned. "You need a little more of the Mother Forest in you, I'd say, to make up for an overblown sense of duty. Come on; if you want to get a quiet hour with Aspen before the feasting starts, you'd better hurry."

It was afternoon before they finished the long walk around Moon Lake, but Shadow didn't regret the time spent; it was a pleasant quiet time with her friend, which happened all too seldom of late, and there was much to see. Even from across the lake, they could see signs of busy preparation for the festival: numerous boats were out on the lake hauling in fish for

the night's feasting; elves, on deer or on foot, were trickling
into the village bearing fresh kills; and the village itself was a
beehive of activity as lanterns were strung, firepits were laid,
logs were dragged in for seating, and other less easily defined
preparations were made.

Aspen was easily recognized even at a distance; his fiery red
hair, uncommon now among elves, was easily visible, appearing intermittently among the many elves, short and tall, dark
and fair, scurrying about through the village. When he sighted
them coming, Aspen stopped abruptly, colliding with three or
four other elves, and waved joyfully.

"My lady!" he said as soon as they were close enough to
hear him over the bustle. "I'm delighted you could come so
soon. And Guildmistress Shadow! Unexpected, but no less
welcome for all that. Can you both stay for the Planting of the
Seed?"

"Just for tonight," Donya said. "I hope there hasn't been
any further trouble with trespassers?"

Shadow winced a little; by elvan standards, it wasn't really
polite for Donya to cut to the main business so quickly, but
Aspen appeared to take it in stride.

"No, there have been no other disturbances," he said. "It
happened at an inconvenient time, but I suppose there's never
a convenient time to deal with trespassers! But this fellow was
a worry. If you'll follow me, I've isolated him somewhat
outside the village."

"That dangerous?" Donya asked curiously. "I wondered
why you wanted me to come."

"Whether he's dangerous or not I can't say," Aspen said,
shaking his head. "What he is, is a puzzle. He was certainly
carrying weapons when he all but staggered into a patrol camp
near Yellow Oak, but he showed no inclination to use them. He
babbled something in some foreign tongue and fell unconscious. The patrol were both puzzled and frightened and
brought him back. He speaks no tongue I've heard, and—
well—you'll see for yourself, my lady."

He had stopped outside the door of a large hut on the fringe
of the village; the door was barred from the outside, and two

elves stood guard beside it. Aspen nodded at them, and they stepped aside.

"Do you mind if I come in, too?" Shadow asked. "I've done a lot of traveling. Maybe I've heard his language before."

"Somehow I doubt that," Aspen said oddly, "but you're welcome, nonetheless." He unbarred the door.

Freedom-loving elves found the concept of "prison" almost incomprehensible, and they usually dispensed their justice on the spot; the village's attempt at confinement was more like a guest cottage than a cell. The windows were too narrow to permit egress but there were plenty of them; a stone-paved firepit, table and chairs, and a few colorful hangings gave the hut a decidedly homey atmosphere. A midday meal, simple but plentiful, sat untouched on the table. A wide sling-bed, comfortably heaped with cushions and furs, apparently held the prisoner, for although he could be seen only as a lump under the furs, his rasping breath could be heard from the doorway.

Donya had drawn her sword when they entered; now she lowered it hesitantly.

"He's ill?" she asked.

Aspen nodded.

"Worse now, much worse than when he came," he sighed. "I pray through no fault of ours. He was yet senseless when the patrol brought him back, and he has never roused."

"I doubt he'd complain if he could," Donya said, glancing around the hut. "He's not armed now?"

"No; we took everything from him to examine, even his clothing and ornaments lest they be bespelled, but I have his belongings here to show you," Aspen told her.

Well, they could talk all day if they liked; the fellow sounded anything *but* dangerous. Shadow moved around to the side of the bed and lifted aside the edge of the furs.

"Doe," she said immediately, "better have a look."

She could understand Aspen's puzzlement and concern; this was no common poacher. No common *anything,* to her way of thinking.

The face she had exposed was darkly tanned and exquisitely fine-boned; if Aspen hadn't said "he," Shadow couldn't have named the face male or female. It was topped with hair exactly the color of polished bronze; how long it was, Shadow couldn't say, as the single braid at the back disappeared beneath the covers. The half-opened eyes were slightly slanted and were the same polished-bronze color.

Whoever he was, he was well fevered; Shadow's hand, clutching the furs, could feel the heat radiate from the man's skin.

As Donya bent over the bed, Shadow pulled the furs down a little farther. One limp hand rested on the slender throat as if he had fought for breath before losing consciousness; the hand was long and heavily callused—sword calluses, Shadow noted—but boasted six fingers, not five.

As soon as Shadow pulled the covers lower, the strange being began shivering so hard that the sling-bed swayed. Shadow hurriedly pulled the furs back up, but not before she saw the strange hand grope restlessly at his throat, as if desperately seeking something. The stranger murmured something unintelligible, shouted once, hoarsely, then subsided again.

"Our healers have attended him," Aspen said helplessly. "He was fevered but not severely so, we thought, when he came. But after we took his belongings and confined him here he worsened quickly. We dared not potion him; elvan medicines sometimes work ill on humans, and whatever he is, he is neither human nor elf."

"He was reaching for something at his throat," Shadow said. "Was he maybe carrying a message?"

"No; it was a piece of jewelry," Aspen said. "Come outside and see."

One of the guards produced a large, fur-wrapped bundle; Donya murmured with surprise as they opened it.

There was a sword nearly as long as Donya's although not as broad, but which was wonderfully light and forged of some odd white metal, as were two daggers. A coat of links of metal so fine that at first glance it appeared to be cloth was made of the same substance. There was some sort of outlandish pipe carved from what appeared to be bone, long and slender. Dark gray trousers and a tunic were oddly cut but otherwise unremarkable. The pack contained a small quantity of journey food and some rolled leather on which was penned a very rough and incomplete map of the area.

"There is what he wore," Aspen said, pointing.

Under the pack was a pendant made of the same white metal as the sword, strung on a fine chain. On the circular disk was depicted a highly stylized eye; it had been inset with countless tiny gemstones of a dazzling purple color.

"That's really something," Shadow said, reaching for it. "It's worth a fortune, bet on—"

Just as she picked up the pendant, a hoarse scream came from the interior of the hut. They quickly turned to look.

The stranger was no longer lying quietly on the bed. He continued to scream and shriek, his arms and legs now flailing at the covers as if desperately scrambling for purchase. The sling-bed swayed precariously.

"Quick, help me hold him," Donya said, striding to the bedside. "He's having a fit."

Shadow dropped the unusual pendant on the table and turned to help, but her help appeared unnecessary; immediately the stranger collapsed back into unconsciousness, his breath even weaker than before.

Aspen gestured to the guard.

"Quickly," he said. "Fetch Roena."

"Roena?" Donya asked.

"Our chief healer," Aspen told her.

"Doe—" Shadow picked up one of the daggers. "Have you ever seen any metal like this? Light as moonbeams, but harder than steel. Got an edge that would split spider silk longways."

"No, I've never seen the like," Donya admitted. "If I would have, I'd have beggared myself to buy it." She hefted the sword. "Weighted—got to be, or it wouldn't balance and the swing would have no force. Hmmm. Strange grip, for six fingers. What I'd give for a sword like this!"

"This is what I'd want," Shadow said, gesturing at the pendant. "The gems, the art—I could sell this to a couple of jewelers I've seen for enough Suns to floor the Guildhall in solid gold." She caressed the eye design. "Think this is religious or—"

Another scream from the bed, this one weaker but somehow

more desperate. Startled, Shadow pulled her hand away— and immediately the stranger was quiet.

"Don't touch that again," Aspen said sharply. "It must be magical. Your handling it appears to be harming him."

"He's getting awfully weak," Donya said worriedly, stepping aside as a tall elvan woman appeared and moved immediately to the bedside.

"He is indeed," Roena said, shaking her head. "His fever is no higher, but it is as if the life is draining out of him."

"What if we give him this back?" Shadow suggested, gesturing at the necklace. "It seems important to him, and magical or not, if it's a weapon he's in no shape to use it."

Roena shrugged.

"I see no harm in trying," she said. "He will die if he continues to weaken, and any potion I might try could well do more harm than good."

Shadow glanced at Aspen, who nodded reluctantly. Shadow picked the necklace up carefully by the chain, carried it over slowly, and dropped it, amulet first, into the man's hand.

The effect was almost miraculous. Immediately the stranger's harsh breathing eased, and the desperate lines smoothed out of his face. His taut muscles relaxed and color flooded back into the skin.

Roena's eyebrows lifted.

"Praise the Mother Forest, his fever's going down," she said. "And his heartbeat is much stronger. He is resting peacefully now. We should leave him be until he awakens."

"Very well," Aspen agreed, motioning the others outside the hut.

"I see now why you asked me to come," Donya said when the door was shut behind them. "A curious business."

"More than that," Aspen frowned. "He appeared almost in the midst of an Inner Zone patrol. How could a stranger, and a sick one as well, pass our Middle Zone patrols unnoticed? Why at all, and why now? This goes beyond a mere case of poaching or trespassing upon our lands, Lady Donya. I doubt this man represents an enemy—or if so, a very foolish one to send an envoy sick and alone into our very hands—but what his presence may portend disturbs me."

"Have you thought that his illness might spread?" Shadow asked.

"When he was brought here, he had already been in contact with a dozen elves, and they with other patrols," Roena said, frowning gently. "There was no possibility of isolating them. They have shown no signs of ill health, nor have his guards, nor have I myself. If he carries a plague, I cannot find it."

Aspen shook his head and smiled.

"But that must all wait, at least until the man can be questioned," he said. "Meanwhile, tonight begins the Planting of the Seed, and I will not let such concerns trouble so important a celebration. Come, lady, and I will show you where you can store your armor—it would be both uncomfortable and inappropriate for the festival."

"I wish *I* could learn to do that," Donya muttered to Shadow as they followed Aspen away from the hut.

"Do what?" Shadow asked, her mind more on what she'd seen than her friend's words.

"Just shrug off worries like that," Donya sighed. "He's as concerned as I am, but by all the gods I've ever heard of, I'd swear he's not even going to *think* about it tonight."

Shadow chuckled.

"Neither should you, Doe," she grinned. "You could use a little of the Mother Forest in you. Worrying at a sore tooth only rubs your tongue raw and doesn't help the tooth, you know. Have some wine and cheer up. There aren't many humans invited to the Planting of the Seed. You may meet the great love of your life tonight, who knows? It's certainly the right place and the right time."

Donya grinned back weakly and shrugged.

"Who knows," she agreed. "Shady, just what goes on at this festival?"

"All the good things—wine, dreamweed, food, dancing, music," Shadow said. She chuckled. "A lot of 'seed planting,' too. Supposedly any children conceived during the festival will be blessed by the Mother Forest. I was a festival baby, you know."

Donya gave Shadow a warning look, and Shadow laughed.

"Don't worry," Shadow grinned. "It's males who get

chosen for High Circles, not females, and certainly not humans. Besides, at the Planting it's traditional for the women to choose the men. I'm afraid if you want somebody, you're going to have to tell them.''

"Here is my hut," said Aspen, who had diplomatically ignored their conversation. ''If you wish to leave your armor and weapons here, they will not be disturbed.''

Donya unbelted her sword and lifted off her heavy chain mail without a murmur. Aspen turned politely away, but Donya watched amazedly as Shadow relieved herself of a small arsenal of knives, daggers, dirks, darts, and the like from various recesses in her clothing. She tucked the bundle out of sight under Donya's mail and smiled brightly at Donya and Aspen.

''All right,'' Shadow said. ''Which way to the wine?''

TWO ≡≡≡≡

Inner Heart, before it had burned during the Black Wars, had once been the home of one of the largest tribes in the Heartwood. When the Black Wars were finished, the village had been rebuilt on the shores of Moon Lake as the center of the allied tribes.

"Fortune favor me, there must be fifteen new huts!" Shadow gasped, looking up into the trees where the woven dwellings hung from the branches or were cradled near the trunks of the massive trees. "How many are living here now?"

"Nearly two hundred," Aspen told her. "Not so many more than when you were here last. Some of the extra huts are guest quarters, others storage huts for fruits, vegetables, smoked meats, furs. There is more trading with the city, now, so we need room to store our goods."

The central plaza, too, had been expanded since Shadow had last seen it; the huts that had rimmed it had been moved back to bare more of the solidly packed soil, and the five smaller firepits fringing the large, central firepit had become ten—all occupied now with roasting meats on spits and vegetables stewing in pots or buried in the coals. Split logs, their flat sides smoothly polished and, tonight, padded with cushions, surrounded the central firepit. Casks of wine flanked the logs at regular and frequent intervals. Aspen winked at Shadow and led them to one of these casks, where an elf Shadow recognized was drawing goblets of rich moondrop wine.

"Welcome, Lady Donya," Laurel grinned, handing her a goblet. "And twice welcome, Shady! Everyone will be so delighted to see you here, doubtless I will have to stand in line to renew our acquaintance."

"Laurel," Aspen chided. "Perhaps you will let Shadow have some wine and food before you begin importuning her."

"With reluctance, I obey," Laurel laughed, drawing Aspen a goblet of wine. "But I hope the moon rises quickly!"

Aspen chuckled and led the women to a quiet corner, out of the bustle of elves rushing back and forth, and they sat down to watch the preparations.

"Aspen . . ." Donya began uncomfortably, fortifying herself with a healthy swig of wine, "there's something I need to talk to you about."

Shadow chuckled. "Should I leave?" she asked.

"No, that's all right," Donya sighed. As she told Aspen her problem, his eyes grew a little rounder and finally his jaw dropped slightly—true amazement, Shadow thought, in an elf who, in many centuries, had probably heard everything.

"My lady," Aspen said at last, "I hardly know what to say. A difficult problem indeed. In your short time in Allanmere you have hardly had time to meet many of our men, nor they you. Despite the traditions of the ruling family of Allanmere, we have no experience here in the wood with—with arranging matings. Until now, thank the Mother Forest, the Heirs have always managed to choose mates during their youth, usually during fostering, as Sharl did Celene."

"But Doe wasn't fostered," Shadow said, nodding.

"That is difficult," Aspen agreed. "But the problem, as I see it, is that Lady Donya also spent little time in court— indeed, little in Allanmere. Celene, as you know, involves herself as little in matters of state as she can, being neither schooled nor inclined for rulership. You, my lady, must find a mate who is prepared to assume his share—perhaps more than his share—of rulership, until at least you have become accustomed to the position. I fear, my lady, that you would be better advised to look among the city elves for a mate. They are more familiar with the city, its laws and its needs. My people of the wood, while honest and true, are perhaps not serious enough to provide a strong High Lord of Allanmere.''

"What about you, Aspen?" Shadow grinned. "Ready to leave the forest and become rich and titled?''

Aspen and Donya both gave Shadow a thunderstruck look; Aspen broke the tension at last with a delighted laugh.

"Ah, but, Shadow, where will I find another foolish enough to take my place here? Will you do it?''

Shadow grinned. "Not till the sky falls, Aspen, bet on it. I was mist-headed to let myself get maneuvered into taking the seat at the Guild. Besides, I'm out of touch with the forest.''

"And I with the city," Aspen smiled. "I know nothing of taxes and laws and politics. Also, it is most likely that I am not fertile, as that seems important to the lady.''

"It's important to the City Council," Donya said wryly.

"I'm afraid I must agree with Shadow's advice," Aspen said, shaking his head. "Finding a mate to meet your requirements is difficult enough; insuring that he is fertile as well is nigh impossible.''

"Surely some of them know," Donya protested. "You do.''

"But that is a rarity," Aspen told her. "Occasionally an unusual woman will want a child she knows is by her mate, as my mate Bria did, rather than a more assured pregnancy with a High Circle. Although she had already borne two children before we were mated, she bore none after. Thus it seems likely that I am not fertile; however, I cannot be certain. Bria had already borne two children and was near the end of her ripening, and it is uncommon for an elvan woman to bear more than twice. So only the Mother Forest can say, and that is as it should be.''

"What about a spell?" Donya asked. "Some kind of divination?''

Aspen was silent for a long moment. "So far as I know," he said at last, "there is no such spell. If there were, it would be forbidden. I know of no elf who would submit to it.''

Shadow nodded at Donya's surprised look. "I thought even you'd know better, Doe," she said gently. "Fertility is a very precious thing to an elf. Can you imagine what such a spell would do here in the Heartwood? Elves wanting it cast on prospective mates before mating, casting it on themselves and then believing they're not fit to mate because they're not fertile, men excluded from the High Circle—no, that's not the way the Mother Forest intended it to be. Even I can respect that, and I *know* I'm barren.''

''Then what do I do?'' Donya asked desperately. ''I have to have a husband, he has to be an elf, and he has to be fertile because I have to have an heir. So far as I know there's no spell to *make* someone fertile.''

''Now, *that* spell would be dearly loved in the forest,'' Aspen smiled. ''No, Shadow has the right of it; choose the elf you want and then come to the forest and dance the High Circle. If you find that unacceptable, then all I can advise is to choose your mate and wait until you are pregnant to wed—and be prepared to choose again.''

''Gods, how do I get into these messes?'' Donya demanded, pounding one fist in frustration against the log. She downed the rest of her wine in a single gulp.

''By being foolish enough to be born noble,'' Shadow said sympathetically, handing Donya's empty goblet to another elf for refilling. ''Look, I'll tell you what—before we go back to the city, we'll make a side trip to the Forest Altars and ask the Mother Forest for an answer. That's what this festival's for, after all. She should be sympathetic to your cause.''

''I thought you weren't a believer,'' Donya said bitterly, accepting a filled goblet.

''I said I wasn't a *worshipper,*'' Shadow corrected. ''I'll be one of Her children till the day my spirit goes back to the earth it came from. For you I'll risk making Fortune jealous—I've felt Her left hand enough, the gods know, to be used to it—and ask for a favor on your behalf. Good enough?''

''Why not?'' Donya smiled wearily. ''The gods seem to love you well enough.''

''Bet on it,'' Shadow said cheerfully. ''I must be fine entertainment! Anyway, try thinking like an elf for a change—leave it in the Mother Forest's hands, if just for one night, and enjoy the festival.''

Donya smiled, a little more genuinely this time, and nodded.
"I'll try," she said. "The gods know it's hard not to, with
moondrop wine in my cup!"

"And harder still if the wine's in your belly," Shadow
laughed, draining her own cup.

"Have a care," Aspen said, chuckling as he sipped from his
own cup. He gestured at the setting sun. "The moon has not yet
risen, and it would be sad if you and your friend were
intoxicated before the festival even began! Come, have a cup of
stew while you wait a little longer."

Shadow rose and stepped over to the indicated firepit, where
a huge caldron over the fire was giving out the most delicious
aroma—a rich meaty smell, tangy with wine and herbs, and
hotly pungent. A soupstone hung in the kettle, enriching the
stew with its special flavoring magic.

"Venison?" Shadow asked, smiling as she recognized
Teria, who had once shared her mate with Shadow when she
and Blade had traveled through the forest.

Teria nodded. "Only the best," she said, "with the first
vegetables and four kinds of tubers, and those new southern
peppers they're trading in town. Very spicy, I warn you. If you
prefer bear stew, Willow is tending that—it is gamier, but
much milder."

"I like spice in my life," Shadow laughed, accepting three
bowls and attempting awkwardly to balance them while Teria
handed her several rounds of bread. Donya, seeing her plight,
came to Shadow's rescue, while Aspen poured large mugs of
chilled ale.

Donya had eaten enough elvan-style meals with her mother
and with Shadow, and at elvan inns in town, that she was
comfortable without eating implements, scooping up the thick
stew as adroitly on the flat bread as Aspen and Shadow did. At
the first bite, however, her eyes bulged and she reached quickly
for the ale.

"Grief of the gods, Shady," Donya gasped. "That's worse
than that illegal liquor I pretend I don't know you buy. Why do
you seem to insist on eating and drinking every substance
that'll burn out your guts from the inside?"

"I like the danger," Shadow laughed, scooping up more

stew. The fire in her mouth seared its way to her gullet—a delightful inferno indeed akin to her occasional death-defying drinks of Dragon's Blood.

"Well, you'll *be* in danger if you ever try to kill me with food again," Donya said sourly, nonetheless scooping up another bite. "To make up for that, I hope at the very least you're going to dance for us tonight?"

"Mmmm, maybe," Shadow conceded. "But if you really want to see something, we should find Aubry's cousin Mist and have him dance. He does a sword dance, from what Aubry's told me, doesn't he, Aspen?"

"Indeed he does," Aspen said, nodding. "And he has promised to dance tonight. Although sword dancing is not precisely appropriate to the occasion, Mist's dancing is, as you say, not something to be missed."

"What exactly is sword dancing?" Donya asked, interested.

"I wouldn't spoil the event by too much foreknowledge," Aspen told her. "But sword dancing is a very old and traditional art, older than the oldest stories known. Shadow's dancing is excellent, true, but Mist remains unrivaled."

"Do I hear my name being praised?" a light voice interjected.

Shadow raised her goblet to greet the newcomer, a middle-sized, wiry elf whose pale skin, near-white hair, and silver-gray eyes more resembled Argent than Aubry. The mischievous tilt of his eyes and his rather lopsided smile were, however, highly reminiscent of Shadow's friend, assistant, and occasional lover. Mist, however, was obviously older than his cousin; the coiled braid of his hair made a respectable knot, and Mist had divided the ends into numerous smaller braids, knotted with gold and silver beads, which hung clacking to his waist. Shadow had never seen a more interesting-looking elf.

"Well met, Mist," she said. "Aubry's told me a bit about you. Not enough, I'd say."

"He has told me a great deal about you, Shadow," Mist said, smiling slyly, "and only whetted my curiosity." He took her free hand, and Shadow thought for a fleeting, confused moment that he might kiss the knuckles as some humans did; but he laid a kiss in her palm, folding her fingers about it, a daringly intimate gesture that made a shiver run down Shadow's spine.

"I hear your dancing's not something to be missed," Donya said, grinning complicitly as she glanced from Shadow to Mist and back again.

"I have studied for a good many decades," Mist told her. "I have been favored with an excellent teacher and kindly audiences." He turned to Shadow. "Will you watch me dance?" The tone of his voice made it an intimate request, a whispered favor asked of a lover in the privacy of darkness.

"*Watch* you?" Shadow grinned, responding to the challenge. "At the very least!"

Then she wrinkled her nose as a sudden familiar stench drifted past.

"What's that—Aubry!"

Aubry laughed and sat down next to Mist, bowl, bread, and goblet in his hands, and the offending pipe in his mouth.

"You used to say you could smell me coming across the city," he chided. "Can it be your attention was distracted? Oh, I can see how the dice are falling—one look at my striking cousin and the world disappeared. Well, cousin, this time I'll have to say you've met your match."

"You intrigue me," Mist said, giving Shadow a sidelong glance through half-lidded eyes.

"I'd like to do more than that," Shadow laughed. "But I'll bet there'll be a dozen women wearing the ribbon tonight. I'll be lucky if they let you finish your sword dance!"

"What ribbon?" Donya asked.

"I told you, during the festivals it's traditional that the women choose the men," Shadow told her. "Women who are ripe wear a green ribbon to show it, and they choose first for the High Circles. Just *look* at him—the women'll be fighting over him like a bunch of humans."

"Well, he can say no, can't he?" Donya asked. "I mean, they couldn't *make* him, right?"

"Say no?" Shadow, Aspen, Aubry, and Mist exchanged blank stares. "*Make* him?" Shadow asked. "Doe, you're talking about a High Circle. Reproduction. What could be more important than that? If the Mother Forest herself called, the men might wait until the High Circle was over! Mist and I have decades to tumble each other, but those women may never ripen again in their *lives*."

"That dance must be quite a sight," Donya said, shaking her head.

"You should know," Shadow said. "You saw me dance it once."

"Not likely," Donya retorted. "I was too busy trying to saw through the thickest ropes I ever hope to be tied up with and praying to at least fifty different gods that nobody'd see me doing it."

"Well, you'll see it tonight," Aubry said, chuckling. "And don't walk into any of the vacant huts or you'll stumble over the aftermath."

"Well, whether or not I am honored to be chosen for a High Circle," Mist said, "no woman should lack for a man to warm her pallet. Even the Hidden Folk, those tribes who scorn humans and the Compact and choose to live secluded in the Heartwood, often come to Inner Heart for the Planting of the Seed."

"Really?" Donya asked delightedly. "I've never met any of the Hidden Folk."

"And you probably won't tonight," Shadow warned her. "They don't like humans, Doe, and they don't like half-bloods any better. They're just as aloof to town-living elves, like Aubry and me. See, there're a few by that caldron. Silver Springs, by the look of them."

Donya was not the only one to give the eight newcomers a few curious looks. These elves wore no bright cloth as did most other elves, nor even the exquisitely tanned leathers for which the forest tribes were renowned; they wore skins—stitched together, indeed, into rich garments, but furred skins nonetheless. They eschewed the metal that some tribes mined and traded to the others; their arrows and daggers, carried despite the festival, were tipped with flint, and their only ornaments were of tooth or bone, feather or shells. Their faces were narrow and feral, exotically carved like Mist's. Two of the Silver Springs were nearly as short as Shadow.

"The taller five are sisters and will likely dance tonight," Aspen said. "Now that will be a sight to rival even Mist's sword dance. But come, I hear the musicians tuning their instruments, and I see a sliver of the moon over the trees. The festival will soon begin.''

Other elves were joining them to sit around the large central fire; most had filled goblets and plates or bowls first. Many were lighting and passing pipes of fragrant dreamweed.

Aspen and Mist excused themselves. Shadow and Donya finished their stew and amused themselves watching the elves; Aubry seemed to have a never-ending stream of kinfolk, most of whom he introduced to them in a blur of names and smiling faces. At last everyone was settled, and Aspen stepped to the center of the circle as near the fire as he could, followed by three other elves: one bearing a covered basket, and two staggering under the weight of a large clay jar.

"Welcome, kinfolk," he said. "Tonight we share food and fire in honor of the Planting of the Seed, to celebrate the renewal of life in the Mother Forest after the sleep of winter. May Her life awaken in each of us, in the loins of our men and the wombs of our women. May we flower and bear fruit in Her rich soil, washed in Her gentle rains, nurtured in Her warming sunlight.''

Each elf emptied his or her goblet on the earth, carefully behind the sitting logs where no one would step in the mud. Shadow hurriedly gulped down most of her wine so that there was only a trickle to spill. Donya poured out her own wine.

An elf picked up the covered basket and approached, holding it out. It contained nothing but acorns, enough to nearly fill the basket.

"Take one," Shadow told Donya, taking one herself. "You're supposed to plant it, and if it grows, you'll be blessed by the Mother Forest.''

Donya took an acorn and pocketed it, shrugging. Shadow tucked her own acorn into her pouch with somewhat more care.

The two elves with the jar walked along the circle of logs, pouring from the clay jar into the upheld goblets. Golden liquid, flower-scented, poured into Shadow's goblet. The elves filled Donya's goblet partway and hesitated. Donya looked at them sternly and they filled the goblet full.

"Watch that," Shadow murmured to her friend when the

elves with the jar were out of earshot. "That's Sun Flower Nectar, and it's got dreamweed juice in it."

Donya nodded and squeezed Shadow's shoulder. Finally the jar had made its rounds and returned to the center, where Aspen held out his own goblet.

"From the seed grows the sprout, from the sprout the seedling," Aspen said. "From the seedling a sapling, from the sapling a tree. One day it is a great tree, dropping seeds of its own. And one day it will fall, its flesh returning to the Mother Forest to nourish the soil so that a part of itself may grow forever, renew itself each time in the endless cycle of life. Thus the Mother Forest grants the magic of life to Her creatures. Through the flesh of Her soil, the blood of Her sap, are we nourished." He lifted his cup and drank. "May the seeds we plant this night in hope of Her blessings grow strong and tall in Her honor."

Silently, the elves lifted their cups and drank—Shadow unhesitatingly, Donya more cautiously. Aspen lifted his cup again in salute, then stepped from the center of the circle.

"That's all?" Donya asked surprisedly as Aspen rejoined them.

"No one comes to the festivals to hear me talk," Aspen chuckled, sipping from his goblet. "Not even the Mother Forest. Especially the Mother Forest. Do you like your nectar, Lady Donya?"

"It's—wonderful," Donya said, taking another gulp. "I've never tasted anything like it."

"Sun Flowers bloom only two places in the Heartwood," Aubry said. "And only for three days. Luckily it doesn't take many to make the nectar."

"It's wonderful," Donya repeated, sipping more cautiously. Shadow, assessing the level in Donya's cup, imagined it was too late for caution.

"Look," Aspen said, gesturing at the center of the clearing.

Mist was there with a leather-wrapped bundle. From it he took a sword and set one edge of the blade carefully into the soil, tapping it into place with a wooden mallet. Eight more swords he produced, setting them meticulously at angles to each other, point to hilt. Firelight glistened off the sharp edges of the blades.

"Nine swords," Aubry said, surprised. "He's improved. Last year he did only seven."

After a few more minute adjustments, Mist appeared to be satisfied with his arrangement. He took off his clothing and walked across the circle to hand it to Shadow, grinning mischievously at her. Shadow grinned back; she noticed that Donya blushed furiously but never looked away.

Mist nodded to the musicians. Slowly they began, a precise pulsing melody that seemed to follow Mist's bare feet as he placed them exactly between the shining blades. His face was calm, not tightened with concentration; his hands moved easily.

The music was slowly building in speed. Mist's feet moved more quickly, the beads in his hair clacking against each other as they swirled.

Mist's feet were moving almost too fast to see now, the sweat running in rivulets down his pale body or spraying from his flashing limbs. Firelight gleamed from his sweat-filmed shoulders.

Shadow glanced briefly at Donya. Her friend's eyes were riveted on Mist, her face still flushed—but this time, Shadow would wager, not from embarrassment. She grinned to herself. Sun Flower Nectar, laced with potent dreamweed juice, was something of an aphrodisiac.

Shadow reached into her pocket and pulled out her handkerchief—green silk, to match her jerkin. She leaned over and whispered into Donya's ear.

"You're not bleeding, are you?"

Donya glanced at her, first startled, then puzzled, then embarrassed.

"No. Why?"

"Good enough." Shadow twisted the handkerchief into a narrow band, then tied it around Donya's left arm, above the elbow. "When the dance is over, grab him."

"Me?" Donya's whisper was incredulous. "But I'm—I thought you—"

"Shhh," Shadow scolded. "I want to watch the dance."

The musicians, now, were sweating freely as they pressed

themselves to one final effort. Mist's feet were a blur of white among the silver blades; at any moment Shadow expected to see the red of his blood. Abruptly the music stopped and Mist leaped free of the blades, landing safe on the hard-packed soil.

There was a moment of silence before the elves began stamping their feet and thumping the logs in approbation. A dozen wineskins were offered; however, Mist, laughing and panting, waved them away and stepped toward his clothes. Shadow offered her half-empty goblet; Mist smiled and took it, draining it at a gulp. He pulled a rag from the bundle of his clothes and began drying himself.

Shadow elbowed Donya and nodded toward Mist. Donya hesitated. Shadow sighed, took Donya's hand, and clasped it firmly around Mist's wrist.

Donya blushed furiously but did not withdraw her hand. Mist looked from Shadow to Donya and grinned.

"I am glad you so liked my dance, my lady," he said.

"Go on, you two," Shadow grinned. "Doe, grab him a skin of wine on the way. And hurry. There's half a dozen green-ribboned women headed this way."

Mist took Donya's other hand and pulled her to her feet, leading her out of the circle.

"Mist," Shadow called after him.

Mist turned.

"When you're done," Shadow said, "come and find me."

Aubry was choking with laughter. Shadow thumped him on the back and refilled her goblet and stew bowl.

"What's bothering you?" she said mildly when she sat down.

"You," Aubry choked, knuckling tears from his eyes, "are the most devious bit of work I've ever seen."

"What *are* you talking about?" Shadow asked innocently. "Just because I generously decide that my friend needs a tumble worse than I do, now I'm devious?"

"You green-ribboned her," Aubry chuckled. "A half hu-man, with a whole goblet of nectar in her? Half an hour and she'll be sleeping like a bear in winter, and by that time the other green-ribboned women will have already picked their fellows for the High Circles, and Mist will be yours for the rest of the night. Devious, I say!"

"Well, she *does* need a good tumble," Shadow said good-naturedly, "and a good night's sleep. This way I can do us both a good turn at the same time."

"Then I trust you will not mind your friend doing *us* a good turn," a female voice said.

Shadow looked up. Two of the Silver Springs women were there, green ribbons tied to their arms. They looked rather irritated; Shadow could well imagine why.

The taller of the two women had reached out to grasp Aubry's wrist.

"Come to our High Circle," she said, "and we will dance for you there."

"I'd be delighted," Aubry grinned. He turned to Aspen. "If you'll excuse me, Grandfather."

"Strong seed, rich soil," Aspen said graciously, waving him away.

"They aren't any too happy with me," Shadow remarked as the Silver Springs led Aubry away.

"Your ploy was kindly, if not entirely unselfishly meant," Aspen said gently, "but perhaps not altogether wise. None of us would have balked the Hidden Folk. They still control many areas of the Heartwood, and we respect their territories. Their anger is slow to fade."

"I didn't know the Hidden Folk were very important these days," Shadow said, raising an eyebrow. "Just a few scattered tribes, aren't they? Less than a tenth of the elvan population in the Heartwood."

"Look there," Aspen said as if in answer. Five of the Silver Springs women, the ones Aspen had identified as sisters, had begun to dance. Although Mist's sword dance was an ancient thing, rooted in the oldest elvan traditions, this seemed more ancient still, and more savage; it put Shadow in mind of the time she had danced with Blade, the most lethal assassin in Allanmere and the strangest creature Shadow could ever hope to meet. Even the odd man in the hut could not surpass her.

Aspen and Shadow watched the dancers in silence for some time.

"In a way they are the purest of all of us," Aspen mused. "Before the Compact, when the elves were separate and often warring peoples, there were fewer of us but more were Gifted. There are more children now that we have mixed but fewer beast-speakers and their like; our lives are longer and safer but our magic is weaker. We have, indeed, paid a price for the Compact. The Hidden Folk are, perhaps, an uncomfortable reminder of a time when we lived closer to the Mother Forest—needing no others, heeding no others. You and I are old enough to remember that time."

"Remember it?" Shadow laughed ruefully. "I'm the one who found even the freedom of the forest too confining. What about Mist?"

Aspen smiled. "What of Mist, indeed?"

"I mean, how old is he?"

"A handful of decades older than you," Aspen told her. "As far as I know. He was born among the Hidden Folk, did you know?"

"Really?" Shadow blinked in amazement. "But—Aubry's cousin? I thought all of Aubry's folk were Redoaks."

"One of his mother's mother's sisters mated among the Silvertips," Aspen said. "Mist is of that branch of the family. Most of the Silvertips were slaughtered in the Black Wars; what was left merged with the Goldeneyes. Mist left the Hidden Folk only a decade ago to join Aubry's folk to the south."

"Explains the accent," Shadow nodded. "And the sword dancing, which is all but a lost art. Also why he's so in demand for High Circles. Is he Gifted?"

Aspen chuckled.

"Many of our women appear to think so," he said. "You must draw your own conclusions."

"All right, his own business," Shadow agreed. She watched the dancers for a few minutes. "Say, Aspen, what *am* I going to do about Donya?"

"What are *you* going to do?" Aspen mocked. "What is there for you to do but let her find her own answers, her own mate? This is a human foolishness, this business of arranged matings and heirs, and elves should not involve themselves in it.''

"Oh, but it's such an interesting foolishness," Shadow laughed. "Short lives they live, but never dull ones!"

"Surely your own exploits are more interesting by far," Aspen told her. "The tales the trading elves bring us have kept us all entertained."

"Oh, I wouldn't have had those exploits if it hadn't been for the humans," Shadow admitted. "Donya most of all."

"But have you no goals of your own?" Aspen asked.

"Me?" Shadow hurriedly reached for a wineskin to fill her cup. "Oh, I'm a person of simple needs, Aspen. I'll see Doe through her present difficulties. One or two more years and I'll have the Guild on its feet and a successor ready to take over."

"Are you so eager to be rid of the Guild?" Aspen asked interestedly.

"Guildmistress is an unenviable position," Shadow sighed. "I hardly get a chance to practice myself anymore. If some two-copper pickpocket isn't trying to cheat me out of the Guild's dues, he's trying to kill me for the seat. No, let someone else have the headaches; I've served my term and past."

"What will you do then?" Aspen said. "Return to the forest?"

"Ah, I see the hook under that bait," Shadow laughed. "You're tired of being Eldest and you're looking for another elf old enough and foolish enough to be tricked into taking over. Well, forget it. After Allanmere it's the open road for me, my friend—new places to see, new wines to drink, new men to tumble."

"What, have you exhausted every pleasure Allanmere and the forest have to offer?" Mist asked significantly, sitting down beside Shadow. "Your friend, I fear, has—at least for this night. Her snores threaten to vanquish the walls of the hut where I left her dreaming."

"Poor Doe," Shadow chuckled. "She's had a tough time of it lately. I hope she didn't fall asleep *too* soon."

Mist smiled lazily, tracing the edge of Shadow's ear with a feather-light fingertip.

"Often a tasty tidbit merely whets the appetite for a feast," he said.

"Do you know, I've got a bit of an appetite myself," Shadow said, grinning as she captured the tickling finger.

"Oh, please," Aspen groaned. "Do take your play elsewhere. As Eldest, it is still some hours before I may leave the festival and attend to *my* appetite."

"So speaks the poor deprived Eldest, who has the enviable duty of cementing the alliance with each chieftess attending the festival," Mist laughed. "Come, Shadow, let us leave this poor unfortunate to his starvation."

Shadow took his hand and stood, only to turn as an abrupt silence fell over the clearing.

A slender figure stumbled into the firelit circle, mumbled something unintelligible, and collapsed. Even from where she sat, Shadow recognized the bronze braid and six-fingered hands of the elves' captive.

"How did he get out of the hut?" Shadow asked, approaching the fallen man. He was unconscious again. Shadow noticed with interest that while he was still naked, he had donned the necklace.

"I have no idea," Aspen said amazedly, "but we had best get him back."

"I will carry him," Mist declared, carefully lifting the stranger.

Shadow had been amazed enough to see him; however, her amazement was nothing to that of the two guards, still stationed outside the door of the hut.

"By the Mother Forest!" one exclaimed as the other hurriedly opened the door of the hut and peered confusedly inside. "How did he escape?"

"I would like to know that myself," Aspen said gently. "How did he pass you?"

"I swear by the very earth he did not," the guard protested, and the other nodded. "We have heard not so much as a cough from him since you left. Arin checked him not an hour ago and he was deeply asleep."

"I see no holes in the walls," Mist said, laying the sick man back on the sling-bed. "He could scarce have fit through the windows, nor yet have flown through the smoke hole in the roof.''

''Well, he got out somehow,'' Shadow said practically, ''and I can't see that he burrowed through the floor like a rootworm. He's too sick to have done much of anything in an hour.''

''Mount two guards inside the door as well as those outside,'' Aspen decided. ''When the Lady Donya leaves, let her take this captive with her if she so desires. I cannot fathom what we will do with him otherwise; we are no murderers of the sick and helpless. If he survives and heals, perhaps the High Lord and Lady will be kind enough to return him to us for judgment.''

''I'll talk to Donya about it,'' Shadow promised. ''Shall I go get her now?'' she added reluctantly.

Aspen noted Mist's disappointed air and chuckled.

''I much doubt we could awaken our lady Heir at this moment,'' he said. ''There is no need for you to forgo your own enjoyment of the festival. I will summon Roena to assure that he sleeps, if she must bespell him to be certain.''

''Then we must find some way to pass the time until Lady Donya awakes,'' Mist grinned, ''and I vow that will be no short time.''

''Think there are any empty huts left?'' Shadow asked with a quirk of her eyebrow.

''Take mine,'' Aspen sighed. ''It seems it will be some hours before I will have any need of it.''

Mist chuckled as Shadow pulled him to his feet and all but dragged him toward Aspen's hut.

''You know,'' Shadow said, ''watching your dancing, I believe there's a step or two I'd like you to teach me.''

''Indeed,'' Mist chuckled. ''That should be a most interesting lesson.''

''And in exchange,'' Shadow continued innocently, ''I do believe there's a dance or two I've learned in my travels that I may still teach you.''

THREE ═══════

"Wake up, Doe."

"Uhhhhh?" Donya rolled over drowsily, knocking Shadow over backward into the furs. "Whazzit?"

"Better wake up," Shadow repeated, scrambling back out of the furs. "It's after midnight. If we're going to stop at the Altars before we go back, we'd better start now."

"Uhhhh. Yehhh." Donya rolled over, groaning and clutching her head. "What in Fortune's name happened?"

"Mist wouldn't find that very flattering," Shadow chuckled. "And I have to agree that I find him pretty memorable. Too much nectar, that's your problem. Well, pick up your head and let's get going. Mist's fetching his belongings and arranging for a sleeping potion for your guest."

"Guest?" Donya grumbled. "What else did I do, invite half the forest tribes home with me?"

"No, Aspen's trespasser," Shadow told her. "He got out of the hut somehow earlier this evening. He'll be potioned to sleep now—Roena didn't want to risk it at first—but Aspen wants you to take him back to Allanmere. Mist will see that he's dressed and ready to travel, and we'll just take him with us now; that way the guards can go to the festival instead of standing by the door all night."

35

"Mist's coming back with us?" Donya asked, apparently remembering something of the evening, for her cheeks were flaming red.

"Don't panic, I invited him," Shadow grinned. "He's never seen the city before, and Aspen would prefer a local elf to go along as his representative with the stranger, so I invited him to be my guest for a few days. If you'll let him back through the Gate, that is, when he's ready to go back. By the way, Aspen wants the fellow back again, if possible, when you're done with him."

"Yes, that's in the Compact." Donya shook her head again. "Got any wine, Shady? A dragon used my mouth for a chamber pot, I think."

Shadow handed Donya a goblet.

"Wine plus a potion," she said. "Your mother's got to get the formula from Roena, I swear."

Donya sipped cautiously, then smiled and drank.

"Not bad!" she said. "But you know, Shady, we don't have to go to the Altars. I mean, if you just want to go back to Allanmere now—"

"No, no, I promised," Shadow chided. "It's only a short ride. One of the beast-speakers here called us up a few deer. There's a stag that I think can carry you. I hope."

Mist was waiting outside the hut with three does and a tall, sturdy stag. The stranger, sleeping heavily, was on one of the does; his belongings were safely stowed with Mist's on Mist's doe. Mist politely made no comment as Donya glanced at him, turned an even deeper shade of red, and hurriedly looked away.

"Ride a *deer*?" Donya said doubtfully, eyeing the stag. "I'm not sure I could sit my warhorse right now."

"If I can do it, you can certainly do it," Shadow grunted, struggling onto her doe's back, behind a bundle containing Donya's armor and sword and her own weapons. "Come on, we'd be half the night walking to the Forest Altars and back."

Donya sighed resignedly and mounted awkwardly, to the great disgust of the stag.

"All right," she said. "Which way?"

It was slow going even with the deer, for Donya's stag wanted to lead; however, his half-human rider, while sharing to

some extent the elves' keen night vision, had no idea of the
route to the Forest Altars. The stranger, ill as he was, could not
simply be thrown across his mount, and no matter how
carefully Mist fastened him upright, he teetered precariously,
and had to be checked regularly for signs of either worsening
or wakening.

Despite the slow pace, they reached the Forest Altars
halfway between midnight and dawn. Firelight sparkled here
and there among the widely scattered stone altars.

"Who's here?" Donya asked, surprised. "I thought everyone would be at the festival."

"Well, there's three days of festival, you know," Shadow
told her. "Most of the ripening women will visit the Altars
sometime during the Planting."

"Oh, to pray they'll conceive?" Donya said.

"It is known," Mist said, "that ripe women who couple at
the Altars will surely bear a child. Such a coupling during the
Planting of the Seed is doubly blessed. Best we skirt the edge
and find a distant altar, or we will be coaxed to join a dozen
High Circles and never find time for your prayer."

"Maybe we'd better go," Donya said uncomfortably. "I
wouldn't want to—ah—disturb anyone."

"I know an altar that's away from the others," Shadow said,
grinning secretly. "I think it's good for our purposes."

The altar Shadow led them to was, indeed, so far from the
others as to seem disassociated and forgotten. It even appeared
abandoned; green goldenbell vines had thickly overgrown it,
their blossoms opening fragrantly in the moonlight.

"This altar looks rather neglected, doesn't it?" Donya asked
curiously, fingering a vine. "Should we clear these away?"

"No, no," Shadow said hurriedly. "I think these are here on
purpose. Goldenbell vines grow on oaks, not over stone
altars."

"That cannot be right," Mist chided. "No one would cover
an altar with vines."

"I know someone who might," Shadow grinned. "At any
rate, if the Mother Forest didn't want them to grow here, they
wouldn't, would they?"

"True enough," Mist shrugged. He had lifted the sleeping

stranger from his mount and settled him comfortably against a tree.

"Well, we're here," Donya said, looking around. "What should we do now? I didn't think to bring an offering from Allanmere. I wouldn't know what kind of offering your Mother Forest might want, anyway."

"It's the intentions that count," Shadow said. "Most of the folks here tonight will probably bring something, but it's not really necessary."

"We're not expected to—I mean—" Donya flushed and glanced at Mist.

"You make it sound such a distasteful chore," Mist chuckled. "I should take offense."

"Have a little pity, Mist," Shadow grinned. "It's her first festival. Her blood may be half-elvan, but she's been raised all human. No, Doe, you don't have to do anything; just sit there at the end of the altar and imagine the mate of your dreams. It's my prayer, on your behalf, and my offering; I'm going to dance."

"Dance?" Mist asked, surprised. "But there are no musicians here."

"I saw drums in your bundle," Shadow said. "Can you play them?"

"After a fashion," Mist said slowly. "I am but a learner. But who will play pipes and strings?"

"Don't need them," Shadow said mysteriously. "I really *do* know a new dance, Mist, one you haven't learned, and I learned it from as unlikely a teacher as you'll ever find. Get your drums, and I'll show you what I want. You may not like my dance, but I'll wager you'll never forget it."

Shadow fussed over Mist for some time but could not seem to get the results she wanted. Blade's black drums had played with the skill of an adept, and Shadow's player was little more than a novice, and then there were the difficulties of trying to re-create, from memory, a complex rhythm. Shadow's memory, fortunately, was, like that of most well-trained thieves, nearly flawless; and the result was, after all, more important than the precision of its creation. At last Mist was creating something like the complex interweaving she wanted.

Shadow picked the pins from her braids, cutting the thongs to let her hair work its way loose, and hurriedly drew off her boots, tunic, and trousers.

She closed her eyes and let memory guide her feet in the slow, catlike steps. She thought of predators: the hawk, spiraling on a high wind above its prey; the forest cat, smooth muscles rippling under its tawny pelt as it poised to spring; the dragon, iridescent scales sparkling in the moonlight; a woman with eyes blacker than night, skin white in the firelight.

Mist was growing easier with the rhythm, and Shadow was losing herself in the dance as she had the night she had watched Blade dance it. Then, she had been drawn into the dance as an insect into the spider's web; this time she spun her own web, and what the Mother Forest might choose to send into it Shadow had no idea.

The world had narrowed to earth and moonlight and the drumbeats that seemed to guide her feet. From far away she heard Donya's gasp, and the drum faltered ever so slightly; then small, callused brown fingers were twining with hers and catlike amber eyes twinkled merrily into her own.

So startled was Shadow that she nearly stopped where she was, but her dance partner would have none of it. Slender brown feet, twined with the designs of sparkling emerald vines, fit as neatly into the dance as a dagger into its sheath; strong, warm hands spun Shadow into an even wilder turn as the dance became something not of predator and prey, but perhaps something of two young wolves, heady with fresh air and swift blood, at play under a spring moon.

Shadow could hear Mist frantically trying to follow the dance, but she could spare him no sympathy; her own feet and lungs were hard-pressed to keep pace. The dance had become the dance of the Mother Forest as Shadow had always thought of Her, an image of fierce young life, of hot blood and swift limbs, of moonlight and moist earth and racing winds.

The question of what would give out first, Shadow's breath or Mist's hands, was solved when Shadow tripped over a root and abruptly measured her short length on the mossy earth. The fall had knocked the remaining wind out of her, and for a moment Shadow simply lay where she was, wheezing. Then small brown hands clasped hers, and Shadow was hauled to her feet by main force.

For once Chyrie's short, curly hair appeared to have been combed, and she was wearing what Shadow guessed was festival best. It would have been a crime to cover with clothing the marvelous twining green vines, some flowering and some ripe with golden berries, that ornamented Chyrie's brown skin, but there were earrings in her ears, bracelets on her wrists, and a pendant of exquisitely carved and polished beryl in the shape of an oak leaf at her throat.

Shadow had but the barest moment to appreciate the presence of her almost mythical friend; Chyrie's slit-pupiled eyes twinkled merrily, she touched Shadow's cheek gently, and then, like a breath of spring wind, she was gone.

Donya and Mist were still sitting rapt, staring at the spot where Chyrie had been. Shadow sighed once, then chuckled ruefully.

"Might as well not wait," she said. "She won't be back again tonight. I'm surprised she came at all."

"Have I gone mad," Mist said slowly, "or was that the wood sprite Aspen spoke of? He said that you knew her, but I thought—well, a spirit of the Mother Forest—"

Shadow laughed.

"She's *not* a wood sprite, nor a spirit of the Mother Forest either," she said, "although I doubt she's insulted by the mistake. She's an elf like you or me—well, I suppose she's not really all that much like you or me. But she's an elf; couldn't you see that? I mean, there was certainly nothing hidden!"

"She looked like an elf," Mist said doubtfully. "But who knows what form a spirit of the Mother Forest might take?"

"All right, then, she's a spirit of the Mother Forest," Shadow shrugged, grinning. "Who am I to say you're wrong? In that case, though, that's really going to be some gift she's left you!"

"Gift?" Mist said blankly. He looked down, then started violently as he saw the small packet lying on top of his drums. "She is in truth a spirit, to place it under my very view without my knowledge!"

"That's not so impressive," Donya chuckled weakly. "I've

seen Shadow do as much. I'd like to know how she came and went. I've seen mages appear and disappear less adroitly.''

"Even I've never seen her come and go," Shadow said. "Come on, Mist, let's see what it is."

Mist gingerly opened the packet, as if he expected its contents to leap out and bite him. Within the folded leather was a carved beryl leaf such as Chyric had worn, but this one hung on a short leather thong.

"Where're you supposed to wear that?" Donya asked curiously. "It's too short for even a bracelet.''

In answer, Mist tied the leaf to the end of one of his many dangling braids.

"Fortune favor me," Shadow groaned. "All you need is something to make you look even finer. Doe, it's a good thing the Gate will put us right into the palace, or else we'd never make it through the streets with him.''

"Please, you will make me vain," Mist grinned. "I would like to believe that my appearance is not my finest quality.''

"I'll have to grant you that," Shadow admitted. "Personally I think your finest quality is your—"

"—dancing," Donya finished firmly. "Shady, what's this?" She gestured at a rather large, leather-wrapped bundle on the altar.

"Well, it wasn't there when we got here," Shadow said patiently, "and I don't believe any of us put it there. Therefore I'd guess, since you were sitting right next to it, it's for you.''

"Why should she give me anything?" Donya asked slowly. "I'm not even an elf.''

"If she's a spirit of the Mother Forest, as Mist thinks," Shadow chuckled, "then it must be something to answer your prayer. But we won't know until you open it, will we?''

Donya prodded the bundle gingerly.

"I want to open this at the palace, where there's better light," she said, "and where I can have Mother look at it. This leather looks odd. Come on, Shady, if you're done, let's get home. This whole business has me very nervous, and the sooner there's someone else to look after our guest, the happier I'll be.''

"But wait," Mist protested. "Is there no gift for Shadow?''

Shadow shrugged, more disappointed that Donya would not open her gift than that she herself had none.

"I suppose not. Anyway, just seeing Chyrie again is enough—rare enough, anyway, and she danced with me, too. Remind me to tell you my story about her, Mist, on the way back. Doe's right, though; I could use a bath and a soft bed. To *sleep* in," Shadow added, winking at Mist.

"Oh, we will sleep," Mist assured her. "Eventually."

Donya packed her bundle carefully with her weapons and armor, on Shadow's doe. This gave Shadow the opportunity to give the leather a surreptitious poke or two; she could feel something long and solid inside, and something tube-shaped, but the leather was too thick to learn anything more.

Shadow sighed and scrambled onto her doe, reaching into her bundle for her wineskin. Something small nearly fell to the ground, and Shadow hastily grabbed for it. It was a small leather pouch that turned out to contain a small bone tube ornately carved with a familiar design of vine leaves.

"Is something wrong?" Donya called, squinting through the darkness. She was already mounted and her stag was moving out of the clearing.

"No, nothing," Shadow said hastily, shoving the small pouch into her sleeve. If Chyrie had concealed the pouch in her bundle instead of giving it to her openly, there must be a reason.

The return trip to Inner Heart was quicker than the trip out; the sky was lightening and the deer moved more quickly, likely anxious to be rid of their burdens. When the deer abandoned them at the fringes of the village, Donya lifted the sleeping stranger, leaving her bundle for Mist.

Inner Heart was a good deal quieter than when they had left. The bustle of preparation had been replaced by a few drowsily stumbling elves on their way to their beds or indulging in a last halfhearted cup or plate. Other elves were asleep where they had come to rest, lulled by an excess of food, liquor, dancing, and/or other bodily exertions. Donya, Shadow, and Mist moved as quietly as they could through the village, stepping around or sometimes over sleeping elves. There was no sign of Aspen; Shadow hoped that the Patriarch had found some enjoyment after his patience, and made a mental note to herself to have a message sent via the Gate when they arrived in the palace.

Donya grumbled that the deer did not remain until they reached the Gate, as the stranger was not much shorter than Donya herself and no small burden; then she grumbled that they had not had the forethought or materials to make a litter. Shadow sighed patiently and ignored it. During the years of their travels together it had usually been Shadow doing the grumbling, as the elf was fond of her comforts; Donya's rare ill temper, Shadow knew, owed much to exhaustion, anxiety, puzzlement, and probably some lingering embarrassment.

Mist apparently felt none of Shadow's apprehension about Gates, for he followed Donya through without hesitation. On reflection, Shadow remembered what Aspen had said—that elvan magic flowed stronger and more frequently among the Hidden Folk; doubtless Mist was accustomed to even more impressive sights.

There were few stirring at the palace, either, but that didn't stop Donya from ringing for the servants as soon as they arrived. She saw the stranger bedded and guarded in an inside guest room, then bulldozed Shadow and Mist into taking a nap at the palace, over Shadow's protests that she should get back to the Guild.

"You might as well sleep here as there," Donya said practically. "You aren't going to be giving any orders or solving any crises for a few hours, at least, and there's no chance you'll get that bath you want at the Guild this time of the morning. I'll send a messenger to the Guild so anyone can reach you here if they need to, and when we all wake up, we'll see what Celene says about our guest and my gift."

Despite Shadow's token protests, she was more than happy to give in and be ministered to by a flock of eager, if yawning, servants. Palace luxury suited her perfectly, and this time there was the added enjoyment of experiencing them with a wide-eyed, awestruck, and often amusingly confused Mist. He had heard of Allanmere's hot springs and bathing pools, magically drilled from deep beneath the earth, but had never actually seen one. He had never been attended by a bevy of servants eager to obey, if not anticipate, his every wish; he had never been clothed in silk nightclothes or been housed in a room large enough to encompass ten of the huts at Inner Heart, where a huge fireplace drove away any hint of spring chill and damp and where a huge down bed could have accommodated an entire High Circle. Mist wandered gingerly around the room while Shadow combed out and braided her damp hair, cautiously sampling tidbits from the snack tray left for them and then staring out the window at the Brightwater River.

"What's the matter?" Shadow said as she coiled her braids into place. "Aren't you ready to sleep for a few hours?"

"Are we not to meet someone?" Mist asked confusedly, plucking at the silk of his nightshirt.

Shadow chuckled.

"Even with an elvan High Lady, almost everyone here thinks like a human," she explained. "Humans have special clothes they sleep in. You don't have to wear them."

Mist grimaced, stripped off the pajamas, then amused himself vastly for a few minutes crawling about the feather bed.

"Never have I slept on a pile of furs so soft," he vowed. "And such a luxury is wasted, for I could sleep equally well now on cold rock. Come and warm me at least, lest I become lost in this huge pillow, and let us sleep as we can before your friend summons us."

Shadow grinned, wagering to herself that she'd get little enough sleep, if any, with such a bedfellow; however, when she pinned the last braid in place, hung her nightgown over a chair, and crawled into the huge bed, she found Mist sound asleep and snoring.

Shadow sighed contentedly, curled close to his warmth, and was asleep before she had time to pull up the covers.

"Wake up, Shady."

Shadow groaned, stretched, and yawned hugely.

"Morning, Doe."

Donya grinned and sat down on the edge of the bed.

"It's noon, or a very little past. Better get up. Celene was in audience this morning, and as soon as she finishes and changes clothes she'll see our guest. I've ordered dinner brought to his room in about an hour. Meet us there then, if you can.''

"All right." Shadow glanced over amusedly; Mist was still sleeping soundly. "If I can roust him out by then, anyway."

"Oh, I'm sure you'll think of something," Donya said, chuckling. She gave Shadow a wink and left as quietly as she had come.

Shadow leaned over Mist and tickled his cheek with the end of one long braid that had come loose.

"Wake up, lover."

Mist only snored louder.

Shadow bent over and began to tickle his nose with the end, only to yelp with surprise as Mist opened his eyes wide and seized her, flipping her over and pinning her to the bed.

"You are a vixen," he chuckled. "Have you no pity for a sleeping man wearied by a busy festival?"

"None at all," Shadow laughed. "And have you no pity for a poor city elf whose friend is anxiously awaiting her presence?"

Mist bent down to kiss her, then mischievously nipped the end of her nose.

"None at all," he said.

Donya and Celene were already awaiting them in the stranger's room, where two guards admitted them. Donya, looking so weary that Shadow wondered whether her friend had slept at all, was helping herself to cheese and wine from a tray; Celene, sitting in a chair beside the bed, was gesturing at a map that their guest, fully awake and babbling animatedly in an odd tongue, was holding.

"There you are," Celene said, relieved. "Come and see, Shadow, if you can make anything of his language. I've never left this area and know only a few foreign tongues. I've managed to puzzle out that his name is Farryn, and that he comes from somewhere to the north, but I think he's starting to get impatient with me."

"In a moment, in a moment," Shadow laughed. "You should know me well enough by now to know that you won't get anything out of me until I've had some wine. This is Mist, Celene, Aspen's representative.''

"Oh, yes," Celene smiled. "I've heard of you—the sword dancer, aren't you? My pleasure, kinsman. I hope you'll forgive my rudeness. Come *on,* now, Shadow, I'm perishing of curiosity.''

"All right, all right," Shadow laughed, grabbing a mug of wine and a chunk of cheese as she joined Celene at the bedside. "That map isn't going to do you any good, Celene; it's the one he brought, isn't it?''

"He seemed so eager to show it to us," Celene apologized. "But of course I can't see what he's trying to tell us. It's badly out-of-date, of course, and not very accurate to begin with. The Brightwater's course is all wrong, the Dim Reaches are far too small, and the shape of the forest is askew. I'd say it dates back to around the Black Wars, wouldn't you think?''

"It might look like that at first," Shadow said thoughtfully. "But look here. The western edge of the forest didn't come out this far even before the Black Wars; my mother said a flood had expanded the Dim Reaches and swallowed that part of the forest hundreds of years before. I'd say this predates even the first human settlement of the area by decades, if not centuries. What would you say, Mist? You probably know more about the historical aspects than I do.''

Mist scrutinized the map.

"It is not inaccurate," he said slowly. "It is simply very, very old—the layout, I mean; this is obviously a new and rather hasty copy.'' He tapped the representation of the Brightwater River. "The river has not flowed thus for well over a thousand years—since the great flood you mentioned. But the shape of the forest is even more significant, for the eastern edge was burned by a great fire long before. I am no lore-keeper, but I would suggest that this map shows the land as it existed twenty centuries or more ago.''

"Two thousand years!" Donya exclaimed, stepping over to look at the map. "Where can this fellow have been that that's the best map he could come up with?''

"Well, obviously somewhere very far away," Shadow said.

"More than that he'll have to tell us himself, I'll wager. Well, let's see, then."

She faced their guest, who had attended their conversation with somewhat desperate eagerness.

"Farryn?" she asked, pointing to him.

"Farryn!" he repeated, nodding vigorously and thumping his own chest with a six-fingered hand. "Celene," he said, gesturing at Celene, although he pronounced it *Saleen*, "Donya." *Don-eee-yah.* He raised his eyebrows inquiringly at Shadow and Mist.

"Mist," Shadow said, pointing to her friend. "Shadow." She pointed to herself.

"Missch," Farryn agreed. "Shad-owww."

"Good enough," Shadow agreed. "You're right, Celene, that sounds like a northern accent. Let's see—Ramant is the largest northern trade city I know. Let's see what he can do with Karnstian." Switching to that language and speaking slowly, she asked, "Can you understand me?"

Farryn listened intently, but only shook his head and sighed sadly when she finished.

"Farther north than Ramant?" Shadow guessed. "Some of the northern merchants speak Ransti. It's worth a try." She tried again, and this time Farryn scowled as if he almost understood her. When she finished he spoke again—a different language than he had used before.

Celene leaned forward at Shadow's surprised expression. "Did you understand him?"

"I don't know," Shadow said slowly. "Almost. Something about houses. It sounds almost like Isseldik—one of the nomadic dialects, maybe. I don't know much Isseldik, though."

"You speak now?" she said with difficulty, in Isseldik.

"You understand!" he said excitedly. "Honor—" something, something, "house. Important that I" something, "find" something, "warn all, very" something "danger. Understand?"

Regretfully, Shadow shook her head. Farryn sagged in disappointment.

"He speaks Isseldik, all right, or some form of it," Shadow

said. "But it's not his native language, and he doesn't speak it
much better than I do. I did manage to understand that he wants
to deliver some kind of warning, and he wants to find
something. It seems important, at least to him. But I don't
know how we're going to find out what he wants, short of a
translation spell or someone who speaks Isseldik a lot better
than I do."

"Better a translation spell, then," Donya said grimly.
"Whatever his warning may be, I don't know that we want to
have it babbled to everyone in town."

"I'm no expert in such spells," Celene said, shaking her
head. "Aliendra is the only mage I know who specializes in
divination and language spells, and because of her usual—
well—clientele, she is usually not amenable to official re-
quests."

"I'll ask her," Shadow said. "I was meaning to visit her
shop anyway. If somebody will reimburse me for whatever it
costs, that is."

"I might have known," Donya laughed. "Well, it *is* a city
matter, Mother; don't you think the coffers can stand the
cost?"

"Of course," Celene chuckled. "It's only fair, after all. But
whatever your private business with Aliendra, Guildmistress, I
don't expect the city to pay for *that*."

Farryn had observed this exchange, his brow furrowed as if
he could make himself understand their words by main force.
Now he put his hand on Shadow's arm as if to restrain her and
burst forth anew, so fast that Shadow caught only the words
"find" and "warn."

"No, no," Shadow said, trying to dredge up the proper
Isseldik words. "Wait. Need—" she shook her head. "Need—
magic to speak."

Farryn's eyes widened and he gabbled something in his own
language, obviously very excited; then he shook his head and
said something equally unintelligible in Isseldik.

"What was that?" Donya asked.

"I don't know," Shadow said, shrugging. "Something
about 'carrying light.' I give up, Doe. Let's wait until we get a
translation spell. I'm doing good to say 'which way to the

privy' in Isseldik. He is looking a lot healthier, though, isn't he?''

"Oh, yes," Celene smiled. "Healer Auderic said he wasn't very ill at all; mostly extreme exhaustion, I gather. He's still weak, though. I was worried that perhaps he'd caught whatever disease is going around Allanmere. It's very serious.''

"Disease?" Shadow asked, Donya echoing her with equal astonishment. "I hadn't heard anything about a disease.''

"The first cases were only reported day before yesterday,'' Celene said, frowning worriedly. "Already it's spreading quickly. Several people have died, and Auderic is worried it may reach plague proportions.''

"Only two days and it's that bad?" Donya asked, aghast. "Where can such a serious disease have come from with no warning at all?''

"I have no idea," Celene said frustratedly. "Auderic's representatives have already questioned and examined all the foreign trade caravans. None of them came from any place with any such sickness, nor did their goods. It seems to have sprung up out of nowhere.''

"That settles it," Shadow said decisively. "I've got to get back to the Guild right now. They weren't expecting me to be gone overnight to begin with, and then I saw Aubry at the festival. I don't want to leave the Guild alone with a threat of plague in the city. Maybe my people have some news, anyway.''

"I hope someone does," Celene sighed. "But please, Shadow, don't forget to see Aliendra. You can imagine how important it is.''

"I can do that on my way back to the Guild," Shadow promised. "Mist deserves a chance to see the city. But, Doe, don't I get to see what was in that bundle Chyrie gave you?''

"Oh, that," Donya said, her face brightening. "Come on and let's see.''

Donya had brought the bundle from her quarters. At Donya's request, Celene ran her hands gently over the bundle before untying the thongs.

"There's a strong preservation spell here," Celene said thoughtfully. "It has an odd—well—flavor, is the best way I can express it, as if the magic was done in an entirely different way than I've ever seen, but it *is* only a harmless preservation spell. Shall I open it?''

''Go ahead,'' Donya said.

Celene carefully untied the thong, then paused.

''Do you know, I've never seen this particular leather before,'' she said, fingering the wrapping. ''It has a very unusual texture—rather like a reptile, perhaps, or that outlandish sea-fish leather I sometimes see southern merchants selling.''

Shadow looked at the leather, sniffed it.

''Just like that, really, or maybe eelskin,'' she said. ''It even has a kind of a musky, marshy smell to it. Smells just like the Dim Reaches, in fact. I wonder how long that particular odor's been preserved?''

''Look at this,'' Donya said wonderingly, flipping aside the leather to expose an exquisitely tooled scabbard of apparently the same leather. The odd designs made Shadow frown, wondering where she'd seen their like before. Nor was the scabbard empty. A plain leather-wrapped hilt, sweat-stained but otherwise in perfect condition, protruded at the top.

''It is unusually long in the hilt,'' Mist commented. ''Such a hilt would be made for a large hand.''

''No,'' Shadow said. ''Anyone that large would have a longer sword. Besides, look. The grasp's a little thick for me, but it's just right for Donya. She's tall, true, but most human men are nearly as tall, and their hands are larger; but look how long the hilt is on her.''

Donya carefully drew the sword, and they fell silent. The strange pale metal and its obvious lightness were unmistakable.

''No wonder the hilt was so long,'' Mist murmured. ''It was made to a six-fingered hand.''

Farryn darted forward, his eyes wide, speaking so rapidly and excitedly that even had he used Isseldik—which, in his agitation, he did not—Shadow could never have understood a word of it. He reached out as if to wrench the sword from Donya's grasp. Donya quickly held it away from him, even as both Mist and Shadow reached automatically for their daggers. Farryn glanced quickly at the three of them and subsided reluctantly to the other side of the room, his face furrowed with frustration.

"Farryn's scabbard was plain," Shadow remembered, slowly resheathing her dagger when it became obvious that the tense moment had passed. "But these designs—by Fortune's right hand, I'd swear I've seen something like it before. I wish I could remember where. Seems like Farryn knows, at least."

"But there's more," Celene said. There was a bone scroll-case in the bundle, carved in similar designs. Donya picked it up, probing at the ends, but could find no opening.

"Want to give it a try?" Donya said, handing it to Shadow.

Shadow scrutinized the scrollcase closely, twisting it carefully this way and that, but could find no crack or catch.

"It would be a shame to damage the case," Mist said, "but doubtless the contents are important, for it to be given you in such a manner."

"Well, let's not *break* it," Shadow said quickly. "I can get it open one way or another."

"Are you still wearing that bracelet?" Celene asked, amazed.

"It's safer on my wrist than in storage," Shadow shrugged. "Besides, I never know when I might need it. Anyway, half of Allanmere knows I own the thing, and most often it's the half of Allanmere I wouldn't want to know it."

"What bracelet?" Mist asked curiously.

"This one," Shadow said, pushing up her sleeve to display the silver filigree set with blue-green skystones circling her left wrist.

Mist touched the delicate-looking design of leaves and vines.

"This is Aspen's work, is it not?" he asked.

Shadow sighed exasperatedly.

"Where were you about two years ago?" Shadow demanded. "You could've saved me an *awful* lot of trouble."

"My lady, I would flay my own hide with a dull knife and bathe in salt to spare you the slightest difficulty," Mist said, sweeping an exaggeratedly gallant bow. "However, two years ago I was deep in the Heartwood and had never heard the sweet music of your name, save for odd tales of a sly and rambling elf

who had departed the Heartwood long ago, leaving it bereft of
its greatest trickster.''

"All right, all right," Shadow laughed. "Point made. Now
let's see about this case." She clasped it in her left hand,
covering as much of the surface as her small fingers could.
"Aufrhyr."

Under her hand the entire tube seemed to shift; the upper half
of the tube divided into quarters, and two of them slid up and
over. Shadow lifted the moved sections off easily, exposing a
tightly rolled sheet within.

The parchment, nurtured by the preservation spell, was as
crisp and fresh as the day it had been sealed in its case. It was
sealed with red wax, imprinted with a design Shadow had seen
before—a stylized eye, such as that depicted on the amulet
Farryn wore.

"Should I break it?" Shadow asked Donya.

"You may as well," Donya shrugged. "It's not going to do
us any good sealed."

Shadow carefully broke the seal, then gently unrolled the
parchment. Besides being rolled tightly, it was folded over
three times, so that the resulting sheet covered the table on
which it lay.

Given the seal and the nature of the sword, Shadow was not
overly surprised to see a map similar to the one Farryn had
brought, in the sense that Shadow's bracelet was similar to one
of crudely hammered tin and glass gems. This was no hastily
penned copy; this was an original, meticulously drawn and
finely detailed in what Shadow supposed was as fine a script as
she'd ever seen.

"Look here," Mist said, pointing to the bottom of the map.
There were two lines of intricate characters there—solid lines,
unbroken by spaces or any punctuation Shadow could identify.
The characters themselves were so intricate and ornate that
Shadow wondered whether they were indeed letters or perhaps
an ornamental border. Farryn left his bed to look over their
shoulders, but did not interfere.

"This map was drawn from the same period as the other,"
Celene said, indicating the shape of the Heartwood and the
course of the Brightwater River.

"What's this?" Donya asked, pointing to the swamp area. Two areas were clearly marked, one with a small cluster of flat-side-down hemispheres, and another, farther to the west, with the stylized eye.

"Maybe directions for good fishing," Celene said wryly. "That part of the Reaches, from what maps I've seen, is wet marsh most of the year. In fact, this part"—she tapped the eye—"is probably submerged entirely during spring floods."

"This is interesting," Shadow said, tapping several symbols drawn at various points at the western edge of the forest.

"What are those?" Donya asked. "Old Olvenic, isn't it?"

"*Old* Old Olvenic," Shadow answered. "You've seen the zone markers, haven't you?"

"Well, yes," Donya said warily. "But they're farther into the forest, aren't they?"

"Indeed they are," Mist answered. "And these are not zone markers, for when these markers were placed, there were no zones. These are original territorial markers for the border tribes. See, here are the symbols for Brightfur, Hilltop, and Windlight. Strange—I thought Swiftwater was more to the north."

"I don't know if there's any elf alive today in the Heartwood who ever saw the forest as it's depicted here," Celene said. "If I should hear that Swiftwater had moved centuries ago, I wouldn't be too surprised. Remember, before the alliance territorial squabbles were as common as brown leaves in autumn."

"This is all very interesting, and probably important," Shadow said, "but I've *got* to start back to the Guild."

"Hmmm?" Donya said, dragging her attention away from the sword. "All right. Send a message if you learn anything important."

Shadow chuckled, leaving Donya admiring the sword and Celene and Farryn pondering over the map.

"Donya with a new sword," Shadow grinned at Mist as they found their way out of the palace. "Might as well turn me loose in the palace treasury, for all she'd care now."

"I still find it odd that one would make a life from stealing," Mist confessed. "Aubry has spoken to me of it many times. I would not offend you, but what pride is there in living off the work of others, giving no return?''

''Pride?'' Shadow thought for a moment. ''Mist, do you like to hunt?''

''Of course,'' Mist answered, as if astonished that she would ask. ''It is my living, hunting and trading the meat and skins.''

''Well, there you go,'' Shadow said. ''What makes a good hunter? As opposed to any old amateur with a bow and arrows, I mean.''

Mist was silent for a moment.

''Skill, of course,'' he said. ''I do not understand.''

''The problem is that it's become so automatic to you that you don't think about it,'' Shadow said affectionately, waving at the guards as they passed out the front gate. ''What do you mean by 'skill'? There's several parts to it, you know—wisdom to choose good weapons; dexterity and accuracy with your arrows; a good eye, ear, and nose; experience and knowledge of the ways of your prey; skill at moving quietly and hiding yourself; a sense of timing; intuition—is it going to dodge this way or that?—and, of course, luck. Not to mention all kinds of related skills, like judging the weather, reading tracks and spoor, knowing the sounds of the forest, and all that. If you're good at what you do, you come back with a full game bag, and you've done well. You get to eat, and you get the fruits of your work—whatever you trade for. And sometimes, when you track down a really difficult target, when you push those skills to the limit, you get something more—the pride of an artist who can do something that most others in the trade can't.

''Thieving's just the same,'' Shadow continued. ''You need a good eye and ear, you need to have the experience to choose the right tools, dexterity and speed, knowledge of your target, a quick and quiet hand and foot, timing, intuition, and luck. If I do all those things well, if I'm well prepared, quick and quiet and smart, I get to eat and I get the fruits of my work—whatever I steal, or whatever I sell or trade it for. And when I take a really difficult mark, I'm just as proud as any artist who can do something that the others can't.''

''But I do not hunt my own kind,'' Mist argued.

"And my prey ends up poorer, but alive," Shadow shrugged. "You take the excess bounty of the forest, I take the excess bounty of the rich."

Mist frowned thoughtfully.

"I see the similarities," he said. "Although Aubry seemed proud of his skill, I could see nothing in it but greed and perhaps laziness or lack of any marketable skill."

Shadow chuckled.

"My reply to that, if anybody else said it, would be to dare you to try to steal something. Oh, there's easy marks out there, just as there's the occasional stupid rabbit that sits there and mopes while you walk up to it and kill it. But there aren't many, and the skilled thieves go for the tougher marks with more money to make it worth their while."

"How can you tell an easy—mark—from a difficult one?" Mist asked curiously.

"Well, there's an example for you," Shadow said, pointing to a knife merchant's stall. "He's a more difficult mark—been robbed before, probably, and he's learned to protect himself. See, his knives are stacked touching each other, so it'd be hard to pull one out without moving the others and making some noise. He's arranged his stall so he can see all of his merchandise at the same time, and you can see he doesn't go to one side or another, he lets the customer come to him at the middle."

"I see," Mist said, taking a second look at the nearby merchants. "Most of them do not take such precautions. How can they watch such a horde of people?"

"They don't," Shadow answered. "That's why large trade cities like Allanmere are a thief's paradise."

"Do it, then," Mist said suddenly. "Steal something."

"What, now?" Shadow asked.

"Now," Mist grinned. "I would like to see you do it."

"Well, if I do it right," Shadow laughed, "you *won't* see me do it. What shall I steal?"

"Whatever you like," Mist said.

Shadow shrugged. "Would you like a meat pie?"

"All right."

Shadow pulled two coppers out of her pouch and handed it to him. "Let's go, then, and ask for two."

The pie merchant smiled expansively at Mist as they approached; then, when he saw Shadow, the smile wavered and his hand went reflexively to his belt pouch.

"Good day, Guildmistress!" he boomed quickly. "What can I do for you and your friend this fine afternoon? My pies are fresh and hot and spiced to please a discriminating customer, and only a copper a pie!"

"We will have two," Mist said rather uncertainly, handing over the coppers.

The merchant quickly scooped up the coppers, never taking his eye off Shadow. Even as he scooped two pies out of the bubbling fat and onto bark platters, he darted nervous glances over his shoulder at his customers. Shadow smiled at him innocently, stepping around two arguing nobles to accept her pie.

Mist looked at Shadow expectantly as they walked away, blowing on their pies to cool them.

"Where is the pie you stole?" he said.

"Steal a pie?" Shadow said, lifting one eyebrow. "I never said I was going to steal a pie."

"But I thought—" Mist began puzzledly.

"Steal a hot pie and burn my arm off?" Shadow laughed. "Not me."

She patted a jingling bulge in her sleeve. "But I did get the purses of both the nobles standing next to the pie cart."

Mist stopped where he was, mouth agape. Then he laughed heartily and bit into his pie.

"As one hunter might drive the prey toward the other," he grinned.

"Rather like that," Shadow agreed. "An old trick, but a good one. I encourage my newer thieves to work in tandem like that. It's much easier."

"But you are the Guildmistress," Mist protested. "Surely you have no need of such ploys."

Shadow shrugged.

"I usually have a little more setup time to study my marks," she said. "You wanted me to steal something right then.

Besides, while I might take bigger chances alone, I couldn't risk getting caught with you there. You're new to the city and wouldn't know where to run if someone raised a cry. Anyway, this way it's partly your theft, too.'' She pulled out one of the purses and handed it to him. "Your share."

Mist looked blankly at the purse.

"I have never had coin before," he said uncertainly. "Besides, you are the one who earned it.''

"If you happened to be hunting with a friend, and he startled the stag toward you so you could get a good shot," Shadow said practically, "wouldn't you give him his share of the meat?"

"I suppose I would," Mist said at last, pocketing the pouch. "But I feel I did nothing."

"If you really want to learn thievery, I'll teach you," Shadow said, "but you have talents enough without. If you're really interested, and you stay in town long enough, I'll set up something complex and let you see how it works. Not take you with me, of course, but you could see the planning and the diagrams and so forth."

"I would like that," Mist said. "Very much." He hesitated. "But should I not be staying at the palace near the prisoner?"

"If Celene and her magic and all the Palace Guard can't keep him in, you wouldn't be much help," Shadow said practically. "Besides, are you so eager to be rid of me already?"

Mist smiled. "Not just yet," he said, taking her hand and placing a kiss in the palm.

He was making a determined attempt to be cheerful, but Shadow could see that the crowd of humanity unnerved him, and no wonder; she doubted if he'd ever seen more than one or two humans at a time in his life, and Inner Heart, while populous by elvan standards, was only a tiny village next to Allanmere. Even the bustle and hurry of the festival was nothing in comparison to the noise and crowds of the market-place, although the market was unusually empty today.

"We'll take a carriage the rest of the way," Shadow said, taking pity on his confusion. It wasn't far to Guild Row, but most of the wagons came in from the south, the direction in which they were traveling.

Mist was more comfortable viewing Allanmere from the protection of the carriage, although both the luxury of the carriage and the entire process of paying someone for transport mystified him. He marveled at the shops, wagons, pushcarts, and booths selling a variety of goods he had rarely imagined, much less seen.

"We'll stop just briefly at Aliendra's shop," Shadow said. "It'd be better if you wait in the carriage, if you don't mind."

"Very well," Mist said, although he looked at Shadow curiously.

Aliendra's shop was much as Shadow remembered it from nearly two years earlier. Shadow found Aliendra in the same place, behind the counter, a dark human woman clothed in gray, with a voice as gray as her robe.

"I once forbade you my shop," she said.

"I'd say the circumstances have changed," Shadow said. "Wouldn't you agree? I've sent a good bit of business your way since then, at least."

"I'll grant you that," Aliendra said tonelessly. "Well, my shop has always been at the service of the Guild of Thieves. How may I serve you, Guildmistress?"

"Two services, for which I'll pay handsomely if you succeed," Shadow told her. "First, a spell of translation to the common tongue. Do you need to know the origin language?"

"It would help," Aliendra shrugged. "A broader spell is more difficult, and will cost you more dearly."

"Then I'll pay more dearly," Shadow said. "Unfortunately we don't know the language. I know the fellow speaks a little Isseldik, but I don't think he speaks it very well, so I wouldn't suggest using that."

Aliendra nodded.

"Such a spell will cost you two hundred Suns," she said. "It will enable the speaker to speak and understand the common tongue."

Shadow grimaced. "Duration?"

"Indefinite. I will enchant an object to hold the spell."

"All right," Shadow agreed. "When can you have it?"

"Tomorrow morning," Aliendra said after a moment's thought. "If your second task does not overburden me."

"It won't," Shadow assured her. She drew from her pouch the small bone flask Chyrie had given her. "I'd like to know the nature of the contents of this vial."

Aliendra sighed explosively. "Guildmistress Shadow—"

"Don't worry," Shadow laughed. "This one won't get you into any trouble. It's an honest gift, I swear it."

"Then why did the giver not tell you its nature?" Aliendra grumbled, nonetheless taking the vial.

"I don't know," Shadow grinned. "Probably her strange idea of a joke."

Aliendra opened the vial and sniffed the contents, raised an eyebrow, and peered into the vial. She moistened her fingertip from it, touched the liquid to the tip of her tongue, then hastily spat it out on the floor. She capped the vial and rinsed her mouth several times with wine.

"A joke it may have been," Aliendra said at last, "but an expensive one, if so. This potion I have heard called Midnight Dew, and it is a powerful love potion."

"A *love potion*?" Shadow asked incredulously. "Are you sure?"

Aliendra scowled at Shadow.

"As Guildmistress, I trust that you know your work," she said irritatedly. "If you wish to patronize my shop, I suggest you trust my expertise."

"I didn't mean to doubt you," Shadow said hurriedly. "I was just—well—very surprised, considering who gave it to me, and considering that she gave it to *me,* it just seemed a little odd. It doesn't seem like something I'd ever use."

"If you don't want the potion, I would happily buy it from you," Aliendra said, looking for the first time almost friendly. "In fact, I would take the potion in whole payment for the translation spell and give you another hundred Suns besides."

Shadow hesitated. The offer was tempting, but since Chyrie had given it to her—

"No, I'd better keep it, at least for now," she said regretfully. "But if I decide not to, I promise I'll come here first. How does the stuff work, anyway?"

"It's a very powerful potion," Aliendra told her. "As little as a drop in a glass of wine is enough. It used to be—and sometimes still is—especially popular with those who were the mistresses of nobles. Upon drinking, in a very short time it will increase sexual desire, although not to an extreme degree. If the drinker beds his lover, however, his affections will become powerfully fixed on her. The potion takes at least several months to wear off, if indeed it does; but that's hard to say, for when I've seen it used and it resulted in the desired match, natural love may have taken the place of the spell. Midnight Dew is illegal, of course, and has largely fallen out of the market, but it is still in demand. If you have a source, we could make a very profitable arrangement."

Shadow sighed.

"No, I'm afraid this is probably a one-of-a-kind item," she said. "I wish I could oblige you. Well, what do I owe you? I'll pay for the translation spell now, if you'll have it delivered to me at the Guild whenever it's ready."

"Very well," Aliendra said. "Two hundred Suns for the translation spell, and you'll have it tomorrow morning. I will charge no fee for identification of the potion, on the condition that, as you promised, if you decide to dispose of it—or any part of it, I might add—you will come to me first."

"Agreed, with pleasure," Shadow grinned. "It's worth it just to have the use of your services again." She counted out twenty 10-Sun pieces and handed them to the mage.

Aliendra half smiled rather grudgingly.

"Despite the excitement you manage to attract," she said, "I am forced to admit that Guild Row is a better—and safer—place to work than before you took the seat, and my clientele of a better quality."

Shadow gave Aliendra the short bow that a Guildmistress might make to one of equal rank.

"Thanks, and Fortune favor you," she said. "I look forward to a long and mutually profitable relationship between the Guild of Thieves and your establishment." She held out her hand.

Aliendra hesitated, then nodded and took the proffered hand.

"Long and profitable," she repeated, "and doubtless very interesting."

Mist was looking rather restless when Shadow returned to pay the carriage and lead him down the street to the Guild.

"Will she do the spell?" he asked anxiously.

"By tomorrow morning," Shadow said. "She'll send it over to us, which means we'll have to take it to the palace. I don't know if she'd have even done it if she'd known it was for the High Lord and Lady, or at least she'd have gouged me for three times the price. Well, come on, and I'll show you around the Guildhouse."

The Guildhouse was only a short distance down the street. Like many buildings in Allanmere, the Guildhouse was made of stone because the Compact severely limited tree-cutting, and because stone could be ferried down relatively cheaply from a quarry not far to the northwest. The Guildhouse was both tall and wide, and since Shadow's assumption of the seat it was an impressive-looking building. The front face stones were scrubbed down every spring; the wooden walkway, shutters, floors, and fixtures were kept polished and a preservation spell laid on them. The battered furniture within had been replaced. A small bar in one corner was all that remained of the Guild's kitchen, but a passageway had been added to open into the kitchen of the inn next door, with which Shadow had made a mutually satisfactory arrangement for meals when necessary.

"What a large building!" Mist murmured. "Most of the inhabitants of Inner Heart could be housed herein."

"Most of the downstairs is the common room, and a bunkroom for Guild members who need temporary housing," Shadow explained. "There're meeting rooms in part of the basement and part of the upper floor. The rest of the upper floor's my quarters and offices, and the rest of the basement's the Guild treasury, the storage room, and the wine cellar."

There were a few Guild members lounging outside or wandering over from the Crusty Bun next door. To Shadow's relief, nothing seemed amiss; most of the Guild members gave her a smile or a wave or called out a greeting.

Estar, a competent thief and Shadow's occasional assistant, was sitting at the desk at the back of the common room; when

Shadow entered, she heaved a huge sigh of relief and came forward.

"Guildmistress! At last! We've been waiting and worrying, you gone with just that little note, and Aubry gone, too, and what with plague in the city—"

"Relax, relax," Shadow said. "Just tell me the news—the *important* news, if you please, and we'll see what to do from there."

"There's three new fellows wanting membership," Estar said. "Two are good enough but the third'll want apprenticing. The guard picked up Molwyn again."

Shadow groaned. "How much did they want this time?"

"Fifty Suns," Estar sighed. "I don't know if they'll ransom him if they pick him up again."

"All right, that's it, then," Shadow said after a moment. "Five times is too many. Tell Molwyn he owes us the fifty, and he can either redo his apprenticeship until I decide he's fit, or his membership's revoked and he can leave town. His choice. What else?"

"Uriss finally paid his dues," Estar said. "In full, with interest."

"Must've hit a fat mark," Shadow said. "Good for him."

"Not so good. The mark he hit was in the Bun. Sterin complained."

Shadow groaned again.

"Fortune blight his balls. Reimburse Sterin and I'll take it out of Uriss's hide when I get the chance. Fortune favor me, I'm away two days and the whole Guild goes to the cesspits."

"I'm sorry," Estar said humbly. "Aubry wasn't here and they just don't listen to me. There isn't anything much else, though."

"Good." Shadow turned to Mist. "Mist, this is Estar; Estar, Mist. Now, what's this about plague?"

Estar frowned again.

"Haven't you heard? There's folks dying, they say. First ones dropped right in the market."

"Any of ours?" Shadow asked.

"I don't know. Nobody's said anything."

"Put the word out," Shadow said. "I want to know where

this started, how many's died and where, where they'd been, all that. I mean, is this just Rivertown-level crud, or did it come in from outside?''

"All right," Estar said. "I'll talk to the usual people. When will Aubry be back, do you know?"

"He's at the Planting of the Seed," Shadow said dismally. "Two more nights, plus two days to ride back, at the earliest. If he takes a caravan, longer. And blight his sorry hide for running off without saying anything, too.''

"I'm sure he didn't mean any harm, Guildmistress," Estar said. "He probably thought you'd be here. I mean, you've never gone to the festival before.''

Shadow sighed again and shook her head.

"Never mind for now. Have somebody bring up a bottle of something good, will you?"

Shadow's rooms had once been several meeting rooms plus Ganrom's quarters; with the removal of a few walls and considerable cleaning, it was now a positively sybaritic suite with a huge fireplace and a bed easily as large as the one they had slept in at the palace.

"This is yours alone?" Mist asked, surprised.

"All mine," Shadow said. "Not alone too often, though, if I can help it. Kind of big and lonesome, isn't it?"

Mist chuckled.

"That is what I would have said. For the Guildmistress of the Guild of Thieves, though—"

"Oh, please," Shadow said dismally. "Don't start. Can you imagine how many thieves want to end up in this room with me?"

"What, to be the lover of the Guildmistress?" Mist asked.

"That, or to stick a dagger into me while I'm sleeping," Shadow said wryly. "Which I don't do all that much of, what with emergencies and ruckus downstairs."

"Then why not stay at an inn?" Mist suggested.

"First, I'm safer here," Shadow said. She opened the door again, picked up the bottle of wine placed outside, and closed the door again. "Second, this way, when the emergencies come up, all I have to do is go downstairs instead of across town in the middle of the night. And if I wasn't available to the Guild whenever they need me—well, you can see what happened in two days.''

Mist grimaced. ''I would not want to be so burdened.''

''Neither would I, my friend,'' Shadow agreed. ''Believe me, it wasn't any intention of mine to do it. I got trapped into it.''

''Then why not stop?'' Mist asked. ''Why not let one of those who want the seat have it?''

''I plan to,'' Shadow said firmly. ''I've been grooming Aubry for the seat since the day I took it—well, since I recovered from taking it, anyway. Has he told you that story?''

''Indeed, in great and I fear exaggerated detail,'' Mist chuckled.

''For once I doubt it,'' Shadow grinned. ''That story doesn't need any embellishing. Anyway, I've spent almost two years cleaning up the mess that Ganrom left the Guild in, and I'm not going to have all that work undone by dumping the Guild into the hands of the first power-hungry pickpocket who wants it. I owe that much to Donya, who has to put up with the Guild in the first place, and to the folks who need it and who've backed me up through this whole nastiness. Call it professional pride, if nothing else.''

''Aubry is a responsible fellow,'' Mist suggested. ''If you took the Guild with no preparation at all and brought it to its present status, why could not Aubry, who has been trained by you, take it now?''

''He's not ready,'' Shadow said sadly. ''He's too nice to kick people when they need kicking and to step on the ones who need stepping on. He's become an excellent thief, but he hasn't got the sense of managing a Guild yet—obviously, if he runs off and doesn't tell anyone where he can be reached or when he'll be back.''

''You ran off to the same festival,'' Mist pointed out.

''Ah, *but*,'' Shadow said triumphantly. ''*But* I did so at an official request from the Heir; *but* I sent a message saying where I'd be and how long; *but* I traveled by Gate so I'd be back the next day. Besides, when a Guildmistress does that, it's called delegating; when a would-be Guildmaster does it, it's called stupid.''

Mist chuckled. "I believe I understand," he said.

"Good," Shadow said. "Now, shall we go over to the Bun for dinner, or shall I have something sent up?"

Mist hesitated, and Shadow read the look on his face.

"I'll have some dinner brought over," she said quickly. "You know, most of the elves are out of town now, and human crowds at the Crusty Bun tend to get a little too loud for my taste. Besides," she grinned wickedly, "I like dinner in bed."

FOUR ⟝⟝⟝⟝⟝

When Shadow woke, Estar was just placing a tray of breakfast and a box on the table.

"Good morn, Guildmistress," she said cheerily, although her brow was creased with worry. "Here's breakfast, and a box for you from Aliendra's shop. And a message from the palace; they want you there as soon as you're able."

"Fortune favor me, I just *got* here," Shadow groaned. She picked up the pillow next to her, uncovering Mist's toes, and jerked one of them. "Wake up, lover, there's a royal summons waiting for us."

"Again?" Mist said, his voice muffled by the layers of covers. "We just *got* here."

"I know." Shadow stretched and scrambled out of bed. "What's bothering you, Estar?"

"Guildmistress, we'd be relieved if you'd take a carriage to the palace," Estar said hesitantly.

"I was planning to," Shadow said. "But why, in particular?"

Estar poured two mugs of wine.

"One of the drudges went out the back door this morning to throw out wash water," she said. "There was a dead man there."

Shadow shrugged. "What's so new about a dead man in the alleys around here?"

"He died of the plague, Guildmistress," Estar said worriedly. "They're already calling it the Crimson Plague in town, because the sick break out in a red rash. There're dozens dead or dying, I hear. There are guards at all four gates, now, and they are letting no one leave the city."

"I suppose I should've expected it," Shadow said dismally. "The City Council can't afford for the plague to spread outside the city. But it's going to cause some panics, I'm afraid. So what about this dead man?"

"The drudge called me to look. I had him hauled away, but best you take a carriage, Guildmistress, if there's plague in town."

"Mmm. Good idea," Shadow agreed. "Pull our folks out of the market, Estar. Especially they should stay away from any visitors from out of town. I'll see if I can learn anything at the palace."

They barely had time to bolt down their breakfast; far from having to order transportation, a royal carriage arrived midway through their meal. Donya emerged from the carriage and trotted straight through the Guildhouse and up the stairs, giving Estar an absentminded wave as she passed, and pounded resoundingly on the door to Shadow's room.

"Come in, Doe," Shadow called at the sound of the familiar footsteps. She was amused to see that her friend had belted on the new sword.

"Aren't you ready yet?" Donya said, pouring herself a mug of wine.

"Have pity, Lady Donya," Mist chuckled. "The spell of translation has only just arrived, and Shadow came home to many matters requiring her attention."

"It looks like it," Donya said wryly, looking at the rumpled bed and the elves' disheveled state. "But our guest is frantic, and we need that spell. Is this it?" she asked, tapping the box.

"Mmm-hmmm," Shadow said around a mouthful of jam-smeared roll.

Donya opened the box and pulled out a simple, hammered-copper torc.

"This is it?" Donya said dubiously.

"Mm-hess-ho," Shadow mumbled. She swallowed. "If it isn't, I wasted two hundred Suns of the city's money."

"Two hundred Suns?" Donya repeated incredulously. "For that, the thing should be solid gold!"

Shadow gulped down a last mouthful of wine.

"If you want to," she said, "you're welcome to go over there and negotiate with Aliendra yourself. If you think you can get a better deal, that is."

"I doubt it," Donya said resignedly. "Come on, Shady, and let's go."

"All right," Shadow said. "But, Doe, I've *got* to be back here tonight. I mean it. There's a lot of problems right now and they need me."

"Just a few hours, I promise," Donya said, and something in her voice made Shadow take another look at her friend. Donya looked, if anything, even wearier than when Shadow had seen her last.

"All right, let's go," Shadow said. Mist grabbed a last bun on the way out.

"What is troubling you?" Mist asked when they were settled into the carriage. "Is it the plague?"

Donya nodded glumly. "You've heard, then?"

"Heard?" Shadow said. "I didn't have to hear. Somebody died on the Guild's back doorstep last night."

Donya sighed and shook her head.

"I'll have to remember to tell my parents," she said. "There hadn't been any deaths farther south than Rivertown that we knew of. It seems to have centered around the market. Mother and Father hesitated about sealing off the city. I guess it was a wise decision."

"That's bad," Shadow said. "I've told my people to pull out of the market, but—well, you can figure out how many will do it, especially if there's a panic about the gates. I hope the elvan merchants haven't taken the plague home to the forest."

Donya looked at Shadow curiously.

"So far, no elves have been taken sick at all," she said. "In the market or otherwise. Only humans."

"How strange," Mist murmured. "I have never heard of such a sickness."

"It's not unknown," Shadow said. "I remember in Wyndemere, only the elves got Balan's Itch."

"This plague is hardly Balan's Itch," Donya pointed out.

Shadow had to admit that that was true. For a sunny midmorning, the market was shockingly empty. Shoppers made their purchases quickly and left as quickly. Vendors haggled halfheartedly or not at all, and many stalls were empty or closed. Even the beggars and the ragged street urchins had eschewed their usual haunts.

"Thinking again, I do believe my people *will* pull out of the market," Shadow said quietly. "There's nothing for them here."

"Nothing but the plague," Mist said suddenly. "Look there."

Shadow looked in the direction indicated by Mist's pointing finger and shuddered. A corpse lay half in and half out of an alley, its extended legs covered with a red rash.

"Mother's had most of the healers and all the better mages in at the palace conferring," Donya said tiredly. "They're looking for a cure, but without any luck so far. Mother thinks Farryn has something to do with it."

"But he didn't die," Shadow protested. "In fact, it looked to me like he was all but well. And we never saw a red rash on him, either."

"And the plague started in Allanmere before he ever came to the city," Mist added.

"But it started not long after the elves brought him back," Donya said quietly. "About long enough for the next elvan traders to reach Allanmere."

"But the elves have not sickened," Mist objected.

"No, she's right," Shadow said thoughtfully. "That's why merchant trains are always suspect—they may carry plague from one city to another, sometimes without even sickening themselves. Sometimes they don't carry the plague themselves, but it travels in their animals or their goods, I've been told."

"That's what Mother suggested," Donya agreed. "Hurry, let's get inside. She and Father are waiting for us."

Indeed they were. Farryn, dressed and appearing well, if weak, was waiting with them in one of the smaller meeting rooms at the palace. The two maps, the crude one Farryn had brought as well as the one Donya had found in her bundle, were spread over a large table. Beside them was another map, a well-drawn modern one. It was this last map that Farryn was scrutinizing, his face drawn with worry.

"At last!" Sharl exclaimed, beckoning them forward. "Did you get the spell?"

"Right here," Shadow said, holding up the box. "What's happened?"

"One of the mages I've had in speaks a bit of Isseldik," Celene said. "We've been trying to get what we can out of Farryn, with sign language and whatnot, but Bron caught a couple of words. One was 'plague' and the other was 'invasion.'"

Shadow removed the copper torc from its box and held it up.

"We haven't tested it," she said. "I didn't know but that it might only work for one person."

Farryn eyed the torc as Shadow extended it, his expression politely curious. He glanced at Shadow again, then reached out to set one slender fingertip to the torc. Immediately he snatched his hand back with a single startled exclamation.

"Shirai!"

"What's that?" Celene asked, glancing at Shadow.

"*I* don't know," Shadow said irritably. "I don't think it's Isseldik. Go on, take it," she said to Farryn, then repeated it in stumbling Isseldik.

Farryn hesitated, scanning each of the faces around him, then reached out to grasp the torc. His odd hand trembled violently and his lips firmed into a tight white line against the bronze of his face, but he took it and, after a long pause, fitted it about his throat.

"Well?" Sharl demanded. "Has it worked?"

At his words Farryn started violently and whirled to stare at Sharl.

"What enchantment is this," he said, his voice shaking, "that enables you to speak my tongue?" His heavily accented voice was as harsh as Mist's was musical, and Shadow noticed for the first time a long scar crossing his throat—a battle wound, no doubt.

"We're not speaking your language," Shadow said, as calmly as she could manage. "You're speaking ours, and understanding it as if it were your own."

"I was right to come," Farryn said slowly. "This is indeed a land of powerful sorcery."

"Can you tell us now," Mist asked, "from whence you came, and why?"

"Indeed I have tried to do nothing else," Farryn said quickly. "I am an envoy of my people, sent here to discover the traces of the people who have gone before."

"Of what people?" Donya asked puzzledly.

"Of the people," Farryn said again, then frowned frustratedly.

"I think I understand," Shadow said. "He doesn't mean 'the people'; that's just what the translation spell turns the name of his folk into. The name of his folk, in his own language, means 'the people,' just as 'human' means to humans. 'Elf' is a human term, you know; we never called ourselves that. If we used a term for ourselves, it was our tribal names."

"Then you are 'elf,'" Farryn smiled, pointing to her, "and Don-eee-yah is human." He pronounced it *yu-mane*.

"And you are?" Shadow prompted gently.

"A warrior of the people," Farryn answered, then growled in frustration. "I cannot say it." He snatched off the torc. "Kresh," he said.

Celene nodded and indicated the maps. "Can you simply show us where your people—the Kresh—live?"

Farryn looked first at the modern map, shook his head, then looked at the map Chyrie had given Donya.

"It is not on these," he said regretfully. He pointed to a spot at the far north edge of the map. "Here, but more north, much more north, in these mountains. That is where my people live now."

Shadow shook her head.

"Even in Ramant they don't know what lies beyond these mountains—they call them Walls-of-the-World there. Only a few nomads are known to live there, and even that's only in the southern foothills. The nomads say there's no way past where it's mapped here, that the mountains are too steep and the rock too friable to hold a road.''

"There is a way," Farryn said quietly. "I have no map to show you, but it is somewhat to the east—where your map ends. It is a narrow pass, and dangerous. My people live near that pass, and through it once they came from the south to our valley home.''

"From the south?" Celene asked doubtfully. "I've never heard of your folk at all.''

"Nor heard I of yours," Farryn said, glancing from Celene to Shadow to Mist and back again. "But that time is so long past it has faded into legend. From the journey of my people we have only a few old records, such as this map, which was copied from one long crumbled.''

Celene glanced at Mist.

"That map must be many centuries old, indeed," she said. "But even twenty centuries ago, how could the elves not have known of your folk?"

"As to that I cannot say," Farryn said humbly, "for there is no account to say. Perhaps your folk and mine simply walked paths that never crossed." He looked at Shadow curiously. "But I feel that I know you—how is it possible that we have met?"

"I don't think so," Shadow grinned. "I'd certainly remember seeing *you*.''

"This map would seem to indicate there were others," Farryn said, tapping the elvan tribal symbols on the map Donya had found. "These runes are not those of my people.''

"The tribal markers were visible to any nearing the boundaries," Mist said. "They were placed specifically to warn other tribes away without necessitating conflict. If the Kresh were uninclined to meet other peoples, they would likely have seen the markers, indicated them on the map as a warning, and never encountered the elves otherwise if they did not venture into the forest.''

"Then your folk drew this map, too?" Donya asked Farryn.

"My folk and not mine," Farryn said, shaking his head. "But that is a long story.''

"If it bears on your presence here, or on the plague," Lord Sharl said grimly, "we'd better hear it."

"Plague?" Farryn asked quickly. "What manner of plague? Does it strike and kill swift as lightning, reddening the skin?"

Donya chuckled mirthlessly.

"I think his story's relevant," she said dismally. "I'll send for lunch."

When the meal arrived Farryn eagerly heaped his plate with meat and bread, looking at the fruits and vegetables curiously but leaving them. He sniffed the wine suspiciously, tasted it cautiously, and to everyone's amazement asked for water instead.

"Long ago," Farryn began, "in a time now passed to legend, the Four Folk lived as one in the far west, in a land of never-ending plains and low, rocky hills. Then came conflict which split our people one from the other, and a battle in which the vanquished were driven forth from our lands while the conquerors remained. Stone Brothers and Wind Dancers were we, and east we came across the burning waste, across sand and dust and mountains which belched forth their flame, until we came to a new land, a land filled with green plants and flowing water unlike any we had seen before.

"At times we saw signs of other peoples here and there, but we passed them silently by, for we were a race of warriors shamed by our defeat and weakened by hardship, and we dared not face those who might not welcome our presence in their land.

"East and east we came, sickening in the wet lands, until many of our people were frail and ill and could go no farther. There we stopped and there we dwelt, in a land wet and sickly but one laid upon strong stone, upon which the Stone Brothers could sing forth our homes and the temple in which we worshipped. In that temple dwelt our Enlightened Ones, keepers of our knowledge, and there they chronicled the great magics, such as we remembered or brought from our home-lands.

"There we lived," Farryn continued, "but there we grew fewer and more frail with each season. Each year the waters rose higher and swallowed the land. Each year our Enlightened

Ones waned in power as if something in this strange land leeched the power from them.

"At last many among us, mostly Wind Dancers, thought we should leave regardless of our weakness and our unfamiliarity with the land. The Stone Brothers disagreed, but they had found strong stone on which to live. Finally the Wind Dancers and a very few daring Stone Brothers left alone, although all of the remaining Enlightened Ones chose to remain at the temple. They went north, and north, and north again, and finally came to a mighty range of mountains. The few Stone Brothers who had left spoke to the mountains and found a pass, and through the pass a valley that was not too wet, and which was habitable. There the wanderers settled, and there we have dwelt ever since."

"That explains everything," Shadow laughed. "Farryn, that's a handsome story, and one I'd love to hear set to music, but it's about as understandable as you were when we first met. What's this Wind Dancer, Stone Brother business?"

"Shadow, the names of their tribes aren't important," Celene said. "I've known elvan tribes with odder names. What I'd like to know more about are these Enlightened Ones. What were they, Farryn?"

"The Enlightened Ones were—" he hesitated, then shrugged. "The Gifted ones," he said helplessly. "They were the keepers of knowledge, who served our gods, and who wielded the gods' power."

"Priests?" Donya guessed.

Farryn frowned.

"That word means nothing to me," he said. "What is 'priest'?"

"Priests are men who speak to their gods," Sharl said. "Or at least whose worshippers believe they do."

Farryn shook his head.

"We did not need someone to speak to our gods, of course," he said. "And our Enlightened Ones were most usually female, although there were some few males born with the Gift. But you have Enlightened Ones yourself, do you not, or whence came this?" He touched the torc.

"Ah, mages," Shadow nodded. "He means mages. Yes, we

have them, too. But, Farryn, your story really doesn't explain anything. What's it got to do with the plague, and why you're here?''

"Forgive me," Farryn said politely. "I had not finished.

"When we settled in our valley," he continued, "we did not trouble ourselves with what lay to the north. When we were well established, we sent a few scouts to survey the lands. They said that the mountains were rough, and beyond them there was a land of white cold where the ground was ice and where only snow fell from the sky. Such a land was of no interest to us, and we paid it no further mind. In that we were careless, but our only Enlightened Ones were but children, born since we left the Stone Brothers, and could not far-see for us or instruct us. Even our few Stone Brothers died over the years, and no new ones had been born—that is often the case in the intermixing of tribes. It did not concern us. Our success made us think overmuch of ourselves, and we thought ourselves mighty in our mountain-walled stronghold and safe in our solitude. We were wrong.

"It was not long before the first of the narrow-handed ones came," he said. "When the ground shook we thought nothing of it. It was a new land. Stone Brothers could have told us of our danger, but there were no Stone Brothers left to tell us. None of us were injured when the land danced, so we laughed and forgot.

"A few weeks later came the narrow-handed ones. They were filthy and dressed in ragged furs, and their weapons were simple and crude. They did not attempt to bargain but charged upon us as if to overrun our land. We easily defeated them; they fought with great strength, but clumsily, as does an unschooled child. Again we laughed at the paltry threat of such stupid creatures. It was we, however, who were the fools.

"Then more came, and more. At first they were in small groups, then larger groups, then still larger. At the last it was difficult to defeat them. Finally the last of them turned back, but we were many weeks fighting the ills and diseases they had left behind—ills and diseases our bodies had never known before, and we had no Enlightened Ones to aid us. We survived.

"In the times that followed we discovered why they had come. Black ash fell upon us. We remembered the fire-belching mountains our people had passed in the west. Somewhere to the north were other fire-belching peaks. When they spat forth their flame, they drove these people from their lands and frightened away the great deer they used for food.

"From what little were able to learn of their tongue from prisoners, and the signs we could find of their habits, it was their belief that the earth danced because two gods warred beneath the earth—their own god, and an evil god summoned up by the people of the south. In response to this attack, at such times it was their way to go south and make war upon these distant enemies, and to raid for food, horses, weapons, and tools. As our valley lay in the only pass through the mountains, thence they came, apparently to return from those southern lands when their stolen horses were laden with loot and when they had killed many southerners in the name of their battling god. Our people, blocking the pass through which they must travel, were nothing more than a hindrance to them, and perhaps a small battle to whet their appetite for greater slaughters to come.

"After much deliberation we decided we would not mount a war with these northern barbarians. We were too few and the land too unknown. Our Enlightened Ones were Gifted, but their Gifts were largely untrained, for none had crossed with us to teach our young when they were born Gifted, and so they did not have the wisdom passed down teacher to student among our Enlightened. Surely the earth could not dance often, and unless it did we were safe. We prayed such an attack would not happen again.

"Adraon answered us, for it was three generations before the narrow-handed ones came again. Again we repelled them, again at a cost. Seven times they came through the years," Farryn said proudly, "and six times we drove them back."

"What happened the seventh time?" Shadow asked with dawning understanding.

"The seventh time the gods punished us for our arrogance," Farryn said unhappily. "When the land danced, more strongly than before, we were forced to flee our valley because of falling rock, and we had no Stone Brothers to save us. We fled deep into the mountains, and when we returned, we saw by their tracks that the narrow-handed ones had passed through unhindered. Their trampling through our village had destroyed what the rock had not, and they had plundered what they could find, but we cared not; we could rebuild, and the narrow-handed ones were gone forever, we thought, to the south. Why should they return when they lived in the mountains so poorly? Again we were careless, and we were wrong.

"Some months later they returned. They were far fewer, but they were unexpected, and we were unprepared, having spent our energies on building rather than defense. Unforgivable in a warrior, and unfortunate in a small people. They came, and they won through, at a great cost in blood to us."

"Farryn," Shadow interrupted, "when would this have been?"

"Over two Great Cycles past," Farryn said.

"And what," Mist said, understanding, "is a Great Cycle?"

"A Cycle is two hands of turns of the seasons," Farryn said. "A Great Cycle is two hands of Cycles."

"What, then, two centuries?" Sharl asked.

"Ah, but no," Mist said quickly. "His hands are six fingers. Twelve times twelve years, twice, and more—near on three centuries, the time of the Black Wars, when barbarians beset us from the north. They near slaughtered all our kind, but were eventually driven back to the north. It has been supposed that such barbarians had come south before even the founding of the city."

"I've heard that, too," Celene said. "Certain elvan legends speak of other such battles."

"I can guess where this is going," Donya groaned.

"Two moons ago the land danced," Farryn said heavily. "When the first of the narrow-handed ones came, we were prepared. We fought them off easily; indeed, it seemed to us they fought more weakly than the records indicated. We hauled the dead from our land and burned them, as was our custom. Many were covered with a red rash.

"Immediately we began to sicken. It was not a fatal sickness, but a debilitating one—it turned strong warriors into weak children, too feeble to wield a sword. Soon there were far too few to mount a good defense, and presently, little by little, the narrow-handed ones became a challenge too great for our forces. Only their own illness kept our enemies from prevailing.

"At last our few Enlightened Ones gathered together and it was decided to send a messenger to the Stone Brothers here. The illness was not unlike one we had suffered when first we came to the wetlands, and likely the Stone Brothers would know of a cure. Whatever our disagreements, they were our people, and many of our own Enlightened Ones had remained among them. It was hoped that they could render aid in some form."

"I doubt it, unless they've learned to breathe water," Donya murmured.

"I do not understand," Farryn said, frowning.

"Much as I hate to deliver the bad news," Shadow said sympathetically, "there's nobody in the swamp. Most of it is underwater this time of year. Nobody's ever been there—to the knowledge of the elves or the humans, at least," she amended. "And I've been through the swamp myself only last spring, and there were no signs of any people there. Well, there were *signs,* but nothing to indicate anyone had been there for centuries."

"What signs?" Donya, Farryn, and Celene asked almost simultaneously.

Shadow shrugged.

"I didn't think it was very important at the time," she said. "Just some old stone trail shelters near the edge of Spirit Lake."

"You told me about Spirit Lake," Donya said curiously, "but you never mentioned trail shelters. Who in the world would have built them?"

"Fortune favor me, how should *I* know?" Shadow said lightly. "I'd never seen anything like them. You couldn't even see where the blocks joined, they were built so neatly. Covered over with these odd carvings, too, inside and out, like—" She shook her head. "Seems like I'd seen something—Fortune

favor me, that's it!'' She pointed to the sword at Donya's side.
''Like the tooling on the leather.''

Donya instinctively touched the hilt of the sword, and Farryn
stared openly, his eyes widening.

''That sword,'' he said, a surprising edge to his voice. ''How
came you by it?''

Donya raised her eyebrows, and her voice had an answering
edge.

''The same place I got this map,'' she said, tapping the
document. ''It was given to me as a gift by a—'' She glanced
at Shadow. ''Someone who makes a hobby of collecting
antiquities. As old as it likely is, I strongly doubt the previous
owner is in any shape to make objection.''

''I—meant no discourtesy,'' Farryn said stiffly. ''Would you
permit that I examine the sword?''

''I don't see why not,'' Donya said, ''seeing that I had the
chance to look at yours.'' She unfastened the scabbard from her
belt and handed the whole to Farryn.

His bronze fingers gingerly traced the tooling before he drew
the sword slowly, with a reverence that seemed excessive. He
eyed the blade without touching it, then as carefully sheathed it.

''This is Idoro's sword,'' he said, ''he who led my people
here from the west.''

''How can you tell?'' Mist asked. ''Did you know him?''

''Know Idoro Deathbringer?'' Farryn asked, amazed. ''Nay,
that was hundreds of generations past. I know it from the
carvings upon the scabbard, the runes on the blade. I might
have guessed it from the blade itself. We have brought forth no
new swords since the last of our Stone Brothers died, but this
sword was brought forth from the stone at the World's Heart,
from whence we came. You can see it in the metal of the blade,
that it remembers the fire in the bowels of the world.''

''It's a wonderful sword,'' Donya agreed. ''So is yours. I've
never seen metal like it. Hard as I look, I can't even see the fold
lines in it.''

''Fold lines?'' Farryn repeated puzzledly, but Celene interrupted.

''All this talk of swords is well and good,'' she said sternly,
''but we have a plague in our city, and now I hear the threat of

another invasion such as the Black Wars. I fear there must be all too much talk of swords in the future, so we can spare it for now, daughter.''

Donya's eager expression faded, and Shadow sighed to herself. It had been a long time since she'd seen Donya so animated. But Celene was right; there was more important business at hand.

"What must we do?" Mist asked. "Must we arm ourselves for another Black War?"

"We can't fight if our people die of the plague," Celene said sensibly. "A cure must be found. My mages are working hard, but so far we've learned almost nothing. What of your healers, Farryn?"

"If my folk had found a cure I would not be here," he said sensibly. "Legend tells that when we journeyed from the west we were afflicted with a similar sickness and the Enlightened Ones found a cure. It was to gain such knowledge from the Stone Brothers' Enlightened Ones that I came."

"But they're gone," Donya said.

"There will be records," Farryn said with assurance. "In the temple they will have made records of their wisdom."

"Temple?" Shadow asked. "Excuse me, Farryn, but I never found anything even remotely like a temple in the swamps. Those odd stone houses, yes, but none of them big enough to be a temple."

"It must be there," Farryn insisted. He pointed to Donya's map. "Do you see? Here is marked my people's village. Here," he said, tapping the stylized eye, "is the symbol of Adraon. There must be the temple."

"Did you ever see that part of the swamp, Shady?" Donya asked.

Shadow shook her head.

"No, we—I stayed as far to the east as I could."

"Even if this part of the swamp isn't underwater," Celene mused, "it's going to be awfully treacherous. I'd hate to send anyone in there not knowing the way, and not knowing where to look, either; and Shadow's the only one I know who's seen the swamp in any recent years."

"Maybe," Shadow mused, "I might know someone who—who might know something."

Donya gave Shadow a startled look; then her eyes narrowed. "Shady," she said warningly, "you can't possibly mean—"

"No one you know," Shadow said firmly. "Remember?"

"What *are* you two talking about?" Sharl demanded exasperatedly. "*Who* are you talking about?"

"Just an old friend," Shadow said vaguely, "who knows a bit about the swamp. If you'll give me until this evening, I'll see what I can find out."

"You," Celene said narrowly, "are a person of many strange friends—forest sprites, beggars, unknown persons of questionable knowledge—"

"Yes, and don't forget sword dancers and mercenaries-turned-Heirs," Shadow laughed. "Well, that's the business of a Guildmistress of Thieves. Come, now, Celene, you and Sharl have profited by my odd acquaintances and their questionable knowledge on occasion, and stand to do it again, so don't crowd me, if you please."

"Shady," Donya said seriously, "surely you're not going to take Mist to meet, well, your friend?"

"I suppose that wouldn't be a good idea," Shadow said regretfully.

"Now you are making me curious," Mist protested. "I would enjoy to meet any of your friends."

"I doubt if you'd enjoy this one," Donya said wryly. "I don't have time right now to show you around the city, Mist, but I know someone who'd make a good guide."

"Oh, really?" Shadow asked. "Who'd you have in mind?"

"Argent," Donya told her. "If he'll leave his herbal shop long enough. And, thank the gods, he'll show Mist the *better* parts of Allanmere—places he'd doubtless never see with you!"

"All right, all right, sheathe your sword, Doe," Shadow chuckled. "Argent's a good choice, if Mist doesn't mind."

"I have met Argent and his sister Elaria, and traded with them on occasion," Mist said graciously. "I would welcome a chance to see them again."

"Hopefully it'll only be for a few hours," Shadow apologized. "I'll meet you at Argent's shop this evening and we'll come back to the palace, or I'll send word if it'll take me longer."

"Why can't your friend simply come here?" Sharl asked. "I can have a messenger and carriage anywhere in the city in an hour's time."

"I don't think that would be a very good idea," Donya said hastily. "This particular friend is a very solitary sort and would *never*—believe me—come here."

"Very well," Celene said reluctantly. "But I don't like this very much. We have too many mysteries now."

Shadow hurried from the palace before anyone could present any more arguments; she was far from confident of her own success in locating the very elusive Blade, and even less in persuading her to help.

Shadow had half expected the flower vendor to be absent from the market; Blade might or might not be immune to the plague, but it was unlikely that her influence would protect her lackey. However, he was at his accustomed place, looking apathetic and subdued, and Shadow could well imagine the cause: he had likely been faced with the choice of possible death by plague or certain death by something considerably worse.

"Lemme guess," he said sourly when Shadow approached. "Black orchids, eh?"

"Right," Shadow said, nodding. "But this time it's a special delivery." She reached into her pouch, fingers sorting nimbly through the coins there. "Here's five hundred Suns for you. There's another five hundred for you, and a bottle of your source's favorite liquor, if I can have my orchids immediately. The sooner the better, and I don't care where."

The vendor looked visibly alarmed.

"Well, it don't just work like that," he said quickly. "I got contacts to make, arrangements—"

"A thousand Suns, then, and two bottles," Shadow said irritably. "On delivery."

The grizzled man's eyes widened and he rubbed his chin thoughtfully.

"I ain't making no promises," he said warily, "but come

back here in an hour and I'll see what news I'll have for you then."

"All right," Shadow said. "One hour, and no more."

That hour gave Shadow just enough time to return to the Guild (sneaking in the back way so Estar could not waylay her), and pick up two flasks of Dragon's Blood, a pouch of hundred-Sun pieces, and a pouch of gems. As an afterthought, she thrust a pen, ink, and parchment into a sack and tied it to her belt.

The vendor was waiting for her when she returned to the market.

"You got your orchids," he said. "They'll be waiting for you at a meeting room at the Golden Gill."

Shadow grimaced but counted out ten more hundred-Sun pieces, making a mental note to get it back from Celene somehow, and trotted off as quickly as she could.

The Golden Gill, despite its name, was in a decidedly disreputable section of Rivertown, near the docks, and Shadow decided on the road that choosing that particular tavern for a meeting place was yet another example of Blade's macabre sense of humor. The plague was running rampant here; there were corpses in several alleyways and, once, even in the street. The Gill was almost empty, and the stony-faced barkeep was grimly silent as he escorted her to a meeting room at the back.

Blade was waiting, which surprised Shadow; she'd have thought it more Blade's style to let her wait some short time—five or six hours, for example.

Blade looked exactly as Shadow had seen her last, nearly a year ago—a study in black and white, ebony hair, eyes and clothing startling against pale white skin. Shadow searched those onyx eyes for some sign of the precarious camaraderie they'd formed, but as usual, Blade was unreadable.

Shadow pulled out the two flasks of Dragon's Blood and placed them on the table.

"I appreciate you meeting me with so little warning," Shadow said.

Blade shrugged, inspecting one of the bottles.

"These days there is little else to occupy my time," she said coldly. "A more deadly killer than I stalks the streets of

Allanmere now, and there is little demand for my services where plague may well lay both sides low. I am gratified by your business and your payment. What is it you want of me now?''

"This is a little unusual—'' Shadow began awkwardly.

Blade chuckled dryly. "From you I expected little else,'' she said. "I hope at the least it is no other mage you wish disposed of.''

"Actually I don't need anyone 'disposed of,''' Shadow admitted. "What I need is information about the swamp.''

Blade was still. Slowly she drew the dead black dagger from its sheath and fondled it idly, tracing patterns on the tabletop with its tip.

"And what,'' she said slowly, "do you desire to know?''

"None of your secrets, believe me,'' Shadow said quickly. "It's someone else's secrets I'm looking for this time.''

Blade opened one of the flasks of Dragon's Blood and took a sip. "And whose secrets might those be?'' she asked.

"When we were in the swamp,'' Shadow said, "you showed me some odd shelters near Spirit Lake, and you mentioned a people who had lived in the swamp long ago. You said there were other traces of them.''

Blade raised one ebony eyebrow. "I had not heard that you had changed your line of work,'' she said idly. "Have you then become a sage, to seek after the remnants of lost peoples?''

"Something like that,'' Shadow grimaced. "On this one occasion. But tell me, did your pe—ah, did you ever hear of any other structures besides those houses? Anything larger, maybe, like a temple?''

Blade was silent for a moment, then shook her head.

"Nothing larger than the shelters,'' she said. "There is, however, the Black Door.''

"Black Door?'' Shadow repeated eagerly. "What's that?''

"I have seen it myself, long ago,'' Blade shrugged. "In truth I do not know why it is called a door. It is merely a rectangular slab of black rock, carved with reliefs such as you saw in the shelters, set deeply into a hummock. So far as I know there is no way to open it. Upon digging at the edges, one encounters more of the black stone. But one does not dig long in the swamp mud.''

"Where is this Black Door?" Shadow asked quickly.

Blade sat silently watching her, saying nothing.

"All right," Shadow sighed. "How much for a map, showing the paths through the swamps, the shelters, the Black Door, and anything else you think we need to know?"

Blade took another sip from the flask.

"Need to know for what purpose? Surely you do not propose to go there alone, and you will not persuade me again to act as your guide."

"That's hardly your worry," Shadow shrugged. "All I want is the map. Tell me your price."

Blade was silent again for a long moment. Then she looked up and frowned.

"You have dealt fairly with me in the past," she said, "so I will speak honestly to you. You may not find the Black Door. At this time of year it is likely submerged within Spirit Lake."

Shadow remembered that dead water and shivered.

"That's not my worry," she said. "But I appreciate your honesty. Will you do the map?"

Blade shrugged. "Why not?" she said. "If you wish to drown yourself in Spirit Lake seeking it, that is your own foolishness."

"What's your price?" Shadow asked, trying not to sound nervous.

Blade laughed coldly.

"What price shall I ask of an elf who must buy?" she mocked. "Once before I found you in such a position, and what I charged you then I may not ask again. Liquor you have given me and gold I rarely need. Will each of your Guild members come forward to give me of their lives that I may give you what you wish?"

Shadow shook her head slowly. "No games," she said. "Not this time."

Blade's eyebrow raised again, but she said nothing while she eyed Shadow thoughtfully and sipped Dragon's Blood.

"Very well," she said. "Dealing with you is always entertaining, if often unprofitable. Here is my price: Before I draw you this map, you will tell me exactly why you need it, and all facts related thereto. And if you go to the Black Door and open it, and if you, O favored of the gods, should chance to return, you will tell me what you found there.''

''Tough bargain,'' Shadow said, grimacing. ''I'm not supposed to say anything to anyone.''

''Secrets for secrets,'' Blade said implacably. ''A fair bargain, is it not?''

At last Shadow chuckled. ''I suppose it is a fair bargain,'' she grinned. ''And nobody actually *told* me I couldn't tell anyone.''

The story took nearly two hours to tell, punctuated here and there by Blade's brief questions and sips of Dragon's Blood and wine. When it was done, Blade laughed again and swigged heartily from the small flask.

''If what you say is true, and I have no cause to doubt it,'' Blade said, ''it is in my interest to aid you, for unless a cure for the plague is found there will soon be no one on whom to ply my trade, much less any to pay me for it. Give me therefore the paper I see in your pouch, and I will do what I can.''

Shadow handed Blade the pen and ink as well, but Blade waved them away; in her leather-gloved hand the black dagger blurred and became a black quill pen. Blade released it, sitting silently as the pen moved of its own volition across the paper. Occasionally it would pause, and Blade would frown and concentrate briefly; then the pen would fly on, leaving its clear black impressions behind on the parchment.

''Here is what I can give you,'' she said at last, pushing the parchment toward Shadow. ''Any warnings I might give are useless, for most hazards of the swamp you have already discovered by stumbling carelessly into them.''

''This is fine,'' Shadow said gratefully. The map was indeed detailed and neat; Shadow thought wryly that it would have been nice to have had such a map the last time she'd had to navigate the Dim Reaches!

''You are ill advised to enter the swamps, especially at this time,'' Blade said, ''but I suppose you will insist on drowning yourself nonetheless. A pity, when you have apparently finally found a fellow who, if you do not lie, may even prove your match in the furs. Still, it will save you pain in the end."

Shadow, who had been rolling up the parchment, looked up. "What do you mean?" she said warily.

Blade shrugged. "We leave home, and the long years pass," she said remotely, and Shadow was surprised to see a hint of pain in her eyes. "When we return, it is often to find that we are not who we were, and home is no longer home."

Shadow swallowed heavily as she realized how closely Blade's words expressed what she herself had thought about the Heartwood. Almost instinctively her hand went out to touch the black-gloved one on the table before her; immediately the hand was snatched away, and Blade's eyes were cold and unreadable as before.

"You have your map," Blade said, and her voice was stone. "I will trust in you to honor your bargain." She rose, sweeping up the two flasks of Dragon's Blood, and was gone.

Shadow chuckled and stayed where she was, finishing the last few sips of wine from the skin at her hip. A story that long deserved wine aplenty, and there was no chance of buying anything decent to drink at the Golden Gill; and besides, if she left too close on Blade's heels, Blade might think that Shadow was following her—a stupid mistake on Shadow's part.

Shadow considered another carriage, but dismissed the notion. The strong probability that elves were immune to the plague would make returning through the almost-empty market on foot a safe, if depressing, endeavor.

What vendors and buyers there were paid no more than half a mind to what they were doing, but Shadow didn't have the heart to reap the harvest of their inattention.

"A conscience," she muttered darkly to herself as she hurried on. "Fortune favor me, what an idiotic thing for a thief to be developing, and after five hundred years, too. Before you know it I'll end up like Donya, too duty-bound to leave a town when I'm sick of it and too nice to pay for a tumble in a brothel. Gods, what a curse."

Almost defiantly she relieved a tray-carrying vendor of a meat pie as he passed, sighing with relief as she bit through the crisp, flaky crust and licked up the gravy before it could run down her chin.

"A conscience," Shadow repeated, but with a chuckle. "A dire illness, but curable if caught early."

"There's one of them now!" a woman's harsh voice screamed.

"Huh?" Shadow looked around quickly, then froze as two things became clear: first, that a large crowd of angry-looking humans, some spotted with rash, were rapidly approaching; and second, that they meant *her*. For a moment she was puzzled— what in the *world* could she have stolen to make them all so angry—then she abruptly decided it didn't matter.

She ran.

The market was almost empty, which made it easier to run, but it also made it more difficult to lose her pursuers. Shadow ducked between the shops, carts, and stalls as quickly as she could, but the mob followed, simply knocking over or trampling whatever they could not dodge quickly enough.

Roofs. Where was the nearest roof?

Not near enough.

Where was the Fortune-be-damned guard? No matter what she'd stolen, even prison was preferable to lynching!

Large hands gripped at her tunic. Shadow pulled free, leaving a swath of cloth behind. Fear lent her a new burst of speed, and for a moment she thought she might make it; then a hoarse voice shouted triumphantly as strong fingers hooked into the heavy coil of her braid and jerked her backward into the hands of her captors.

"All right!" Shadow yelled. "Whatever it was, I'll give it back!"

Then, "Kill her!" several voices roared.

"No, bleed her!" others argued.

"Whoa, wait a bit!" Shadow shouted. "At least take the time to rob me first!" Wriggling one hand free, she ripped loose her belt pouch and flung it as hard as she could. It hit the cobblestones several yards away and the broken ties opened, spilling coins and gems across the ground. Some of the shouts changed tone and a few of the hands released her; the others loosened in surprise.

It was enough.

Shadow twisted wildly, her already-torn tunic yielding readily. Leaving the tunic in the hands of her captors, Shadow slid down through the mob for a safer level—ground level. No time to be nice; she pulled out two daggers and used them, slashing desperately at feet, shins, calves, and thighs indiscriminately. Humans screamed, stumbled, and fell, tripping over her and each other, grabbing at Shadow, the coins and gems, or their own wounds. A boot caught Shadow squarely in the side of her head while another slammed into her belly; Shadow *whoofed* out what air remained in her lungs and rolled as best she could, praying that the wildly stamping feet would not crush her skull on the stones. Then she saw a gap in the forest of legs and crawled for it desperately, only spurred on by a knee in the ribs. A heavy foot came down on her lower leg, and if the human hadn't stumbled and fallen, doubtless the small bone would have been crushed. What frightened her more, however, was the knife that came flashing down, missing her face by only a fingerbreadth.

She rolled again, and then she was up and running— stumbling, rather—away as quickly as she could. The mob behind her, however, were confused and unsure just where their quarry had vanished to, and Shadow was able to duck under the shelter of an abandoned cart before the humans realized that their prey had won free. By the time they started searching puzzledly, Shadow had crept quietly into an alley and from there to the safety of a rooftop—even if they heard her clumsy progress, the tiles were too fragile for the weight of the humans—and collapsed, panting for breath.

She had to chuckle a bit when she had enough wind to do so. Less than two years ago she had lain, similarly tunic-less, on another rooftop not far from here.

"And I thought a few loin-hungry men were an inconvenience!" Shadow breathed to herself, watching the mob in the market slowly dissolve. "Fortune favor me, I've got to remember to tell Donya that this plague makes humans lose their vine-rotting minds!"

Mist and Argent were waiting for Shadow at Argent's shop, where Mist was inspecting Argent's special reserve of dream-weed resin.

"Shadow!" Argent said, shocked at Shadow's battered and half-clothed appearance. He hastily pulled off his own shirt and draped it around Shadow's shoulders. "Are you all right? Shall I send for a healer?"

"No, they're all at the palace, and that's where I'm going anyway," Shadow said wryly. "I'll just trouble you for your shirt, if you can spare it, and get Mist back there as quickly as I can. I ran into some plague-crazed lunatics in the market."

"So I see," Mist said worriedly, examining the bruise already forming on Shadow's side. "Are you sure you are well?"

"Argent can tell you I've looked worse," Shadow chuckled. "I'll tell you sometime about the day I dropped down his chimney. No, let me clean up a little, and I'd rather we don't say anything to Donya about this. She worries enough, and this was just a bunch of crazies, panicking because of the quarantine and the plague."

"As you say," Mist said, troubled, but he changed the subject. "I knew Argent was an herbalist of renown, but you failed to tell me that he was an artist in producing the finest dreamweed resin to be had."

"No, no," Shadow groaned, "that's not the way you do it, Mist. Now that you've praised his resin to the skies, he'll charge you an outrageous price. You're supposed to say what poor stuff it is, and find all sorts of fault, so you can bargain down the price."

"But it is *not* poor stuff," Mist said innocently.

"I can imagine," Shadow said to Argent, "how you bilked this poor naive elf in a trade, you scoundrel."

Argent sighed. "How could I cheat my own folk in the forest, and take cruel advantage of their inexperience in bargaining?" he said woefully. "Your accusation wounds me, Shady, and you should've known better. At any rate, after bargaining with you, sweet thief, the best haggler is only a novice."

"Flattery's a sweet wine," Shadow said, laughing, "but I won't let you get me drunk on it, Argent. Come on, Mist, they're waiting for us at the palace."

"I'd like to come with you, if I may," Argent said, picking

up a satchel. "I've gathered some more medicinal herbs for Celene and her healers to try on the plague, and some of them are so strong I'd like to discuss the amounts to be administered, and find out if any of the herbs I sent yesterday have done any good. Besides, Shadow, I'd like to see you arrive safely after your adventure."

"In that case, let's get a carriage," Shadow said. "The market isn't a very pleasant place to walk through right now."

The Mercantile District was no better, nor was the Noble District. From their carriage, however, Shadow could see that at least the Temple District was thriving as peasants and nobles alike thronged to the temples to beg their gods for protection from the plague. Priests and novices, armed with heavy staves, roughly pushed away those obviously already infected who hobbled or crawled to the temples seeking divine healing.

It was also obvious that the City Guard was taking no chances with the safety of the High Lord and Lady. The guards around the palace were doubled, and each citizen seeking audience was closely scrutinized for signs of the plague. Those refused clustered outside, assaulting the carriage as it hesitated at the gates. One of the gate guards thrust his head through the carriage window, recognized Shadow, Mist, and Argent, and hurriedly waved them through, pulling away the sick peasants clinging to the carriage.

"I don't like this," Shadow said uncomfortably. "It's spreading too fast. It's only been a few days, and already they're starting to panic."

"Some of these herbs are powerful," Argent said comfortingly. "Perhaps one of them will be the solution. Healers say that for every disease there is some cure. Sometimes it takes more time to find it."

"It'd better not take too long," Shadow muttered darkly as the carriage passed through the gates.

FIVE ══════

Donya and Farryn were already awaiting her in the meeting room. Sharl was with the City Council and likely to be there for some time. Celene was closeted with the mages and healers, and Argent found a page to convey him to them, promising that he would send Celene as soon as she could come.

Waiting until Argent was gone, Shadow pulled the map out of her pouch and added it to the maps already laid over the table.

"Here's what I could find out," Shadow said. She pointed to the temple symbol on Donya's map, then the drawing of a door on her own. "Bl—nobody knew anything about a temple in the swamp, but there's supposed to be a black door, a door of black stone, set into a hillside here. It looks like the same place to me."

"A door alone," Farryn nodded eagerly. "Yes, that would be the temple. That is the place I must go."

"I'm not sure you can," Shadow said. "Look. This whole area is covered by Spirit Lake in the spring. There's only one trail through the area, and that goes right around the edge of Spirit Lake. It may be submerged, too."

"It's been a dry spring, and the swamp's had time to drain a little," Donya said quietly. "It may be above water by now."

Shadow shook her head doubtfully.

"Even if both the door and the road are above water, the trail will be—well, I don't even want to think of it. All but impassable. Last year it was later in the year, and I never would've made it if it hadn't been for—well, help from someone who knew the swamp as well as anybody ever will."

"I'm afraid we're running out of choices," Celene said from the doorway. Argent was beside her.

Shadow grinned at the tall elf sheepishly.

"I didn't know whether they were going to tell you about all this or not," she said apologetically. "I was afraid to say anything."

"I think we'll have to take Argent into our confidence now," Celene said. She led Argent into the room and bent over Shadow's new map. "Now show us what you were showing my daughter and Farryn."

Shadow quickly reiterated what she'd told Donya and indicated the location of the Black Door and the single trail that led there.

"Now we have a double reason to go," Celene sighed when Shadow finished.

"Huh?"

"Moonwort," Argent said as if in explanation.

"Who, or what," Donya said exasperatedly, "is moonwort?"

"It's an herb Argent brought me yesterday," Celene told them. "One of my healers' trainees tried substituting it for agrimony in an experimental healing spell. The spell *seems*," Celene emphasized, "to have slowed the progress of the Crimson Plague in the volunteers we treated with it. Even if the effects are only temporary, as I suspect they will prove to be, it puts us on the road to finding a cure."

"So, what?" Shadow asked excitedly. "Do you need more volunteers? There must've been fifty at the palace gates."

"No," Celene said softly. "We need more moonwort."

"It's a swamp plant," Argent explained. "It needs wet soil. What I've managed to get I've gotten from a few adventurous gatherers among the elves who forage at the forest edge of the swamp. Moonwort is never common, and now that the water is receding, the plants at the edges of the Reaches are dying out. No one competent is willing to go deeper into the swamp to gather more, and unless the plant is gathered at the proper stage, and properly stored, it quickly loses its strength.''

"Oh, please," Shadow protested. "You don't mean to think that *you're* going to go on some half-witted expedition into the Dim Reaches? Argent, have you *ever* been outside of Allanmere, except for going into the forest with some traders or the like?''

"That's not important," Argent said quietly. "I can't trust an amateur to gather and prepare the moonwort. That leaves Elaria or me, and Elaria hasn't handled the fresh herbs.''

"Fortune favor me, you're as bad as Donya and Farryn," Shadow groaned. "You want a plant that may or may not be there and may or may not do any good; and Donya and Farryn want to go looking for some stone door that may or may not be there, and if it's there, may or may not be under five manheights of swamp water. Who in Fortune's name are you going to find who's mist-witted enough to take you three idiots into the Dim Reaches?''

"You are," Celene said firmly.

"Oh, no," Shadow said with equal firmness. "I saw this coming; that's why I got you the map. I appreciate your misplaced faith, High Lady, that I can work miracles, but there's a plague in the city and my Guild needs their Guildmistress here for once. And you and Donya know exactly how much I love being able to say that!''

"You're still a citizen of this city," Celene said sternly, "and a subject of its High Lord and Lady. I have a right to command you, and to expect your obedience.''

"You can *expect* anything you want," Shadow returned, an unfamiliar coldness in her voice. "But if you *expect* that I'm going to leave my Guild without its Guildmistress when there's plague in the streets and a war threatening, you're badly mistaken. If Aubry could handle the Guild under this kind of pressure, I'd be long gone from that seat, and probably from this town, too.''

Celene frowned darkly and opencd her mouth to reply, but Donya laid her hand on her arm.

"Don't, Mother," she said quietly. "You can't expect to appeal to Shady's sense of duty on one side by asking her to abandon it on another."

"Respectfully, I must agree, noble lady," Farryn added. "For one to abandon those who rely on her leadership in a time of danger would be heinously dishonorable."

"It's hardly a matter of honor," Celene said flatly. "If Farryn can't get back to his people with a way to stop the barbarians from the north, we'll have an invasion on our hands. If we can't find a cure for the plague, there'll be no army to stop them. Other than a handful of desperate criminals and stupid fishermen who have gone into the Dim Reaches and never come back out, Shadow's the only one who knows anything about that swamp. Guild or no Guild, those are the facts, Shadow."

"Well, here's some more facts," Shadow said irritably. "I'm no fighter, nor herbalist, nor mage. I'm neither a fisherman nor a tracker; Donya can tell you I can't even *cook*. All I managed to do in the swamp was nearly get myself drowned once, eaten once, and swallowed up by Spirit Lake once. I couldn't tell you a single landmark, even if there were any left after a year, which I doubt. By Fortune's sweaty armpits, what in the *world* do you think I could do?"

"No, Mother, she's right," Donya said unexpectedly. "Shady's needed here, and besides, she'd be no use."

"That's right," Shadow said a little warily. What was Donya playing at now?

"Farryn's got to go, of course, but he's obviously a skilled warrior and well able to defend himself. Mist's got to go to represent the elves' interest, since Farryn is technically an elvan prisoner," Donya mused, "but he's a skilled hunter, which will be useful. Argent's got to go to collect the moonwort, and his knowledge of plants should help us find food. I'm not bad at hunting myself, and I'm a mean tracker and, if I say so myself, a pretty fair warrior. Shadow would just be dead weight, somebody we'd have to look out for."

"Now, wait a minute," Shadow said, recognizing this game. "You're not going to shame me into going, Doe. I'll even agree with you: you're right, I'd be dead weight."

"I have no intention of shaming you, Shady," Donya said affectionately. "You're more than competent in your own areas. It's just a matter of using the proper people with the proper expertise."

"Well, that's true," Shadow admitted.

"So we've simply got to find someone with more expertise to guide us," Donya finished. "In other words, Shadow's guide and the originator of this map."

"An excellent idea," Farryn agreed, and Mist nodded.

"Perfect," Celene said, relieved.

"Whoa, whoa, whoa!" Shadow said, alarmed. "Doe, have you been at Argent's dreamweed resin? You can't possibly be serious!"

"I'm perfectly serious," Donya told her. "Obviously she's the only one who knows the swamp—how to get through it, how to survive in it."

"Perfect," Celene exclaimed. "Who is she?"

"Now I *know* you're not serious," Shadow said with satisfaction. "You couldn't even find her if she didn't want to be found, and I can guarantee she doesn't, especially by you."

"I don't know about that," Donya said speculatively. "I admit I don't have your contacts about the city, Shady, but I've been building my sources even longer than you."

"Who is *she*?" Celene repeated.

"You've gone totally moonstruck," Shadow exploded. "Don't you know what she'd do if you *did* find her?"

"I have some idea," Donya said softly.

"No, you don't, you have no idea at all," Shadow snapped. "What do you think you're going to do if she pulls out that—Well, never mind."

"Who," Celene shouted suddenly, *"is she?"*

Startled, Donya and Shadow whirled to face her.

"Nobody," they chimed simultaneously.

"Well, for *nobody,* she's more trouble than the plague," Argent said exasperatedly.

Shadow and Donya looked amazedly at each other. Then Donya coughed a cough that sounded suspiciously like a chuckle, and the corners of Shadow's mouth twitched. Then Donya laughed weakly; then she and Shadow fell on each other, hugging and roaring with laughter until they gasped for breath.

"All right, damn you, I'm in," Shadow choked.

"I never doubted it for a moment," Donya grinned.

"Wine," Shadow said. "Horses, tents, skins, blankets, rope. Trail rations, medicines, fishhooks and line, pots, pans, tea, wine."

"You already said that," Donya said patiently as she scribbled.

"And I'll say it again. Wine," Shadow said firmly. "Flint and steel, lanterns, oil. Rain cloaks. Waterproofs—good waxed skin bags—for everything. Spare horses."

"What for?" Donya asked. "If we find the temple, we're not there to loot the place."

"Speak for yourself," Shadow said. "If I'm going to all that trouble, I intend to get something out of it. Besides, we'll need the extra horses when the first ones break their legs in that damned soap-slick mud or step into quicksand and disappear. Hopefully without us. Seriously, walking through that slop wears a horse out fast, so it's good to switch even if you're as light as me. And believe me, get the sweetest-tempered nags you can find. We're going to need it."

"Spare horses," Donya noted resignedly. "What else?"

"Needles, thread, cloth, leather," Shadow said thoughtfully. "Soap. Oh, something to fend off bugs; whatever Argent can come up with. Food for the horses. Wine."

"Wine, for the third time," Donya sighed. "Shady, we're looking at a caravan here. Sure you don't want a wagon while you're at it?"

"If I thought we could get one through the slime, I'd take it," Shadow said grimly. "We may need a Fortune-be-damned *boat* for all I know."

"All right, all right. What else?"

"I don't know what you'd call it," Shadow said, "but some kind of magic so I can talk back and forth with Aubry."

Donya put down the pen exasperatedly.

"Shady, you've got to be joking," she said tiredly. "Where do you think I'm going to get something like that?"

"From your mother and her pet mages, where else?"
Shadow said brightly. "Look, Doe, if she hasn't already
thought of it, she's going to think it's a great idea. After all, the
Heir going off and risking her life in the swamp? Come on,
now. She's going to want regular reports, anyway, and we're
going to need to hear news from the city, too, so message birds
won't do. Just ask her and see if she doesn't jump at the idea.
But I'm telling you, Doe, I'm not leaving until I have some way
to talk to Aubry."

"Communications," Donya wrote. "All right, this gives me
something to get started on. Argent's already getting whatever
he needs from his house and his shop. You'd better go to the
Guild and fetch whatever you want. I want all of us at the
palace until we're ready to leave."

"There's one more thing," Shadow told her. "I need
somebody to go through the Gate—me, if necessary—and
fetch Aubry back if he hasn't already left. He needs to be back
with the Guild before I leave."

Donya looked at her blankly.

"He's already back," she said. "He came back through just
a little before you got here this morning, and headed straight
back for the Guild. I thought you'd run into him when you went
back."

Shadow groaned.

"I was only there for a few moments, and I sneaked in at the
back," she said with a sigh. "He's probably combing the city
for me—or if he's smart, he's shaking in his boots and hiding
from me."

"Don't be too hard on him," Donya said, rolling up the
parchment and thrusting it into her belt. "After all, you *didn't*
tell him you were going to be away from the Guild."

"I didn't *know*," Shadow grumbled.

"Well, then, that's my fault," Donya said wearily. "So
lecture me, if you want. But show Aubry a little mercy."

"The Guild won't show him any mercy," Shadow sighed,
"when it's his. Fortune knows it hasn't shown me any. And
certainly the Royal Family hasn't."

"Barb accepted," Donya said, slapping Shadow's shoulder
absently—Shadow rocked under the impact. "Now go get your

things. And take Mist with you. He's wandering around looking as lost as a frog in the desert.''

Mist was hovering about in the hallways, looking every bit as ill at ease as Donya had described. Shadow grabbed his hand.

"Come on," she said. "Let's find a carriage. I need to snatch a few belongings and leave some last instructions.''

"I am glad you could take me with you," Mist said awkwardly. "I feel useless here.''

"You're not," Shadow said. "I'm going to be the useless one, if anybody, as soon as we leave Allanmere. Just wait till you try my cooking.''

Mist was obviously impressed that Shadow would blithely order the Palace Guard to bring a carriage round, and even more impressed when they obeyed.

"Don't look so awestruck," Shadow laughed as the carriage pulled out of the palace gates. "I couldn't get dust off their boots if it wasn't for Donya. Well, I take that back. I *am* the Guildmistress, after all. I suppose I could get the dust off their boots.''

Mist chuckled.

"Poor Argent," Shadow sighed after a moment. "You know, he's going to be even more miserable than I am, if that's possible. I don't believe he's ever even gotten muddy.''

"Perhaps not." Mist's tone was somewhat subdued, and Shadow was surprised to see the uncomfortable look on Mist's face. He smiled, but it seemed forced.

"Mist, what's bothering you?" Shadow asked, concerned. "Is it the plague, or does the city bother you that much?''

"Neither." Mist shook his head. "Argent is your lover, is he not?''

Shadow raised her eyebrows.

"Sometimes. Not too much anymore, but he's a great friend.''

"And Aubry, he is your lover, yes?''

"On and off," Shadow shrugged. "More on than off. What is this, Mist? I've never heard anything sounding so close to jealousy coming from an elf before, especially a forest elf.''

"Jealousy?" Mist gave Shadow a startled look. "No. I

suppose—envy, perhaps, that they can both share your bed and earn your respect. Argent has a successful business and is well thought of in the forest for his skill, and Aubry—you think to make him Guildmaster after you.''

Shadow chuckled. ''I thought it was usually humans who had these problems with their pride. Mist, what do you think you need to prove to me to gain my respect? You're my elder by quite a few years, you're a skilled hunter and a renowned sword dancer, not to mention a considerable talent between the furs. Fortune alone knows what other accomplishments you've learned over the centuries of your life, but I intend to find out as many as you give me time to. I hope you'll find more to *me* than a title I gained because I was too unlucky and too stupid to avoid it.''

Mist smiled, and his smile this time was genuine.

''Thank you,'' he said.

''It's nothing,'' Shadow reassured him. ''You're just feeling out of your element, and no wonder. Wait till we get out of the city, and then I'll be the one looking to you for comfort. Not to mention food. I hope *you* can cook.''

''I can do that much, at least,'' Mist said, laughing.

''Well, I'll tell you what else you can do,'' Shadow said as the carriage pulled in front of the Guildhouse. ''You can come with me and help me keep a rein on my temper so I don't tear your enviable cousin to shreds with my sometimes oversharp tongue.''

Aubry was waiting for them inside the Guildhouse, pacing the floor nervously with mug in hand. When he saw them enter, he took a last great gulp from the mug, as if to fortify himself, then came forward.

''Shadow,'' he said awkwardly. ''I'm sorry I left the Guild unattended. I didn't know you were leaving, you never go to the festivals, and I should have—''

Shadow held up her hand, silencing him.

''The fact is I didn't know I was going,'' she said. ''I went at the Heir's request. You should've let me know you were leaving, though, since you *are* my assistant and the festival would've kept you away nearly a week, with travel and all. If I hadn't been busy with the Guild treasury and accounts I'd have known, but that's beside the point. I also should've checked personally to be sure you could take over before I left, instead of just sending a message, but that's also beside the point. The point is that a Guildmistress has the right to presume on her subordinates, and that's you. Said subordinates *don't* have the right to assume that their Guildmistress can get along without them. Understand?''

"Understood," Aubry nodded.

"Said subordinates are to *be here* unless they tell me otherwise, come fire, flood, or plague, and said subordinates *still* are stuck with the place until they know it's in shape to be left. Because if said subordinates ever pull such a disappearing act again, said subordinates can wave good-bye to any chance at the seat, and also to certain treasured portions of the anatomy. Got it?''

"Got it," Aubry said humbly.

"Good. End of lecture, and I hope you were single-handedly responsible for a half-dozen babies," Shadow said, her tone much milder. ''That wasn't too bad, was it?'' Shadow added, looking at Mist.

"Admirable," Mist chuckled. "Remarkable restraint."

"Good." Shadow turned back to Aubry. "Now the bad news. I have to leave you in charge again.''

Aubry gaped. "You can't mean it," he said. "There's plague in the city—people are rioting—''

"I mean it," Shadow said ruefully. "I'm going in quest of a mythical plague cure. If it's any comfort, it took nothing less than an order from the High Lady to make me leave. Well, plus some underhanded blackmail from Donya.''

"But how long are you going to be gone?" Aubry asked worriedly.

"I don't know." Shadow shook her head. "No way to tell. But I told Donya that a condition of my going was that she come up with some magic that would let you talk to me at intervals. Whatever that is, I'll see that it's sent before we leave.''

"Well, that'll help," Aubry sighed. "Is Mist going? Does this have something to do with that man the elves caught?''

"Shut up," Shadow said, glancing around. No one had

heard him. "That's between Aspen and the High Lord and
Lady, and nothing for you to be bandying around town, all
right?"

"All right," Aubry said, subdued. "But other elves know
about him, and there's talk in the market, you know. Even with
the plague, there's talk."

"Well, don't add anything to it," Shadow said. "Yes, Mist
is going. And Donya, and Argent. We'll be looking for an herb
that may help with the plague. Hopefully. Come with me while
I get my things together and I'll give you a few last instructions."

Shadow found a well-waxed pack and began stuffing clothes
into it.

"About new Guild members," she said. "Check them all
yourself. Be conservative. Any doubts, apprentice them or give
them a probationary membership until I can check them out.
You know all the good people who can handle apprentices.
Molwyn's reapprenticed or he's out. Find someone who can
put up with him."

"What about Uriss?" Aubry asked. "Estar said he robbed
someone in the Bun."

"Right. Uriss." Shadow rubbed a hand over her face.
"Uriss will reimburse Sterin twice over and spend a week at
the Bun doing whatever Sterin tells him—sweeping floors,
scouring out spitpots, and the like. Tell Sterin not to be too
kind. Then reinstate Uriss with full privileges and put him in
Mertwyn's territory for the time being, at least until I get
back."

She tossed Mist a fur.

"Get in the bottom of that cabinet," she said. "There're five
small bottles in there. Wrap them carefully in the fur, then pack
them in that bag."

"You know, that stuff's very, very illegal," Aubry said with
a grin. "If Donya's going with you, maybe you should leave
your Dragon's Blood at home."

"What few comforts I can take with me, I'm taking,"
Shadow said grimly. "If Donya's going to drag me along, the
least she can do is look the other way and let me enjoy a little

liquor of an evening. Say, Aubry," she said suddenly, "do you know any elves around here with a soupstone?"

"I have one," Mist said unexpectedly. He pulled out the plain brown stone, suspended on a long cord, from his pouch. "Most of the Hidden Folk treasure the traditional magics of our people."

"Well, that's to the good," Shadow sighed, remembering some of the more distasteful game she'd eaten in the swamp. She preferred it anonymously cooked in a stew where she didn't have to think too much about what she was eating.

"Aubry," she said, "make me up a waxed-skin packet for my bow and a quiver of my best arrows, spare bowstrings, spare arrowheads and fletching, and oil and wax. Blast it, where are my spare boots?"

"Muri was mending them," Aubry said. "I'll get them and make sure they're well waxed. Anything else?"

"A pot of tallow," Shadow said ruefully. "A *big* pot of tallow. And my wet-weather cloak."

"Money?"

"Why bother?" Shadow shrugged. "Maybe a little for gambling."

"Going into the swamp, eh?" Aubry said.

Shadow whirled. "Why do you say that?"

"Because," Aubry chuckled, "you're taking the same things you did before, plus a few extra comforts I presume you learned from experience. And you have just about the same expression on your face, too, as I recall. Don't worry, I won't tell anyone where you've gone if you don't want me to."

"I suppose it doesn't matter," Shadow said at last. "Yes, there's an herb, as I told you, that may do some good. It's not a cure, but it may slow the plague. And by the way, if any of our people fall sick, send them to the palace. Maybe Celene's mages will take them as volunteers. Nothing to lose, anyway."

"Any idea how long you'll be gone?" Aubry asked casually, but Shadow could hear the undertone of worry in his voice.

"I don't know," she confessed. "No longer than I have to be, bet on it. Probably not as long as last time. I don't have to go so far, and I don't plan on stopping by the forest on the way back.''

"Better not take too long," Aubry warned, "or it'll be too late for herbs.''

"We will get little out of the Compact if there are no humans to honor it," Mist said gently. "Including the military assistance it guarantees.''

"I don't think military assistance is very important right now," Aubry grimaced.

Silence. Shadow looked at Mist, and Mist looked somberly back.

"I said, I don't think military assistance is very important right now," Aubry repeated slowly, staring at them.

"It's not important—right now," Shadow agreed. "Come on, Aubry, we don't have time to speculate and I don't have the answers you want. Get my stuff together and out to the carriage, and see how many skins of wine you can fit into those bags there.''

Shadow took a self-inventory, patting pouches, pockets, and sleeves.

"Tools, daggers, cord, garrote, flint and steel, moly," she said. "Good enough.''

"But what are you going to need that stuff for in the swamp?" Aubry asked.

"I don't know," Shadow said simply. "But I know that if I don't have it, I'll be sure to want it.''

"Are you going to take—" Aubry hesitated. "You know.''

"What, the bracelet Aspen made and Evanor enchanted?" Mist asked with a grin.

Shadow chuckled. "It isn't much of a secret," she agreed. "And yes, I'm taking it. What did you expect me to do, give it to you, Aubry? Uh-uh. I want the Guild back when I come home.''

"And you'll get it," Aubry said, hurt. "You should know me better than that, Shady, after all this time. If the day ever comes when I think I'd be a better Guildmaster than you, I'll call you out fairly, knife to knife, not stab you in the back.''

"Ah, I didn't mean it." Shadow put down her bundle and gave Aubry a quick hug. "Don't be so touchy just because I gave you a lecture. Take good care of my people for me, and of yourself, too, and I'll hurry back as quick as I can.''

"I hope so." Aubry kissed her quickly and turned to Mist. "Make her eat—something she didn't cook, too. And count your coins after every tumble.''

"If you dare say 'Take good care of her,' I'm going to vomit," Shadow warned Aubry. "Come on, shut your mouth and pick up a bag. Mist, you take that one. Now, where's my bow, and my spare boots?''

"I'll get them, I'll get them." Aubry squeezed Shadow's shoulder. "Why don't you take Mist over to the Bun for dinner, and by the time you're done, I'll have everything bundled up and loaded into the carriage.''

"That's a good idea," Shadow nodded. "What with Donya dragging us out of bed in the mornings Mist's had no time for a proper meal, and it's likely to be a long time before we have another.''

Mist was agreeably impressed by the Bun, which had not suffered too badly from the plague because of the elvan patronage from the Guild. They sat in a corner, lunching on cheese, chicken pie, and a delicate southern wine, and enjoyed the music. For an hour the harsh outside world of plague and imminent invasion vanished in a taste of peace and pleasure similar to that Shadow had enjoyed at the festival.

It seemed all too soon that Aubry came in and, rather apologetically, told Shadow that the carriage was loaded and the driver becoming rather impatient. Shadow chuckled as she thought of the driver, a member of the Palace Guard, guarding a gilded carriage sitting in front of the Guild of Thieves.

"All right," she said, and stood to hug Aubry again. "Take care of yourself and the Guild. And remember, I just did an accounting of our funds, so I know just how much to expect in the Guild treasury when I come back, and I know just what's in the wine cellar, too.''

"Oh, come now," Aubry protested. "You wouldn't begrudge your harried assistant a skin of wine?''

"I don't begrudge you ten, so long as you stay out of my private stock," Shadow said sternly. "Drink up the Guild's cellar and you'll have to restock it, that's all. Why do you think I took my entire cache of Dragon's Blood with me?''

"Ha! You had nothing to worry about," Aubry said with a grin. "I can't afford so expensive an addiction. Anyway, that stuff's got much too much kick for me."

"What is this Dragon's Blood?" Mist asked innocently.

"Wait till tonight, and I'll show you," Shadow said with a grin. "Come on, let's get going. Fortune favor you, Aubry."

"The Mother Forest shelter you," Aubry responded, giving Shadow a last kiss. "Whatever Celene comes up with to let us talk, just have her send it around—with instructions, please."

"I'll see to it before I leave," Shadow promised.

When she and Mist reached the palace, Celene was closeted with her mages, Sharl was nowhere to be found, and Donya, according to the steward, had gone out to buy supplies and horses. Argent had not yet returned. The steward had been instructed to show them to their rooms, or—the steward looked away timidly—would one suite suffice?

"One suite's plenty," Shadow said innocently. "If we invite more than twenty guests, we'll have another bed brought in."

The steward chuckled weakly and showed them to a suite even more luxurious than the guest room they'd previously stayed in. Servants, he said, would bring their belongings along presently.

Shadow learned that Farryn was still in the same rooms and still heavily guarded, but that Donya had left permission for Shadow and Mist to see him if they liked. Since the alternatives were staying in their suite, roaming around the palace alone, or going into town in search of Donya or Argent, Shadow opted to visit with Farryn.

To their surprise, there was but a single guard stationed outside Farryn's rooms. The guard informed them that four other guards had taken Farryn to one of the palace baths shortly before; he could tell them which one, or they could wait, if they wished.

Shadow and Mist exchanged a glance, and Shadow shrugged.

"We'll go," she said. "I've been meaning to show Mist the

palace baths, anyway, and if Farryn's too embarrassed, we'll leave.''

Since the baths were in an inside room with no windows or other means of egress, the guards had considerately stationed themselves outside the door. Shadow knocked on the door, then opened it a crack.

"It's Shadow and Mist," she called. "May we come in?"

"By all means," Farryn said, sounding rather surprised. "Join me and welcome."

Shadow and Mist slipped in and shut the door behind them. Farryn was in the largest bathing pool relaxing against the edge, his chin resting on his crossed forearms, which were propped on the edge of the pool. A chilled bottle, its sides misty with condensation, was beside him, and a goblet was in his hand. He had released his bronze hair from its braid, and wore nothing, so far as Shadow could see, but the torc and the amulet with the eye design.

"This place reminds me of my home," Farryn said, indicating the bath. "Our last Stone Brothers called forth the hot waters from the bowels of the earth in pools such as this. Did your Enlightened Ones so create these baths?"

"A long time ago," Shadow said. "When the city was first built. Most of our mages have lost such powerful magics now. I've only seen a very few other cities with baths like this. Do you mind if we join you?"

"Mind?" Farryn repeated puzzledly. "Do I—mind?"

"Humans are known to be very modest of their bodies, and do not bathe in company," Mist explained. "We know nothing of your people's customs."

"Ah, by 'mind' you mean 'object,'" Farryn said, nodding. "Nay, I have no objections. My folk often share bathing pools, especially in the cold seasons, when we sit in and around the warm pools and tell stories. In any wise it is not mine to say, for this is not my place, and I am in fact his prisoner"— nodding at Mist—"and under his word."

Shadow chuckled as she laid her clothes on a bench.

"Now you've put poor Mist at a loss," she said, testing the water with one foot. "The elves don't know what to do with a prisoner, as you'd probably guessed if you were lively enough to look around the hut where they were keeping you.''

"I—'' Farryn frowned and shook his head. "I do not remember. I was too ill.''

"You were certainly ill," Mist agreed. "We feared for your life. But it was not the plague, was it, with which you had sickened?''

Farryn sipped from his goblet before answering.

"What you call the Crimson Plague does not affect us as it did our invaders, or the folk in the city," Farryn said thoughtfully. "To us it is serious, even debilitating, but fatal only to some of the very old and the very young. I was not sick with it when I left, but the journey weakened me greatly and I fear the sickness struck me down while I was exhausted. And then—'' he hesitated, frowning. "I dreamed that my soul had been reft from me for a time. If that is so, I was indeed near the final crossing.''

"Your soul?'' Mist prompted.

Farryn shook his head and sighed, touching the amulet around his neck.

"It was only a fever dream," he said at last.

"Farryn, what *is* that thing?'' Shadow asked, easing herself into the hot, bubbling water.

"My soul keeper?'' Farryn asked inquiringly, touching the amulet again. Then he looked at Shadow and Mist, and his eyes widened.

"You have none!'' he said amazedly. "Where then do you keep your souls, or are you soulless creatures like those who invade our land?''

"Now there's a question for the sages," Shadow laughed as she unbraided her hair, Mist helping her. "We keep our spirits in our bodies, of course, where the Mother Forest puts them when we're born. How do yours get outside your bodies and into your—what did you call them?—soul keepers.''

"We are not given our souls at birth, but at the age of twelve years, the age of responsibility,'' Farryn said. "Our Enlightened Ones ask Adraon to grant our young ones souls upon completion of their trials at their passage ceremony, when they swear the Code of Honor and take up their swords. None of the people''—again Farryn grimaced at the spell's automatic translation—''may be given souls until they have proven themselves worthy and sworn heart's blood to the Code of Honor. Then we are given our soul keepers, where Adraon guards our souls safe from whatever defilement may befall our bodies.''

He stopped in amazement as Mist coaxed the last braid free and the full length of Shadow's shining black hair floated on the water. Mist had already loosened his braid, and the pale lengths, twining with Shadow's hair in the water, contrasted beautifully in the clear, bubbling liquid.

''You are indeed a wondrously beautiful people,'' Farryn said without embarrassment. ''Do you know, when I first saw you, Lady Shadow, I thought you perhaps a child, so small were you, and wearing no sword. But you can be no child, to have the years to grow so marvelous a train.''

''That is why we grow it so,'' Mist acknowledged. ''Its length shows our age, and our age gives us status.''

''But about this soul-keeper thing,'' Shadow pressed. ''You weren't dreaming, you know. Aspen didn't know that that was anything but a piece of jewelry, and they'd taken it off you. You got awfully weak; maybe that's why. Then when I picked it up—''

''You touched it?'' Farryn said, his head jerking up in amazement. His face flushed darkly.

''Sorry,'' Shadow said with a shrug. ''None of us knew. It hurt you, didn't it?''

''That it did,'' Farryn said, averting his eyes. ''It might have meant my life.''

''Is it not dangerous,'' Mist said slowly, ''to wear one's spirit so openly, when but a touch does you harm?''

''It does me no harm unless it is removed from my body,'' Farryn corrected. ''Only an Enlightened One might remove a soul keeper, and then only for special reasons. To touch the soul holder of another''—he flushed again, glanced at Shadow, and glanced away quickly—''is a great intimacy, a meeting of spirits meant for—''

''I think I understand,'' Shadow said, chuckling. ''Do you know, that's the first time I've ever had anyone complain!

Well, I'm not accustomed to forcing my attentions on the unwilling—in fact, I'm not accustomed to the unwilling—but at least I managed to get them to let me put the thing back on you.''

"You returned my soul to me?" Farryn asked slowly.

"Well, yes," Shadow said. "But don't worry, after I saw what happened to you when I touched it, I picked it up by the chain.''

"Then I am in your debt," Farryn said soberly, touching the amulet, then pressing his fingers to his lips. "By my heart's blood I swear that I am without honor until I can repay you.''

"Oh, that's not necessary," Shadow said hastily, taken aback by the seriousness in Farryn's eyes. "Just thank Fortune that it occurred to me to give it back to you at all. You warned us of the possible invasion, you're helping as best you can, and certainly you're a model prisoner!''

"I have been treated most honorably," Farryn said graciously. "We have had little experience of other peoples, other than the northerners who attack us. It is good to learn that all other folk may not be judged by their example.''

"If you expected no friendship," Mist said thoughtfully as he soaped Shadow's back, "why did you come to elvan lands?"

"I did not know the forest to be inhabited," Farryn confessed. "Neither my poor map nor our legends contained such knowledge. I thought only to arrive in these lands outside of the territory of the Stone Brothers, if they remained, and approach making signs of peace, that they might not immediately slay me as an invader. That your people did not do so is greatly to their honor. I knew that after I danced the many leagues I would be too spent to defend myself.''

"It is as well you did not attempt the swamp alone," Mist said. "Your people are no longer there, and you would surely have died without even the gain of delivering a warning to us.''

"It is a poor gift indeed, if with the warning I have brought plague upon this city," Farryn sighed.

"A cure will be found," Mist said confidently. "Already progress has been made toward finding a cure.''

Farryn was silent for a long moment.

"The warrior," he said at last. "The woman Don-eee-yah. She is a very great warrior, a warrior of renown?"

"As good as any I've seen, or better," Shadow said affectionately. "And I've seen plenty, bet on it. As for renown, she's not much to brag on her deeds these days, although she's got every right. Ah, but to see her in battle—now that's a sight to stir the heart!"

Farryn sipped from his glass and glanced sideways at Shadow.

"From respect, I did not speak to her of it," he said slowly. "But for her to carry Idoro Deathbringer's sword is— dishonorable. We are given swords at our time of passage, or sometimes as a gift by one who can no longer wield it, or when we have bested the wielder."

"Well, it was given as a gift, if that makes any difference," Shadow said, shrugging.

"Not by its owner," Farryn said disapprovingly.

"No; but it was given by someone who's a pretty shrewd judge of character," Shadow said after a moment. "I suppose you'd call her an Enlightened One, in her own way. If you don't think Donya's earned her sword, you're wrong, bet on it. At any rate, it's not your place to judge her worthiness, especially when you don't even know her."

"That is truth," Farryn acknowledged without rancor. "I did not wish her dishonored out of ignorance, that is all. It would take much to earn Idoro's sword."

"She's earned it," Shadow repeated, "and she'll doubtless do it again. We'll all have some trials ahead of us, bet on it."

"In that you are correct," Farryn agreed. "The gods do not give great gifts without a great price."

"If that's true," Shadow murmured, "I'll either bargain them down, or pick their pockets."

SIX

"It already stinks," Shadow said glumly.

"Oh, Shady, it's not that bad," Donya said almost merrily, and Shadow gave her a sour look.

"Admit it, Doe," Shadow said. "You're just glad to be out of the city, taking your chances on the road again."

"Oh, really, Shadow," Donya said, scowling. "With a plague in the city and war threatening—" She stopped, shrugged, and grinned. "All right, I admit it, I'm glad to be out of the city, taking my chances. But there's no road, just this pitiful little trail."

"This *is* the road," Argent said, looking at the map, "such as it is. And as it's a long, smelly distance to the first shelter marked hereon, I suggest we make all haste in following it."

"All right, Shady, you're in the lead," Donya said.

"Me?" Shadow pulled her pony to a halt. "Why me?"

"Because you've been here before," Donya said patiently.

"I think I'm going to get awfully tired of hearing that," Shadow mumbled irritably. "I suppose I should be the first to disappear down a fell-beast's maw, because I've nearly been there before."

"What?" Donya said.

"Nothing," Shadow sighed. "All right, you're the leader and I'm in the lead."

"The swamp is low for this time of year," Mist said encouragingly.

"Only until it rains," Shadow said sourly. "Then the level of the swamp will rise five feet above the level of our camp, bet on it."

"Are you going to be this cheerful all the way through the swamp?" Argent asked impatiently.

"No, because we aren't going to make it that far," Shadow grumbled.

"Argent, you don't want her more cheerful," Donya warned. "When she's cheerful, she sings."

"Where should we look for this plant, this moonwort?" Mist asked, diplomatically changing the subject.

"It grows around the edges of pools, rooted in the water," Argent said. "This mud isn't wet enough. Only the young plants, before they flower, are at full potency."

"Well, this mud is wet enough to send your horse sliding," Shadow warned. "Stay on the trail, in a single line behind my horse, and for Fortune's sake don't let your horse drink out of any of the pools we pass. Some of them are deeper than they look, and sometimes they have things living in them. Big, hungry things that have a taste for elves."

"They obviously share that with the insects," Mist said unhappily, swatting at midges.

"Rub this on your skin," Argent said, tossing Mist a jar. "The smell is unpleasant, but fortunately the insects don't like it, either."

Mist opened the jar and sniffed the contents, wrinkling his nose dubiously. Several midges later, however, he surrendered and rubbed the cream over his exposed skin. The jar quickly circulated through the group.

"I see why my kinfolk abandoned this place," Farryn muttered darkly as he anointed his bronze skin with the cream. "How can one fight an enemy too small to strike with a sword?"

"With a smell that's even deadlier," Shadow chuckled. "Don't worry. There's few enough places here I'd dare to bathe, so we'd all smell this bad soon enough anyway. I already miss those bathing pools."

"Those pools have their own dangers," Argent laughed, giving Shadow a merry glance.

"If that is the case," Farryn said innocently, "it is well that Shadow and Mist bathed with me. I did not realize I was in danger."

Shadow looked back at Argent and laughed until the tears trickled down her cheeks while Mist, Farryn, and Donya looked at them blankly.

"I'm glad you find something so entertaining," Donya said at last. "But what shall the rest of us do to pass the time?"

"We could sing songs," Shadow grinned.

"Why don't we have a story instead," Argent suggested hastily. "Shady, why don't you tell us a story from your travels?"

"A story?" Shadow turned around to look at Donya, then glanced at Farryn. "All right. What about our first dragon, Doe?"

"Oh, my," Donya chuckled. "All right. Farryn, if your people live in the mountains, do they ever hunt dragons?"

"Frequently," Farryn said, his eyes sparkling. "They are the most challenging of game—strong and cunning, an honorable opponent."

"I'll bet you never saw them hunted like this," Donya said with a grin.

"How *do* your folk hunt them?" Shadow asked Farryn.

"We go to the edge of their territory and call a challenge," Farryn said. "How else could it be done?"

"Well, that wouldn't work here," Donya said. "For one thing, we're far from the dragons' home territories. They fly down here mostly to raid for sheep or cattle. So we call in all the herds and stake out a fat cow when there's a dragon in the area. It doesn't fool the dragon, of course, but they seem to like the sport as much as we do, and I gather they find humans—or elves, for that matter—especially tasty. A special snack to brag about back home, I guess."

"Donya and I had just finished guarding a caravan traveling from Berwil to Makon's Ford, or Mackinsford, as they're calling it now. It was late in the fall," Shadow remembered, "and we figured on wintering there in town. We had a good little stake then, and figured we could live soft till spring on what we'd saved, plus whatever I could pick up in the market. We'd settled into the best inn in town, the Blue Counterpane.

"It wasn't long before we started getting bored," Shadow continued. "Being harvest season, most people were out getting the crops in, and there wasn't much to do. Doe took a few odd jobs, guarding moneychangers and the like, and I was milking that little market until the local guards were getting itchy, so when a few other wintering-over warriors said they were going to hunt a dragon that'd been raiding the local herds, Donya jumped at the chance and I went along to watch. I took my bow, though, just in case, thinking I might get a safe shot off from a good distance and earn a share myself."

"A bow is for hunting animals," Farryn said disapprovingly. "Not for honorable combat."

"Talk to a dragon about 'honorable,'" Shadow shrugged. "They certainly don't balk at breathing fire and taking on opponents twenty times smaller than they are."

Farryn grimaced, but said nothing.

"There were some rocky hills near the ford where the dragon was raiding herds," Shadow continued. "So we staked out our bait there and hid in the rocks. I separated myself from the warriors—no point getting in the way—and climbed to the top of a rocky outcropping. There were boulders there to hide between and a good clear shot down into the gap, so I settled myself in comfortably with two wineskins and my bow to let Donya and her friends do what they liked.

"We didn't have much of a wait. The local farmers had pulled in their herds a week before, and the dragon was hungry. It was irritated, too, I'll bet, and a few armor-baked humans were probably just to its taste, not to mention the cow we'd staked out. Anyway, it was only a couple of hours before we saw the dragon, circling widely but drawing in; I figured it was probably counting the warriors and trying to decide whether the meat was worth the trouble. I guess it was, because the next thing we know the Fortune-be-damned dragon's stooping right over our heads, not over the cow as we'd expected. It grabbed one of the warriors and swooped back up with him, ripped him into about three pieces.

"It knew that trick wouldn't work again; the warriors knew where it was and were ready to duck under rocks. But that was one of our six warriors. It came back around, dispatched the cow with one swipe of a foreclaw, spit a little fire over the boulders where the warriors were, just for show, and roared its challenge to the skies.

"I'm here to tell you, that thing was *beautiful*," Shadow said, Donya nodding agreement. "It was a prime buck dragon, three or four man-heights tall at the shoulder and eight or ten nose to tail tip. It was red—coming on to mating season, I imagine—but its scales sparkled with gold, orange, and yellow fire and its wings made molten gold look dull. Its eyes were yellow as the sun. It was too beautiful to kill.

"By that time, of course, we didn't have any choice," Shadow said regretfully. "If we didn't kill it, it would just pick us out of the rocks like south-coasters pick boiled curl-tails out of their shells. It had a cow and a man to sup on at its leisure, and none of the warriors had more than a day's water and food. The dragon swallowed the piece of warrior he was holding, just to taunt us, and the other warriors attacked.

"As you all probably know," Shadow said, "a dragon has two stomachs, and it belches fire out of the second. Having just swallowed a piece of meat, it would be a few minutes before it could bring the heat up again and make fire. For those few minutes we had the advantage—if you want to call it that—that all we had to fight was the dragon's superior strength, speed, teeth, and claws. That's all."

Shadow chuckled and took a swig from the wineskin in her hand.

"Donya was the first to reach the dragon," Shadow remembered. "She was fighting it head-on, no shield—even she had to use two hands for that damned giant of a sword—while the other four worked toward the sides, trying to get in a strike when the dragon was distracted. My arrows just bounced off those scales, and I thought if I missed I might hit Donya. So there wasn't much I could do but watch, which suited me just as well, anyway.

"So this big fellow was making stew out of the warriors. They'd wounded it in a couple of places, and Donya had gotten in a good whack on the neck, I could see, but one flip of its tail smashed a warrior into jelly against a rock, and another warrior was wounded badly and couldn't stand.

"Then Donya sank her sword into the dragon's neck almost to the hilt, right behind the head. The dragon roared and threw its head back, ripping the sword right out of Donya's hands. It was badly wounded, but it wasn't dead yet, and now Donya was unarmed. I whipped off two arrows quick as I could, and by Fortune's grace I hit the beast right in the left eye, but the arrow didn't pierce the brain. Cheap bow." Shadow snorted, patting the long bundle behind her. "With this one I'd have made it.

"Anyway, now the dragon was mad with fury and pain," Shadow continued. "One of the other warriors had slashed its left wing so it couldn't fly, but there was nothing hindering the rest of it. It jumped backward, landing right on the crippled warrior, poor fellow, and crashed sidelong into the cliff I was sitting on. The rocks in front of me shivered, and that gave me an idea.

"'Left flank!' I yelled at the warrior on that side. He drove his sword right into the dragon's left hind leg. It swung its tail to swat at the warrior, he dodged, and the full strike went right into the cliff. At the same time I wedged my bow under one of the supporting boulders and jumped on it. My poor bow snapped like tinder, but the boulder teetered on its support. Not quite enough, though, so I ran, jumped, and pushed as hard as I could. The boulder went, all right, and a few of its kin, and I went with it. I fell, thinking I'd never open my eyes again until I reached the Mother Forest, but I fetched up almost right away—right on the dragon's head.

"Well, the largest boulder dropped on the dragon's wing and broke it, so probably the dragon didn't realize right away that it had an elf-shaped hat," Shadow grinned. "Also, Donya had picked up one of the dead warriors' swords, and she was trying for the heart while the dragon's head was clear. She stabbed and missed the heart, but it must've hurt; the dragon roared, almost threw me off its head, and swatted Donya aside with a foreclaw like—well—like a swamp midge!

"Meanwhile I had one foot braced on the hilt of Donya's

sword, which, thank Fortune, was solidly planted, and the other wrapped around the dragon's neck, while my hands were hooked on its brow ridges. Still, when the dragon tossed its head, I nearly took a lesson in wingless flight, and I couldn't reach any of my daggers, because that would've meant letting go my hold and twisting around to reach for belt or boot. Mist-witted elf that I was, I wasn't wearing a forearm sheath in those days—''

"Why would you wear a weapon so dishonorably concealed?" Farryn asked with a scowl.

"Well, for one thing, in case I ever find myself riding a dragon again," Shadow chuckled. "Anyway, about this time the dragon had figured out it was wearing a cap and was trying to shake me off. I just hung on, not that there was much choice, and hoped that the distraction might give someone a chance to get in a good strike.

"Out of the corner of my eye I saw one of the warriors close in at the side just as the dragon's head dipped down that way. I yelled a warning, but too late; just as he sank his lance into the dragon's side, it sank its teeth into his chest and picked him up at the same time. It bit him nearly in two, and blood squirted all over me—yech!—but there was his belt dagger, right by my hand. I grabbed as quick as ever I have, and sank that dagger into the dragon's right eye. This blinded the dragon, but it also gave me a good, strong—if slimy—handhold. A good thing, because the dragon screamed and threw his head straight back. My feet slipped loose from their holds and my left hand almost slipped off the brow ridge, and for a minute about all that was holding me on there was that dagger, jammed into the dragon's eye. Then the dragon threw its head forward and my hand slipped right off the brow ridge and grabbed the first thing it could—the arrow already sunk in the dragon's left eye.

"I wasn't in any position to see what was going on below," Shadow said ruefully, "so I didn't know that when the dragon threw its head forward, that was because Donya had gotten to her feet, had seen the predicament I was in, and rushed the dragon's chest again. I heard her war cry, though, and thought the dragon had her, and that it was just about up with both of us. So I braced myself against the neck with my knees as best

I could, grabbed hard on the dagger hilt and the arrow shaft, and shoved both of them inward with every muscle I had, just as Donya buried her sword in the dragon's heart.

"The dragon gave one last roar and fell forward, and Donya just got out of the way in time as it landed right where she'd been, and I flipped loose. I must've gone three man-heights before I touched earth, and you've never seen an elf so glad to eat dirt, bet on it. I didn't know the dragon was dead, so battered as I was, I was on my feet and running before you could say 'dragon chow.'" She chuckled ruefully. "I didn't get ten man-heights before I twisted my foot and went down again, and by the time I got up, I realized nothing was coming after me and turned to look. The dragon, praise Fortune, was barely even twitching then, so I gathered my wits and went to see what'd become of Donya.

"To give Doe credit," Shadow grinned, "she *did* check to see I was all right before she retrieved her sword. There was me and her and two others left standing, everybody wounded, more or less, and this big dead dragon."

"We'd arranged for four wagons in case we were success-ful," Donya chuckled. "It took seven. We traded part to a butcher in exchange for his services, along with six of his apprentices, and we sold most of the hide to pay for the wagons and a preservation spell on the meat; but Shadow and I took the head, since we'd made the kill, and we divided the profits of the meat between the four of us. The four of us made hundreds of Suns apiece, and we had all the dragon we could eat for weeks, and the owner of the Blue Counterpane traded us our full winter's board for the head, stuffed and mounted it, and renamed the place the Red Dragon."

"And that," Shadow said grandly, "is the story of how I rode a dragon, and how Doe and I became heroes and got stinking rich in one afternoon."

"Stinking rich for a few weeks," Donya laughed. "You went through that money so fast that if we hadn't traded for our board for the winter we'd have frozen on the streets."

"*I* went through it?" Shadow protested. "At least when I gamble I usually win!"

"Yes, and *I* didn't 'loan' two hundred Suns to that sorry

pickpocket Melvan just before he jumped town two breaths ahead of the local guard,'' Donya returned.

"I could use a good slab of dragon right now," Shadow sighed wistfully.

"So when we get back," Donya said cheerfully, "I'll get a few good warriors together, and you and I can go get one."

"No, thank you," Shadow said tartly. "I'll let someone else ride the dragon from now on." She thumped her pony's back. "*This* mount's taller than I like. I like my feet flatly planted on the good solid ground, if you please."

"Hold!" Argent called. "Stop for a moment, please."

Shadow pulled her pony to a halt. Argent dismounted and approached one of the many muddy pools that could be seen on either side of the narrow trail.

"Wait a moment," Shadow said, sliding off the pony. She walked back to the rear of the train and unfastened a long spear from her supply pony. "Let me check that first."

Standing back a safe distance, Shadow thrust the spear point into the pool, probing the bottom.

"All right," she said. "Just making certain it wasn't deeper than it looked."

Argent knelt beside the pool, oblivious to the muck. He carefully pulled up several plants growing in the pool, stripped off the leaves, and placed them in layers in a wooden box, laying a strip of cloth soaked in a pungent-smelling oil between each layer. He took a waxed bag and, to Shadow's surprise, shoveled in several handfuls of swamp muck before he placed the moonwort roots therein.

"Perhaps they can be cultivated," Argent said in response to Shadow's inquiring glance. "Ordinarily I would harvest only a few plants, to ensure that the supply could be replenished in the future, but in this case I must harvest all I can. If the Crimson Plague ever returns, and this proves to lead to a cure, we'll need to be sure of a supply."

"There's more over there," Donya said helpfully, pointing to a hummock several feet away.

"Hey!" Shadow said sharply. "Wait a—"

Too late. Argent turned and quickly stepped toward the

indicated pool. He cried out as he sank quickly over his knees, the sucking mud imprisoning his feet.

"Grab the spear!" Shadow said, extending the shaft. Argent obeyed, but he had already sunk past his waist by the time Donya, Farryn, and Mist reached him with rope.

"Tie the rope under your arms, quickly," Donya said, throwing him the end. "I'm going to tie the other end to Ambaleis's saddle. When you're ready, yell, and we'll pull you out."

"Ready!" Argent called. The quickmud was already up to his armpits.

Donya urged Ambaleis forward slowly. The tall warhorse, unaccustomed to pulling a load, danced nervously, but it dug its broad hooves into the black muck and pulled. The rope grew taut and Argent gritted his teeth as the thick mud resisted the pull. Mist and Farryn edged as close to the quickmud as they dared, and as soon as they could reach Argent's hands, they added their efforts. At last Argent crawled from the mud and collapsed, panting, in the muck.

"I think Shadow's right," Argent wheezed. "From now on she checks the ground first."

"Well, before you celebrate your escape, let's see how many leeches you picked up in your swim," Shadow said grimly. "Mist, there's a pouch of salt with the cooking gear."

"Leeches." Argent shuddered when Shadow found two muddy brown blotches on his bare forearm. "I hadn't thought of leeches."

"They're probably the least nasty denizens of the Dim Reaches," Shadow said dismally, sprinkling the leeches with salt to make them detach. "Scrape off what mud you can; it'll itch as it dries. Let's go."

"But the moonwort," Mist protested.

"We can't go through the quickmud to get it," Shadow shrugged. "We'll have to hope there's more later."

"I can fetch it," Farryn volunteered, "if Shadow will lend me her spear."

"It's too far to jump," Shadow said skeptically, but she handed the spear to Farryn.

Farryn hefted the spear experimentally, then threw it skill-fully. It thunked solidly into the hummock.

"I needed to be sure the hummock was solid," he told Shadow. "I suppose I should have tied a cord to it first, so we could retrieve it if the ground was too soft."

"Well, it's solid," Shadow said. "Now what are you going to do?"

"I will need room," Farryn said apologetically. "If every-one will give me a clear path, I must start from a distance." He retreated a few feet down the path, waiting until everyone had moved out of his way.

"*Is* he going to try to jump?" Mist asked, puzzled.

"I don't know," Shadow shrugged. "Better have the rope ready, Doe, just in case."

Farryn had closed his eyes and was breathing deeply. He opened his eyes and started forward at an easy lope—

—and he *flickered*.

Shadow blinked and rubbed her eyes. Surely she had not seen Farryn, blinking in and out of visibility, skip *over* the surface of the water. But there he was on the hummock, carefully using the spear tip to dislodge the moonwort roots from the mud. When he finished, he tossed the spear back, shaft first. Donya, gaping rather blankly, caught it.

Shadow watched carefully this time, determined not even to blink, as Farryn moved back to the far side of the hummock. This time Farryn only took a deep breath before he moved, and Shadow was certain he actually winked in and out of sight as he ran. Not even ripples spread out from where his feet passed over the surface of the water.

Then Farryn was there, solid as ever, handing the plants to Argent. It had taken the barest fraction of a breath.

"I tried to keep the roots intact," he said.

Argent took the plants quietly. He prepared the leaves as quickly as he could, tucking the roots into the mud-filled bag without a word.

"Would you like to tell us," Donya said to Farryn in a quiet, calm voice, "just what you did?"

Farryn looked at her, his eyes widening.

"I thought you wanted the plants," he said. "No one spoke or moved to stop me."

"You didn't do anything wrong," Shadow said with a grin. "We were just—well, surprised, that's all. Is that how you got out of the hut in the forest?"

"Hut?" Farryn frowned. "I remember—something—"

"I think that means yes," Donya sighed. "But how do you *do* it? Is it a spell?"

"Spell?" Farryn's brow furrowed. "You mean like this?" He touched the torc. "I am not an Enlightened One. All of my folk dance the wind."

"Dance the . . . " Shadow suddenly burst out laughing. "You could've escaped anytime you wanted! You could've walked right out through the Fortune-be-damned palace walls!"

"Not so," Farryn protested. "I must see or know where I go, and I cannot dance through stone or even thick wood. Long travel weakens me greatly. In any event, it would have been dishonorable to attempt to escape. I had been fairly taken prisoner."

"You could go ahead," Mist suggested, "crossing the swamp instead of skirting it, and find this temple and begin searching for a cure to the plague."

Farryn sighed patiently.

"I fear you did not understand me," he said carefully. "I cannot dance my way past a stone door, and such it has been called. If it is submerged, when I reach the place I shall surely drown, for I do not swim and I cannot dance the wind from under the water. I do not know how to pass the temple door any more than you. And finally, as your prisoner it is my place to remain in your custody, and I will not abandon my sword, which has not been returned to me."

"I think we'd be wise to remedy that last," Donya said after a moment. "As Shady said, if he was minded to escape, he'd have done it. Still, Mist, I'd rather Farryn remain with us. Even if he succeeded totally and found a cure for the plague, his people need that cure as much as ours do." She held up her hand as Farryn began to protest. "Honor or no honor, if it were my people dying I'd take the cure and go as fast as I knew how.

I believe in his good intentions, but I don't want to put him in the position of making that choice. We'll need his knowledge if—when we reach the temple, and we may need every sword we have to get us there.''

She glanced at Mist. "So, if you don't object—''

Mist shrugged. "You are more cautious than I," he said. "I would have given it to him long ago.''

Donya thoughtfully unfastened the bundle of Farryn's belongings from her supply horse.

"As the Heir, I'm empowered to accept your parole," she said slowly. "Under the understanding of fair treatment and my protection, will you give your word that you won't attempt to escape or to hinder our cause, or to do us harm by word or deed, silence or inaction, until you are released?''

Farryn touched the amulet at his throat.

"Lady, by my heart's blood I swear it," he said.

"Then by my authority as Heir to the High Seat of Allanmere, and with the permission of the envoy of Aspen''— she glanced at Mist, who nodded—"I accept your parole.''

She laid the bundle in Farryn's hands.

Farryn opened the leather and matter-of-factly donned the light mail and belted on his sword and the two daggers.

"Thank you, my lady," he said gratefully. "It is good to be a warrior again.''

"Yes, well, be a warrior on a horse, will you?" Shadow urged. "While you two are playing oath games, folk in Allanmere are dying of the plague, and what's left of the guard is getting ready for a war.''

"Don't I know it," Donya said irritably, stepping back to her horse. "How do you think I got away without half the Palace Guard with me?''

"I had wondered," Argent said gently.

"You can only support so many by a little trail food, hunting, fishing, and foraging," Donya said, watching as the others mounted, then motioning Shadow to start. "If I'd brought guardsmen, we'd have needed extra horses for food and supplies. The larger our group gets, the slower we move, and the longer it takes us to get back. All the City Guards are human; elves don't go in for that sort of career. That means any guardsman could already be infected, and might pass it on to me or the other guards. Mother's just as glad I'm getting out of the city. Besides, what guards aren't already sickening with the plague are needed in the city, to keep the plague from leaving the city and to start mobilizing an army in case it does come to war. If anybody can be spared, they'll be sent to the forest to start coordinating with the elvan forces.''

"Still," Argent said doubtfully, "surely Celene would have sent a small company with us. You are, after all, the Heir."

"Of course she would have," Shadow said ruefully. "Especially if we'd left at two hours after sunrise, as we were supposed to, instead of an hour before dawn."

"We were to have left two hours after dawn?" Mist asked puzzledly. "But Lady Donya herself roused us before—" His face cleared. "Ah, I see."

"Our early departure," Donya said adamantly, "kept word from leaking out to the citizenry. I don't want to raise false hopes, and I don't want the citizens rushing blindly into the swamp in search of moonwort, or storming the palace thinking my mother's concealing a cure."

"Our early departure," Shadow mocked, "kept word from leaking out to your parents, who would surely have saddled you with at least a dozen guards and spoiled your grand adventure."

"That it did," Donya admitted, barely smiling. "Well, it won't spare me a lecture." She patted the small leather box tied to the saddle at her knee.

"If the Fortune-be-damned things work," Shadow grumbled, reaching into her saddlebags to be sure her own box was safely padded with soft fur.

"Mother tested both sets," Donya said patiently. "As long as the mirrors aren't broken, they'll work. Mother doesn't even think there's a distance limitation. You should be proud. Mother and her mages all but *invented* that spell for you."

"How marvelous," Shadow said sweetly. "Now I can *see* my Guildhouse falling down around Aubry when I talk to him."

"Shady, what *is* the matter with you?" Donya demanded.

"I've never seen you this grouchy, not on all our journeys together, and no matter how nasty it got."

"I've never had anyone else's lives hanging on me, either," Shadow said exasperatedly. "Let alone a Guild that I'm responsible for, or a whole city full of plague-ridden humans about to be trampled over by a barbarian horde. This isn't the free and open road, Doe, and we're not happy-go-lucky hire-swords anymore. This is a nasty, smelly swamp, and Fortune's left hand is just waiting to give us a good whack."

"Shadow," Mist chided. "Tomorrow's woes will come of their own accord. Let us not invite them."

Shadow sighed. "You're right, Mist," she said at last. "And I'm sorry, Doe. You're right, there's no point making this trip any worse than it is. I'll try not to be such a rumpled badger. See what comes of rousting me out of bed before my morning tumble?"

Mist laughed, Argent chuckled, and Donya smiled; Farryn frowned uncomprehendingly, which made them all laugh the harder.

"Why don't you pass around some of that wine," Argent suggested.

Shadow took a good swig, then passed the skin along.

"Wonderful," she sighed. "I think this calls for a song."

"Farryn," Donya said hastily, "just what is that metal the swords are made of?"

"We call it 'Adraon's tooth,' which means 'Adraon's tooth,'" Farryn said, then scowled irritatedly and snatched off the torc. "Adraonyn." He replaced the torc. "This magic speaking of your people is not without its flaws."

"Never mind," Donya said. "Just tell me about it. I've never seen metal like it anywhere, even in the far north. What about you, Shady?"

"May I see one of those daggers, Farryn?" Shadow asked, as if in answer to Donya's question.

Farryn drew one of the two daggers and looked inquiringly at Shadow over the horses and riders separating them; Shadow nodded, and he tossed the dagger. The sunlight flashed off the blade like fire, and Shadow caught it deftly by the hilt. She eyed the blade critically and touched her tongue carefully to the flat, testing the edge against her thumb and yelping when it drew blood with unexpected ease. She hefted the dagger thoughtfully, then flipped it rapidly a few times before tossing it back to Farryn.

"I've never seen anything like it and never hope to," she said ruefully. "If the strength of the metal matches the edge it can hold and its lightness, it's priceless. It feels almost too light to throw, but with the point and edge that stuff can hold, it'd pierce just about anything. I'd beggar myself for a dagger like that."

"They are not common even among our people," Farryn agreed. "No new blades, sword or dagger, have been made since our last Stone Brother died. Only they could call the metal forth from the earth. Were we not few, some of us would lack blades at our naming."

"But you've got three blades, and the armor besides," Donya observed.

"The sword is mine, given me at my naming," Farryn said. "The daggers and the mail were given me by our Enlightened Ones to protect me on my journey. There are many relics from our past, such as these weapons and armor and the map, which are held by our people and not owned by any one."

"I still don't understand," Donya said. She had drawn the sword Chyrie had given her and was surveying the blade. "I've never seen forge-work like this. And if the metal's as hard as it seems, how could anyone work it?"

"The Stone Brothers call it forth from the earth," Farryn repeated. "They shape it into the living blades we carry."

"Living blades?" Mist asked.

"A part of Adraon lives in each sword," Farryn said. "By his might our swords bring us victory, if wielded by a brave and honorable hand. No sword, however fine, surpasses the quality of its wielder. That is why we must prove ourselves worthy of Adraon's blessed blades, that we do not dishonor Adraon who dwells within them."

"Is it possible," Mist said slowly, "that these Stone Brothers have a gift such as you have, that you may walk not wholly in this world?"

"Aye, their gifts are otherwise," Farryn said. "As the Wind

Dancers walk the breath of this world and the other, so the Stone Brothers are one with the bones of the world.''

"They call the metal forth from the earth," Donya repeated, her face rapt. "By the gods, what I'd give to see that!"

"Most of my folk say the same," Farryn said sadly. "The last of our Stone Brothers is long dead and it seems there are none to be found here. It will be long before any Wind Dancer sees a new blade, if ever." He paused. "If any Wind Dancers will remain, indeed."

"Look," Argent interrupted, pointing. "Is that an old campsite?"

Shadow looked.

"Yes, that's it," she said. "Better stop now."

"But it's hardly getting dark," Donya protested.

"Yes, we made better time," Shadow nodded. "The swamp was wetter before, and the horses were slower. But we can't get anywhere close to the next site before dark, and believe me, there's no way the horses can go on after dark."

"I don't like stopping while it's still light," Donya frowned.

"If we ride on," Shadow said patiently, "we'll stop, either when we lose the light or when one of the horses breaks a leg—maybe your monster of a warhorse—just as you please, and then there won't be a good campsite where we can have a fire and sleep on dry ground. Let's stop now, Doe, and we'll have time to catch some fish and maybe an eel or two for supper. We may as well save the trail food as long as we can. And if my memory serves, there's clean water nearby."

"We've ridden the whole day at a slow walk," Donya said dismally, "and you say we've arrived *early*. How are we ever going to get through the swamp at this pace?"

"We're making excellent speed, believe me," Shadow assured her, "and that's only because it's stayed dry. Farryn may be able to run across mud and water, but the horses can't. Tempt Fortune's left hand and believe me, we'll go a lot slower! Enjoy it while you can. This is still the wet season, you know."

"I will set lines," Mist volunteered.

"I'll get the water, if you'll show me where," Argent said wryly, gesturing at mud-covered clothes and skin.

"We'll do both together," Shadow corrected. "With the spear. And some rope."

"Then Farryn and I will start a fire, take care of the horses, and set up camp," Donya said resignedly.

Shadow chuckled.

"Do you know," she said, "I think Doe prefers the old days, when she'd be worn out with fighting and I had to do all the work in camp. Then we'd spend a merry evening, Doe complaining about my food and boasting—exaggerating, rather—about how many enemies she'd killed, while I sewed up her wounds."

"A grand life indeed," Farryn said, absolutely serious. Mist, Argent, and Shadow looked at him amazedly, then had to laugh. Even Donya had to chuckle.

"I think only another warrior could appreciate a soldier's life," Donya said, loosening Ambaleis's girth strap and sliding the saddle from his back. "Oh, well, Shady, those days are gone, probably forever, and all you've got to put up with now are bug-infested swamps. Hurry with the water, will you?"

"All right, all right," Shadow said, pulling the empty waterskins from her supply horse while Argent fetched the rest. Mist took hooks and lines from his own horse, and carried the long spear.

She remembered the pool where they'd gotten fresh water before, but she was grateful that Mist knew more than she about picking good spots to set lines; she would much have preferred to avoid those other dank-looking pools altogether. She gave Mist the spear and stayed at the water pool with Argent, guarding him while he scrubbed the mud from his skin and clothes. Neither he nor Shadow thought it wise to enter the pool, so he sat beside it, his clean skin white against the murky browns and grays of the swamp, rubbing his soiled clothes against a rock to clean them. He made such a fetching sight that Shadow was tempted to try to persuade him to delay their return to camp; but before she could speak, a startled cry drew her attention. She glanced around, but Mist was nowhere to be seen.

"Mist!" Shadow called. "Where are you?"

"Here!" came his voice from somewhere to the west. "Help! There's—ulghph!"

Shadow ran in the direction of his voice, pulling the coil of rope from her shoulder as she ran, a naked Argent scrambling behind her.

Mist was half in and half out of one of the pools, one hand clutching desperately at the stake by which he had anchored one of his eel lines, his other hand scrabbling wildly in the mud for purchase. A heavy black tentacle had wrapped around his waist; a second had wound around his throat, silencing him. Just as Shadow saw him, his stake pulled loose and he slid back into the slimy black water.

Shadow threw the coil of rope to Argent, retaining one end. She tied the loose end around her waist as she ran, then drew a dagger. She had time to take one deep breath as she dived.

Thick black muck closed over her head, and she could see nothing, but there was no need. Something hit her hard in the face—was it a fell-beast's tentacle or one of Mist's limbs?— and tentacles tangled her arms and legs. Shadow slashed at the tentacles, groping for Mist; unexpectedly she felt his long braid and wound it around her hand as firmly as she could.

The rope around her waist had gone taut, and she hoped Argent had kept hold of his end. Mist's hand flailed through the water and seized the wrist twined in his hair, clasping it gratefully. Shadow prayed he had a dagger in the other hand.

Shadow slashed at the tentacles again, trying not to slash Mist as well. She was running out of breath, too; hopefully Mist could manage until he could get free.

There was suddenly another body in the small pool, a body too awkward in the water to be the fell-beast. Donya? Shadow prayed not; she needed the tall warrior's strength at the end of the rope to pull them out. Then her elbow jarred against fine metal links: Farryn, then—but hadn't he said he couldn't swim? Even in the murky water the odd pale metal of his daggers glinted. Shadow cut through a tentacle clinging to her waist, sawing as quickly as she could at the tough flesh. She saw Farryn's daggers slice through several tentacles, and Shadow felt some of those wrapped around her loosen as if in pain or surprise.

Then the rope was pulling her strongly upward. Shadow gave a tentacle one last severing cut, then dropped her dagger, groaning to herself as she did so; desperately she reached through the muck toward Farryn's flailing arm and grabbed it as tightly as she could. For a moment Shadow felt she would be pulled in two, the rope dragging at her waist as it fought the pull of the fell-beast on Mist and the combined weight of the two men. Farryn resisted for a moment, surprised, then reached to clasp her arm even as his other hand sliced through the last tentacle holding Mist, whose grip had grown alarmingly slack. Then there was a sudden strong pull on the rope, nearly cutting her in half at the waist, and her head was above water. Shadow coughed out mud and water, and then Argent was there, pulling her to the shore and helping her drag Mist up, while on her other side Farryn, coughing and choking, heaved himself onto the mud as quickly as he could.

Mist was utterly limp, and for a moment fear seized Shadow's heart; then he coughed and wheezed weakly. Shadow and Argent hurriedly rolled him onto his side as he spewed muddy water, hoarsely choking down a little air. Donya and Argent dragged them away from the pool, back to the spring where Argent had gotten their water.

Shadow was the first to get back enough breath to speak.

"Got any wine?" she wheezed.

Donya laughed. "Sorry, I left it all at the camp. What about some water instead?"

"No thank you, I've had quite enough," Shadow returned, spitting out mud and picking a strand of swamp weed out of her face. "What about you, Mist?"

Mist coughed hoarsely, then gave a weak chuckle.

"You were wrong, Shadow," he gasped.

"About what?" Shadow said, lying back limply on the mud.

"I was nearly the first to slip down a fell-beast's maw, not you," he replied.

Shadow laughed until the ache of her lungs brought tears to her eyes. Even Farryn gasped out his mirth until the three of them lay still on the mud, regaining their breath in amused, if pained, silence.

"At least you had the good sense to tie a rope on yourself

before you tried to dive headfirst down its throat,'' Donya said
mildly, coiling the rope. She swatted Shadow's hands away and
untied the knots with surprising gentleness.

''Well, I couldn't let Mist go swimming without me,''
Shadow said. ''But, Farryn, whatever possessed you to dive in?
I thought you said you couldn't swim.''

''I cannot swim,'' Farryn admitted. ''But Donya was heavily
armored and her strength was needed at the rope, and Argent
was unarmed. I could not let you and Mist fight alone.''

He was silent for a long moment.

''You loosed your dagger to pull me out, did you not?'' he
asked.

''I can get another sometime,'' Shadow shrugged.

''You leave me ever deeper in your debt,'' Farryn sighed.
''At least this debt I will repay.'' He pulled one of the two
daggers from its sheath and tossed it. Shadow was too tired to
catch it, and it thunked, point first, into the mud by her hand.

Shadow plucked the dagger from the mud and grinned, eyes
sparkling.

''Are you serious?'' she asked, amazed and delighted.

''Such a courageous spirit deserves no less,'' Farryn said.
''Our Enlightened One would approve.''

Shadow wiped the blade reverently and tried it in her sheath.
It fit a little tightly for a quick draw, but a little careful work on
the sheath would do for this trip. Afterward she'd commission
a new sheath, something special and expensive.

''There you are, Shady,'' Donya laughed. ''The finest
dagger in Allanmere, and you didn't even have to steal it.''

''Steal!'' Farryn exclaimed, outraged. ''How can you say
such a thing of one who acquitted herself so bravely!''

''She wasn't insulting me,'' Shadow assured him. ''I guess
nobody told you. I'm Guildmistress, you know, of Allanmere's
Guild of Thieves.''

''And the greatest thief in Allanmere,'' Argent said gal-
lantly.

''A . . . thief?'' Farryn said disbelievingly. ''*You* are a—a
thief?''

''By profession,'' Shadow acknowledged. ''Also an excellent gambler, a Fortune-be-damned good knife fighter, and not bad in the furs, either, by all accounts.''

"A thief," Farryn muttered, his face pale and his lips a thin white line. "A *thief* has touched my soul?"

"Oh, Fortune favor me, I've stained his precious honor," Shadow sighed. "Do you want your dagger back now?"

"I would not have it," Farryn said disgustedly. "To stand in debt to a *thief*—how can I return to my people with such dishonor on my soul?"

"Damn all, she could've left you in that pool with the fell-beast for company!" Donya exclaimed angrily. "What kind of honor is it that lets you spit on someone who's likely saved your life?"

"Now, now, Doe," Shadow said calmly, "don't let it bother you. I don't. I've run into plenty worse in my travels, especially in cities without a Guild. Remember Vikram and Bobrick? At least Farryn's not trying to slit my gullet."

For a moment Donya and Farryn glared at each other, sparks all but flashing from their eyes; then Donya shook her head and took her hand from her sword hilt.

"I can't challenge someone who's sworn parole," she said disgustedly. "And only fools fight on a sinking ship. Shadow, Mist, if you want to clean up a little, we'll wait, and we'll all go back to camp together. I'm sure Argent would like to put on dry clothes, and after that adventure, I could use some of Shady's wine."

Farryn scraped most of the mud from his armor and clothing, but Mist and Shadow chose to strip down as Argent had done, scrubbing the mud from their hides and then sloshing their clothes clean in the relatively clear water of the spring. Donya filled the abandoned waterskins and carried them back.

Donya had no more than started on setting up camp when she'd had to drop what she was doing, but the horses were unloaded, tethered, and fed. Everyone pitched in, glad of action to fill the tense and hostile silence. Too soon the tents were pitched and bedrolls laid out, the fire laid and lit and a pot of water heating over it. Then there was nothing to do but look over the trail food while Mist—with Argent and Farryn—went to check his lines.

"You're still angry," Shadow chuckled as she peeled potatoes and dropped them into the pot. "It's not like you to let an ignorant, opinionated stranger get you so heated."

"I'm sorry," Donya said with a sigh. "I just can't stand to hear you insulted, especially by—well—an ignorant, opinionated stranger who has no idea of what you're made of. When I think of all the times I'd have been worm food on our travels if I hadn't had you at my back—"

"Oh, Doe, don't set me up beside Fortune and the Mother Forest," Shadow chuckled. "If the truth be told, at your back was the safest place to be in a fight because I knew *nothing* would get past that monster of a sword, not to mention that it was the next best thing to having a wall at my back!"

"All right, all right," Donya chuckled.

"I know why Farryn gets you so bristly," Shadow chuckled. "You're hot for a tumble with him, that's what."

"Shady!" Donya blushed bright red. "He's not even human!"

"Neither was Mist," Shadow said knowingly. "And neither are you, just half. And he's not that far off from human, give or take a finger or two. Remember, *I* saw him frog naked at the festival, and in the bath, too."

"Shady, really!" Donya said, blushing even more deeply.

"Oh, please, Doe," Shadow said wryly, reaching for another potato. "A month after we met I had to stitch another bedroll to yours to make it wide enough that your partners wouldn't roll out onto the ground at night. Fortune favor me, when we wintered at Makon's Ford one of your lovers, that fellow Sylvan, snored so loudly that if we hadn't bartered for the full winter's board the innkeep would've thrown us both out. Truth to tell, after a couple of nights with the pillow over my ears I wouldn't have minded if he had! Anyway, what's wrong with a good dance in the bedroll with Farryn?"

"He's not human."

"He's not ugly, either," Shadow said.

"He's narrow-minded," Donya insisted.

"He moves like a dancer."

"He doesn't respect anyone's life-style but his own," Donya protested.

"But he *is* brave," Shadow said, testing the dryness of her clothes where they hung by the fire.

"He's as judgmental as High Priest Vikram," Donya said dismally.

"But he's got a much better rump," Shadow grinned. "Not to mention a pretty good—"

"Shady!" Donya interrupted, shocked. She jerked her head, indicating the returning men.

Shadow chuckled and reached for another potato.

Mist had four large eels and a turtle from his lines, and Argent had a small sack full of plants and tubers.

"This root-blighted turtle ate every fish off my lines," Mist said disgustedly. "So he will repay us in flesh. Did you find my soupstone, Shadow, where I left it for you?"

Shadow nodded and indicated the thong hanging down into the pot.

"What've you got there, Argent?" she asked interestedly. "Medicinal plants or herbs for the pot?"

"Both," Argent said, holding up a few moonwort plants and handing the rest of the sack to Shadow. "Those can go in the stew."

"Perhaps some wine?" Mist suggested.

"Hah!" Donya laughed. "You don't know Shady as well as I do. The wine was the first thing to go in."

Mist cleaned the large turtle while the others dealt with the eels, and soon the pot was giving off a delightfully meaty aroma, fragrant with wine and herbs.

"I can't wait till it cooks," Argent said wistfully, sniffing the pot. "A day on a horse has given me quite an appetite."

"Me, too," Shadow said. She looked at Mist wickedly. "But I wouldn't mind some food, either."

Mist smiled back, raising one pale eyebrow.

"I could well forgo the food," he said. "But there is no need to choose between the two, thank the Mother Forest, and the food will soon be ready. In the meantime, I brought some dreamweed to pass the time; can we broach another skin of your excellent wine?"

"Save the dreamweed. I can give you even better," Shadow

chuckled. She pulled out one of the small crystal flasks of Dragon's Blood.

Donya groaned. "Shadow, are you trying to kill me?" she protested. "I just recovered from that crazy festival!"

"If you've recovered, then it's time for another one," Shadow laughed.

"What is this?" Mist asked curiously as Shadow handed him a tiny cup.

"Dragon's Blood, an illegal concoction Shadow pays outrageous prices for." Donya grimaced, but she accepted her own cup. "Mind you, I'm not supposed to know she's buying this stuff."

"Medicinal purposes," Shadow said stoutly. "Keeps the swamp vapors from giving you lung-rot."

"I do not care for your wine," Farryn started to decline when Shadow offered him a cup. He would not meet Shadow's eyes.

"It's not wine," Shadow said. "It's harmless."

"Harmless!" Donya barked with laughter.

"Oh, go on," Shadow said, seeing that Farryn still hesitated. "You're not afraid of a little liquor, are you?"

Farryn frowned darkly, but he took the small cup.

"I've heard of this," Argent said, sniffing his own cup. "I admit to some curiosity. Well, will we have a toast?"

"Of course," Shadow said, raising her tiny cup. "To roads, and friends, and dragons conquered!"

Everyone drank. Shadow swallowed her own small sip and watched with amusement the various reactions: coughs, choking gasps, sputtering, and, from Donya, even a strangled oath; but when she offered the flask again, even Farryn accepted a second cup. Wine followed, to ease the inner fires, and Mist surveyed his pouch of dreamweed a little dubiously.

"The dreamweed had best wait for another night," he said at last, tucking the pouch away with considerable difficulty. "Otherwise none of us may awaken in case of danger."

"If anything attacks us in the night," Argent said dazedly, "all we have to do is give it some of Shadow's liquor. That should disable even a dragon."

"Best eat some of this stew before we forget it entirely,"

Shadow said, "or that poor turtle will have given his life in vain, and we'll all have skinned those nasty, slimy eels for nothing."

None of them were very sober, but Shadow carefully ladled out bowls of hot stew and everyone took them, setting the bowls on the ground because nobody could hold the bowls straight.

"We should set watches," Farryn said sternly, and then belched resoundingly, looking horrified at himself.

"There's really no need," Shadow said, shrugging. "The only large swamp creatures I know of live in the water and won't come on land, or near the fire. There's no one to attack us."

"No, I think Farryn's right," Donya said. "You said yourself you don't know that much about the swamp, and when you were here before you were safer because of—well, the company you kept would scare just about anything off." She grimaced. "With five of us, we can all get plenty of sleep. Mist can take the first watch, and then you, Shady, so you two can get some—rest. But in the meantime, let's give those mirrors a try, shall we?"

"That's a wonderful idea," Shadow said stoutly. She got up and stumbled to her saddlebag, pulling out the box. It contained a small, silver-edged mirror, carefully padded in cloth and furs. "Who first, Aubry or Celene?"

"Aubry first," Donya said after a moment's thought. "If he's got any special news, I want to tell Celene about it."

Shadow drew out the mirror and looked at it blankly.

"What's the words for this thing?"

"They're scribed around the edge of the mirror," Donya said patiently. "I *knew* you wouldn't remember them."

"Oh." Shadow read the inscription, turning the mirror as she did. "Arbris, tersi, elandriko, roo!"

For a moment the mirror remained blank, reflecting only night darkness and firelight; after a few moments, Aubry's scowling face appeared.

"You should've told me when you were going to call," he said crossly. "I've been sitting in front of this damned thing all day waiting for it to light up, afraid to use the privy for fear I'd miss you.''

"All right, I'm sorry," Shadow said humbly. "From now on I'll call about two hours after sundown, all right? And if you don't answer in a minute or two, I'll call back every hour until you do. Or you can call me. So what's the news?"

"Oh, everyone wonders where you've gone again, of course," Aubry said, sighing. "Most people figure you're off to the forest again, maybe getting Lady Donya away from the plague. Everyone expected that much. As far as the rumors go, nobody's heard anything they shouldn't.''

"You don't sound happy," Shadow said. "What's the matter? The plague?"

"It's bad, Shady," Aubry said soberly, shaking his head. "The riots are getting worse. The Guild may be hit next."

"Why?" Shadow asked worriedly. "I could see healers and mages, maybe, or herbalists, but why the Guild?"

Aubry hesitated.

"It's all over town now that elves don't have the plague," he said. "Some folk are saying that the elves have a cure and won't let the humans have it—there's even a rumor that the elves started the plague, to clear the humans away from the forest.''

"I might've expected that," Shadow said unhappily. "What else, Aubry? I can tell when you're holding something back."

"There's another rumor that elves are immune to the plague," Aubry said slowly. "This morning two elves turned up dead in the alleys in Rivertown, all the blood drained out of them. Seems some humans think that by drinking elvan blood they can avoid the plague, or maybe cure it, I don't know.''

"Mother Forest shelter us," Mist whispered.

Shadow swallowed heavily and reached for her wineskin.

"By all the gods," she whispered, remembering the mob in the marketplace. "So that's what they meant.''

She shook her head briskly.

"Encourage elves to go back to the forest if they can get past the guards at the gate. If I know the High Lord and Lady they've probably told the guards to shut-eye for elves, anyway; nothing to lose. Don't let too many loiter around the Guildhouse at a time, but encourage them that if they go out, they go out in pairs or groups. What else?"

"The guard's doing something," Aubry said thoughtfully. "They've called in their reserves, and I've heard they're drilling on the palace grounds. Maybe it's because of the riots."

"Probably," Shadow agreed. "Is there anything else?"

"No." Aubry hesitated. "Take care of yourself, Shady. We need you back."

Shadow smiled. "I'll call you tomorrow," she said. "Two hours after sunset."

When Shadow had put away her mirror, Donya took hers out and recited the short spell. Celene's drawn face immediately appeared in the mirror as if she, too, had been waiting for the call.

"Donya!" she said gladly. "How are you faring?"

"Muddy but well," Donya said reassuringly.

"Better than you deserve," Celene said dryly. "I imagine you learned your slyness from Shadow there beside you. If you were here and I stood tall enough, I'd beat you black and blue for creeping away without your escort, without so much as a good-bye for your poor parents."

"If I were there," Donya said practically, "you'd have nothing to beat me for. If we make it back safely, I promise I'll let you beat me as hard as you like. But the guards would only have slowed us down. We're making such good progress with the dry weather."

Celene frowned.

"Our seers have foreseen storms approaching," she said. "The first rains may arrive tomorrow. I was waiting to warn you."

"The trail's pretty high above the water now," Donya said. "We've got a good margin for safety. But how are you and Father doing?"

"Well enough," Celene said firmly, although her hollow cheeks and dark-ringed eyes made Shadow wonder. "Of course with the trouble in town—"

"We heard about the riots," Donya said. "And the elves."

Celene shook her head. "It's becoming harder to keep

order," she said. "The guard has all it can do, and of course so many of them are infected themselves. The guards at the gates are watching each other as suspiciously as they are the other citizens."

"It's rumored in town that the guard is drilling," Donya warned her. "But they think it's because of the riots."

"In large part it is," Celene said worriedly. "They've had no time to begin conscripting the army."

"Is there any *good* news?" Shadow asked over Donya's shoulder.

"The mages have made a potion using the moonwort that seems to do some good," Celene said. "Several of the volunteers are—are holding out well." Her voice shook slightly. "Are you finding more moonwort, daughter? It is so very important to us now."

"We've already got a box full of the treated leaves," Donya assured her. "Do we need to send somebody back with them?"

"No." Celene shook herself briskly. "We'll have to make do with what we have until you come back. It's more important now that you continue on as quickly as you can, and I want every one of your companions with you to protect you."

"High Lady," Argent said, peering over Donya's other shoulder, "I could wrap the box in a waxed case and leave it here. If you could dispatch a few guards to retrieve it, they could have the moonwort back in Allanmere in two days or less, and if the guards stay on the trail they will be safe; but they must be cautioned to carry their own food and water and not leave the trail for any reason. And even if you can send no one, the box will be safe here until our return."

"That's a good thought," Celene said relievedly. "I'll dispatch a small party at first light. Leave the box as high above water as you can, however, and marked with something bright. Daughter, is there anything else? If not, I need to return to my mages."

"I'd like to talk to Father, if I can," Donya said. "I'd like to apologize since I didn't say good-bye before I left."

Celene's brow furrowed. "He's with the City Council," she said hesitantly. "It's an emergency session. But wait a few moments and I'll fetch him. He wouldn't want to miss your call.''

It was quite some time before the mirror lit again, so long that furrows of worry had appeared on Donya's brow. When Sharl's face finally appeared, it was even more drawn and pale than Celene's, but his eyes were bright—too bright, Shadow thought uneasily, but she said nothing.

''I'm glad you called so soon,'' Sharl smiled. ''Celene and I were worried when you left so abruptly. Still, it's as well you're out of the city now. The riots are worsening.''

''I've heard,'' Donya said. ''We talked to Aubry at the Guild first.''

''Don't concern yourself with it,'' Sharl said firmly. ''Don't concern yourself with anything here in the city. If you can bring us more moonwort, or even a cure for the plague, that's more valuable than anything you could do here. But the greatest concern, Donya, is to keep yourself safe. Remember that. Allanmere will need you one day.''

''I'll be all right, Father,'' Donya told him. ''It's you and Mother I worry about.''

''Don't worry about us.'' Sharl's voice faltered slightly, then firmed. ''Keep safe, daughter, and know that no matter where you are, no matter what happens, my love goes with you.''

''Thank you, Father,'' Donya said fondly. ''I love you both. I'll call about two hours after sunset every day, if that's all right with you.''

''That's fine,'' Celene said gratefully, her face appearing beside Sharl's. ''Good night, daughter, and fare well.''

Donya wrapped the mirror and put it away thoughtfully.

''I'm worried,'' she said at last. ''Mother and Father were upset about something.''

''They've got plague in the city, an invasion threatening, the people are rioting, and the humans may turn against the elves,'' Shadow said patiently. ''Their daughter's chasing legends in a swamp so dangerous that even criminals won't hide in it. What could they possibly be upset about?''

''That's true,'' Donya said doubtfully. ''I suppose that's it.''

''If there's trouble in town, there's nothing you or I can do about it, any more than your parents can help us here,'' Shadow said practically. "We're doing what has to be done, and the people in town are doing the same. So have a cup of wine and let it go."

Donya sighed and took the proffered wineskin.

"If humans are attacking the elves," Argent said slowly, "what will become of the Compact?"

"Nothing's going to happen to the Compact," Shadow shrugged. "If they have to, Sharl and Celene will tell the people about the invasion. There may be a panic, but that'll keep the elves and humans from trying to kill each other. At least it'll get everyone's mind off the plague. If the elves are smart, they'll all leave for the forest until things are settled, one way or the other—until the humans calm down, or until so many of them die that they're no longer a threat."

Argent sighed. "Five hundred years ago," he said, "the Black Wars ravaged the forest. Now the plague is ravaging Allanmere, and who knows what's to come?"

"What is to come," Mist said patiently, "is that you will cover the stew, drink a little more wine, and go to sleep. I will take the first watch, and in a short time I will wake Shadow, and then *I* will go to sleep. And then when Shadow's watch is done, she will wake one of you, and then we will *not* sleep. That is what is to come."

"I like your kind of prophecy," Shadow laughed. She held up the flask of Dragon's Blood. "Anyone need a sleeping potion?"

Argent groaned. "Mercy on my poor head," he said. "Already I couldn't sit a horse to save my life, and if I tried to mix a burn poultice I'd probably apply itchweed instead."

Donya chuckled bitterly.

"At least you have an elvan tolerance," she said. "I don't seem to have inherited Mother's. All the while I was talking with Mother I was trying to guess which of her three faces was the real one. I'm going to be spitting my stew back into the swamp tomorrow."

"Waste of a good turtle," Shadow chuckled, fastening the lid of the pot down with the lid hooks. "Stumble off to your bedroll, Doe."

"I think you're right," Donya said wearily. She accepted a

last swig of wine from Shadow's skin, then staggered off to one of the tents and collapsed inside.

Farryn glanced back at her, then looked at Mist.

"You and your mate will share a tent?" he asked.

"My—mate?" Mist asked surprisedly, glancing at Shadow.

"Mist and I will be sharing a tent," Shadow said smoothly. "Where will you sleep?"

"The lady should have her own tent," Farryn said stonily. He turned to Argent. "I will tent with you, if you do not object."

"If you snore," Argent warned sternly, "I swear to you that I'm so drunk I'll sleep right through it."

Shadow took a last tremendous swallow of wine and crawled off to her own bedroll.

"Wake me when you're ready," she called to Mist. "I've left you the wine. Whatever Donya thinks about night watches, it's bound to be pretty dull and gloomy. I know."

Shadow felt she'd hardly closed her eyes before Mist was shaking her gently—as gently as he could, that is, considering that he'd demolished most of the remaining wine. He fell into his bedroll and was snoring even before Shadow could rub the sleep out of her eyes.

Mist had relaid the fire to burn low to save wood, although they were still close enough to the forest and high enough above the water that firewood was easy to find. Shadow pushed another stick or two into the fire, pulled a piece of sap-sugar candy out of her pack to nibble, and settled back comfortably for a very boring couple of hours.

It was a little after midnight when Shadow tweaked Argent's foot under the blanket.

"Your watch," she murmured when he opened a bleary eye. "I'll let you wake one of our sword-happy warriors when you're ready."

"Oh, thank you," Argent groaned. "Gods, I'm dying."

"Have some wine," Shadow offered charitably.

Mist had stopped snoring when Shadow crawled into the tent beside him, but he was sleeping so soundly that even vigorous shaking did not wake him. Shadow sighed, curled up next to his warmth, and slept.

SEVEN

Celene's prediction of the weather had been dismally true. When Shadow awoke, the early light—if it could be called such—was leaden gray and a few sprinkles of rain were already falling.

"We'd better get started," Donya murmured, "before the trail gets too slippery."

"Or the water gets too high," Shadow agreed, grinning sympathetically as Donya winced at the sound of her voice. "Is there time for a cup of stew before we go?"

Donya turned a little green at the suggestion.

"I don't think so," she said. "The mud's already getting slick, even with the little rain we've had."

"All right." Shadow yawned, stretched, and shook Mist gently as Donya moved to Farryn and Argent's tent.

"Wake up, lover," she said affectionately. "Although you've done nothing much lately to earn the title. Time to ride."

"By the Mother Forest, I am perishing," Mist moaned. "It was poison you gave us to drink last night."

"More like a sleeping potion," Shadow said, laughing. "Come on, the rain and mud are waiting eagerly for us."

With the five of them working together, it took little time to roll the tents and pallets and pack everything on the horses, keeping out their wet-weather cloaks. Argent carefully wrapped the box of moonwort leaves in a waxed leather, tied a strap of white cloth around it, and secured it firmly in the fork of a dead tree standing beside the trail.

True to Donya's warning and Shadow's worries, the trail was indeed slick and growing slicker. There was no question, however, of trying to wait out the rain; the trail went downhill from here, and if the swamp flooded, the road could become blocked entirely until whenever it might drain.

They rode much more slowly now, the horses floundering on the black mud. Shadow watched the water level of the swamp anxiously, but it had not yet begun to rise, although the rain was slowly growing heavier and the clouds blacker with every hour. There was no question of stopping at midday, either; in any event, there was no shelter or even dry ground to sit on. They ate cheese, tough cured meat, and journeybread in the saddle, occasionally dropping part of their dinner into the mud when their horses slipped or stumbled.

Carefully Donya edged Ambaleis around Shadow's supply horse and rode as close as she dared.

"You marked a trail shelter on the map," Donya said, wiping rain out of her eyes. "Any idea how much farther? Argent's not used to these conditions, and the horses are pretty tired."

Shadow squinted through the rain, but shook her head.

"I can't tell where we are," she said ruefully. "We're lucky to be staying on the road. Any idea how long till sunset?"

Donya peered up at the dark gray sky.

"Who can tell?" she said dismally. "Seems like we've been riding a year, but I'm sure it's more like ten or twelve hours."

"Anytime, then," Shadow said. "We were riding in the rain before, and we found the trail shelter around sunset or a little before. It's just off the trail on the right; even in the rain we can't miss it."

"I hope not," Donya said grimly, reining in Ambaleis to fall back into line.

As if determined to add to their worries, the clouds darkened even more, and an ominous peal of thunder warned them that their spring rain was about to become a spring storm. Soon they slowed to an even slower crawl, the horses stumbling nose to tail while Shadow paused occasionally to wait for a flash of lightning to illuminate the trail ahead.

They did not miss the trail shelter; in fact, Shadow nearly collided with it. She reined in sharply and her horse slipped and slid; the supply horse shied, and Shadow heard Donya curse as Ambaleis nearly lost his footing.

"Here it is," Shadow called back cheerfully. "Anyone want a dry bed and a fire?"

There was no possibility of stabling ten horses in the ramshackle lean-to, so Farryn and Donya loosened several poles and used the tents to form a makeshift roof for the unhappy animals to shelter under. By the time they had finished sheltering, unloading, and feeding the horses as best they could, Farryn and Donya were wetter than the horses and glad to warm at the fire Shadow and Argent had built in the shelter.

"Well, you're the herbalist, Argent," Shadow joked, hanging her cloak near the fire. "Are we all going to get lung-rot?"

"That or drown," Argent said wryly. "I prescribe hot stew and hot wine mulled with some herbs and spices I happen to have, and a good night's sleep for all. In solid walls there's surely no need to keep watches, Donya, is there?"

"I suppose not," Donya said with a sigh. "Help me with my armor, Shady, will you? My fingers are so soaked and swollen, I can't manage the buckles."

It had been years since Shadow had helped Donya remove her armor, but the act brought pleasant memories.

"I suppose you want me to polish it for you, too," Shadow chuckled as she laid the last piece down to drip dry.

"I won't refuse it if you offer," Donya said in the same vein, shivering violently in her tunic. Shadow frowned worriedly, but Donya smiled reassuringly and squatted by the fire.

"Ahhh, that's good," the warrior sighed relievedly. "I've gotten soft, Shady, living in town these last couple of years."

"Soft or sick," Shadow said worriedly as Donya still shivered, although Donya's skin was not abnormally warm to the touch.

"Don't fuss, Shady, I'm fine," Donya said firmly. "Just wet and cold."

"Well, at least dry your wet clothes," Shadow told her. "Somewhere in that pack there must be drier clothing. By the time you're done changing, the stew and wine will be hot."

"I thought of it first," Mist chuckled, hanging his wet clothes to dry. "Everyone can change, and I will tend the food and wine."

"Wet journeybread," Argent groaned as he peered into his pack. "I thought this was tied shut."

"Give it to me and I will make dumplings for the stew," Mist said comfortingly.

"A little Dragon's Blood will warm everyone up," Shadow suggested, holding up the flask.

"No thank you," Donya retorted. "I think we've all had enough of your 'sleeping potion.' We'll rely on stew and mulled wine to warm us tonight, or we'll never wake up tomorrow!"

"Stew, mulled wine, and—music?" Argent asked, pulling a well-wrapped bundle out of his bags. He carefully unwrapped a small lute.

"I have drums," Mist added eagerly, lifting out the small drums he had played at the Forest Altars.

"You play something, don't you?" Donya asked Farryn. "I saw it in your bag. A kind of pipe, is it?"

"A pipe?" Farryn asked, his brow furrowing. "Such as is smoked?"

"No, no," Mist said. "The instrument is so named, for it is also held to the lips to play."

Farryn went to his bags to fetch the long, thin roll of his instrument.

"I will play if you wish," he said, "but I do not know your songs."

"None of us are skilled musicians," Argent smiled. "Start a tune and we will join in."

To Shadow's surprise, Farryn put his mouth to the blowhole sideways, arranging his fingers along the holes in the long pipe. A rich, sweet sound emerged, less complex than that of the multiple pipes Shadow was accustomed to but far smoother and with a lower tone. He set a sprightly tune and Mist joined in on the drums; after a few bars Argent was strumming a dancing harmony.

The music was merry and infectious as music should be; Shadow found herself tapping her foot and then clapping her hands. She put down her cup and stood, beckoning to Donya.

"Come on, Doe, and dance with me," she said. "This'll warm your blood."

"I've ridden all day long," Donya protested, but she was standing even as she spoke.

"So have I," Shadow laughed. "All the more reason to get off our bottoms and onto our feet. Dance!"

This was not elvan dancing, graceful and artistic; this was a jovial human pub-hop, happy and fast and careless. Donya swung Shadow around so fast that the elf's feet left the floor and her braids flew out of their pinned coil; Shadow whooped and matched her friend step for step, dancing dizzying circles around the warrior until Donya wobbled on her feet. Abruptly Shadow tripped over the end of her braid and measured her length on the packed-dirt floor, and Donya collapsed beside her, laughing delightedly. The men gave up shortly after, Mist and Farryn wheezing for breath and Argent shaking his fingers.

"Nothing matches the grace of elves," Donya chuckled heartlessly. "I'll take some wine now, O delightful dancer friend of mine, and a big bowl of stew, and a double helping of breath, if you've got it."

"No, somebody stole all of mine," Shadow gasped, reaching for the ladle. "But at least we're warm now."

"That we are," Donya admitted, wiping sweat from her face. She accepted a cup and bowl and attacked both with the ferocity of a true warrior.

Farryn, despite his dislike of wine, accepted a cup of the sweet, hot mulled drink after a stern order from Argent; no one else had any inclination to abstain. By the time the five of them had emptied a kettle of mulled wine and sopped up the last drop of gravy from the stewpot, everyone was in better spirits. Donya shook her head, however, when Mist started to pack a pipe with dreamweed.

"Not tonight," she said. "Tonight we plan."

She unrolled their map on the floor and traced their path.

"According to your account, Shady, you left the swamp trail for the forest and then doubled back later," she said. "How long did that take you?"

"Two nights," Shadow said after a moment's thought. "But we came back to the swamp not far north of where we'd left the trail, at least according to this map. I don't know, Doe. According to this map, it's farther to the next campsite than we came today, and we got an early start while the trail was still relatively dry. I've never seen this part of the trail in between. If it's still raining tomorrow, I don't know if we can make it before dark."

As if in answer, thunder roared as a flash of lightning momentarily lit the shelter.

"What's this?" Mist asked, tracing a large, ill-defined area marked with dotted lines.

"Spirit Lake," Shadow said, grimacing. "Starting day after tomorrow, probably, we'll be traveling along its edge. If it hasn't risen, that is, and swamped the trail, in which case there's no way to get through. And that's another thing, Doe. I don't like trying to navigate around Spirit Lake when I can't see. It'll be misty around the lake—thick mists—and it was bad enough last time, with a fairly dry trail."

"I don't see that we have much choice," Donya said, looking at the map. "The temple's at the north-northwest edge of the lake, and the trail will meet it at the southeast edge. We'll have to circle around the whole edge of the lake, probably two days ride after the shelters."

"Doe, if the storms don't stop tomorrow the whole trail will be underwater," Shadow insisted. "And the temple, too, if it isn't already. And then we'll be *swimming* in Spirit Lake."

"We could turn east and travel through the forest," Mist suggested. "We can cross the river at the north, circle around, and come back down."

Donya shook her head. "That'll take us at least two days, probably three, out of our way," she said. "Even if we could build a raft big enough to carry five people and ten horses, we couldn't navigate it across the flooded rivers, and there's two rivers to deal with: the northern branch Shadow mentioned, and the Brightwater itself. We can't do it.''

"If the swamp rises too far, and we've advanced into the lower trail,'' Argent observed, "we won't be able to turn back, either. Mist's idea has merit.''

Donya shook her head again.

"No," she said. "We can't spare one day, we can't spare one minute. While we're delaying, folk are dying in Allanmere and the northern barbarians may be walking through Farryn's village."

Farryn put his cup down decisively.

"You are fools to argue now," he said stonily. "The rain and the trails will make our decisions for us soon enough. We know where we must go, we know which road to take. When the time comes our heart will tell us what to do.''

"Isn't faith a wonderful thing," Shadow said sarcastically. "My heart's telling me I should be back in Allanmere with my Guild."

"Allanmere!" Donya exclaimed. "The mirrors!"

"Might as well use them," Shadow said sourly. "We're pissing into the wind arguing here.''

Aubry was waiting when Shadow called. Like Celene, he looked gaunt and harried.

"Hello, Shady," he said tiredly. "I'm glad to see you're all right."

"I am, but you don't look like you are," Shadow said. "What's happened?"

"There was a riot here today," Aubry said. "The guard broke it up, but not before three of our members were killed. Elves, naturally. Now there's guards posted all up and down Guild Row."

Shadow grimaced.

"That won't do much for the trade," she sighed, "but at least it'll keep our people safer. What about the human members?"

"Several we know are dead," Aubry said slowly. "Unfortunately our people spend so much time in the market that they were exposed to the plague that much sooner. There's at least a dozen we haven't seen for a few days, which may or may not mean they're dead.''

"Fortune favor us," Shadow said, shaking her head. "Is there any *good* news?''

"The High Lord and Lady have started informally evacuating elves to the forest," Aubry said. "At least I assume they're doing it. Nothing official, but the guard's been coming around to all the businesses and guilds that have a large elvan population and hinting that if elves want to form caravans and move back to the forest while the plague's in the city, they'll be allowed past the gates and given guard escort to make sure they reach Inner Heart safely. Some of our people have already gone, and a couple of groups are leaving tomorrow. Of course, the fact that the elves are being allowed to leave—although they only go to the Heartwood anyway—and the humans can't isn't helping the general temper.''

"Before you know it, somebody will start a new industry in smuggling folks out," Shadow said glumly.

"It's been tried already," Aubry told her. "The guard's patrolling the wall as best they can, but they're spread pretty thin already." Somewhere behind him, Shadow heard a knock on the door. "Listen, Shady, I've got to go.''

"All right," Shadow said. "I'll check in tomorrow.''

Donya's mirror, however, remained stubbornly blank until a strange face appeared in it—a middle-aged human whom Shadow had seen before around the palace but had never met.

"Councilman Elwyn," Donya said surprisedly. "I thought Mother would be waiting for my call.''

"Celene is with her mages and healers," Elwyn said. "They've had little success, I'm afraid.''

"What about my father?" Donya said.

"Lord Sharl is with Celene," Elwyn said. "I'm afraid they can't be disturbed now. Celene asked me to carry this mirror and await your call, lest you interrupt her in the middle of a spell." He looked away. "I'm afraid I must ask you to excuse me, Lady Donya. I see I am being summoned." Abruptly the mirror went black.

"Well!" Donya said surprisedly. "They must really be frantic at the palace, if Elwyn just dismissed me like that.''

"You caught Aubry's mention about the guard 'escorts,' " Shadow said grimly.

"I don't understand," Argent said.

"They are sending guard envoys to the forest to treat with Aspen and mobilize the elves," Mist said slowly, "in the guise of escorting the elves to safety. It has begun, then."

They were all silent for a moment.

"All right," Shadow said quietly. "We take the north road as soon as there's enough light for me to see by. If necessary, we'll tie the horses together and I'll lead them blind. Rain or no rain."

Donya said nothing, but she reached over to squeeze Shadow's hand.

"I think," Argent said at last, "this calls for more wine."

"I won't argue with that," Shadow said shakily. She raised her cup. "Fortune favor us," she said. "Fortune favor us all."

Silently they all drank.

EIGHT ═══════

"I can't see a Fortunc-be-damned thing!" Shadow shouted over the rain. "Can you?"

Donya rode as closely beside Shadow as possible, knuckling rain out of her own eyes and letting Ambaleis pick his own trail.

"No, I"—Donya paused while thunder rolled deafeningly over the swamp—"don't think we're close enough to see the lake," she shouted back. "We're still probably three miles or more from the southernmost edge."

"I wouldn't bet on it," Shadow said dismally. "For all I know we could be *in* the lake."

"I thought you said anything that touched the lake dropped dead," Donya said.

"Uh-uh." Shadow spat out rain. "The water's poisonous, I know that, and Bl—I was told that if it got into a cut it would cause infection or disease. I don't think it'll kill you just to touch it. But that won't help us if we're flooded. We can't all run over the water like Farryn."

"Hmmm," Donya said thoughtfully. "That gives me an idea."

"Well, tell me, please," Shadow said gladly. "I'm glad *someone's* got one."

Donya shook her head. "It'll wait," she said. "Hopefully we won't need to use it. But Farryn running across the water isn't a bad idea."

"Huh?"

"Scouting," Donya said. "I'd like to be sure we're heading in the right direction. I can't even tell if we're on the road."

"You'll know if we get off the road," Shadow retorted grimly. "I'll be the first to go down in a pocket of sucking mud."

"Don't you recognize *anything*?" Donya asked worriedly.

"I can't *see* anything, let along recognize anything," Shadow said.

"All right, that's it," Donya declared. "Stop here. I'm going to see if Farryn can scout ahead. We can't risk losing the road."

Shadow stopped obediently, taking advantage of the rest to pull out a wineskin and fortify herself against the cold drench. Donya had ridden back to Farryn and was leaning close to speak to him, but Shadow couldn't hear anything over the rain; the falling curtains were so thick that Shadow could, in fact, hardly see them. At last Farryn dismounted, and Shadow was alarmed to see that the muddy water was swirling around his knees.

The trail had dipped lower and lower since they had left the trail shelter the day before. Thankfully the rain had stopped around midday and the weather had improved, a few glimpses of sun showing around the clouds, before they camped, exhausted, on the tumbled stone blocks of a ruined shelter. The only complication had arisen shortly after noon, when Donya's supply horse had fallen in the mud. The horse, with two broken legs, had to be killed; but worse, Donya's mirror had been crushed beneath the animal's fallen body. Shadow had told Aubry to send a message to Celene explaining why Donya did not call. At least the water had lowered slightly, and Shadow had dared to hope that they could ride through safely and that they had exhausted their bad luck.

This morning, however, the clouds had spit forth a storm the likes of which Shadow had rarely seen. Lightning reached down fingers several times, and had there been anywhere to go to escape them, Shadow would have done it. The thunder was so loud that Shadow's ears rang, and the water was rising again.

Shadow squinted through the rain, but for the moment rain and horses conspired to hide Farryn. Suddenly a silver-coated blur flashed by Shadow's side and vanished into the storm. Shadow shook her head and took another healthy swig of wine, grimacing as a little rain diluted the heady purple liquor.

"Fortune-be-damned swamps," she muttered darkly.

Almost immediately Farryn reappeared beside her, sinking into water and mud as he flailed his way to a stop at her side. Shadow leaned precariously in the saddle to hear him.

"The road appears to run straight toward the lake," he shouted over rain and thunder. "We have not strayed from it yet, but you must bear a little more to the east. It is another hour's ride to the lake, and another hour or a little more to the shelters."

"Fortune save us, it's getting dark," Shadow shouted back. "Turn my horse the right way. We've got to hurry."

"If you wish," Farryn said, "I will take flint and steel and a pack of dry wood and go ahead, clear a shelter and start a fire."

Shadow was sorely tempted, but she thought of Spirit Lake and shook her head.

"We can't lead both your horses on this narrow trail," she said. "And it's not safe for you to be alone by Spirit Lake, not even for a couple of hours. If there's trouble we couldn't help you. Besides, if we run into trouble here, we may need you."

"As you say, then," Farryn said stonily. He turned her horse gently to indicate the proper direction.

Shadow sighed to herself as her poor horse headed patiently into the rain. No amount of wine was going to keep her warm in this gale, especially with two more hours to ride. She pulled her cloak around her a little more tightly and, like her horse, tucked her head down against the driving rain.

They rode, and rode, and rode, and still there was no sign of Spirit Lake. Shadow's vision had narrowed to a short circle no farther than her horse's ears. Looking behind her, she could just make out Argent's dark cloak behind her supply horse; she hoped she would be able to hear over the rain if anyone was in trouble.

More riding into the wind, and now Shadow was wondering dismally if she'd strayed from the trail somewhere. Surely Spirit Lake should've been visible by now, even in the storm. She looked down and saw, to her horror, that the water was swirling halfway up her horse's legs. Just as she made this alarming observation, her horse suddenly plunged forward, almost throwing Shadow from its back; a wave of foul-smelling water washed over her, and Shadow desperately held her head up and pulled her horse back as sharply as she could.

"Get back!" she shouted as loudly as she could. "I've gone into Spirit Lake!"

The supply horse snorted and danced back as far as the line would allow; Shadow quickly drew her dagger and cut the rope with one quick slash. Her own horse was sinking quickly, its struggles growing feeble, and Shadow suspected it had probably swallowed or snorted in some of the water. Hurriedly she cut loose her saddlebags.

Suddenly Donya was there, not too far behind Shadow's horse, water swirling around her thighs.

"Jump!" the warrior shouted. "I'll catch you!"

Shadow threw the saddlebags first, gave Donya a moment to pass them on, then sheathed her dagger and jumped. Donya's arms closed reassuringly about her and swung her around, handing her up to Argent. Shadow scrambled up behind the tall elf while Donya caught the floundering supply horse. Shadow's horse gave a last panic-stricken scream and vanished under the swirling water.

"I assume," Argent called back, "that we're now the lead horse."

"Bear east," Shadow said, shivering miserably but touching Argent as little as she could, and that only through his rain cloak. "And *slowly*." She spit to one side, hawked, and spit again.

"You didn't swallow any of the water, did you?" Argent asked worriedly.

"Uh-uh, but I'm wearing a fair amount," Shadow said. "Just keep riding while I strip."

"Strip?" Argent asked, aghast. "In this storm?"

"I don't dare keep these clothes on me, not full of poisoned water," she said. "Just keep going, and watch out for the shelters on your right."

She pulled off her clothes as best she could, tying them into a bundle with her boots, and knotted them to the skirt of the saddle. Icy rain sluiced down on her, and she shivered uncontrollably but bore it until she could no longer smell any trace of Spirit Lake on her skin or Argent's cloak. Then she pulled the back of Argent's rain cloak over her head and huddled shaking against his warmth. Her legs still hung outside, but she was warmer than she'd been all day, and she stayed where she was in the comfortable darkness until Argent's horse stopped.

"I think this is it," he said.

"Thank the gods," Shadow sighed, peeping from under the cloak. The large stone mounds were just as she remembered them.

"Better wait," Argent said as Shadow started to pull his cloak back over her head. "Donya's checking the largest."

A few moments later Donya patted Shadow's leg.

"I'll take her in," Donya said. "Just slide down and let me catch you, Shady, your legs are probably numb."

"Numb? They're Fortune-be-damned *gone*," Shadow said, obeying gratefully. Donya caught her, but, to Shadow's embarrassment, simply wrapped her own cloak around the elf and carried her to the stone shelter.

"Don't be ridiculous," Donya said as Shadow protested. "The water's over my knees, and you're frozen. Good thing these crazy stone houses are built on hills."

Then they were inside, and the sudden relief from the rain and wind and the noise of the rain and thunder was utter luxury. Donya put Shadow down.

"Now just sit here in that cloak until we get a fire going," the warrior ordered sternly. "I want your skin covered better than a monotheistic monk's until this place warms and we have dry clothes for you."

"Yes, Mother," Shadow sighed, huddling comfortably in the cloak as Donya stepped back out into the storm.

Mist and Argent arrived next, bearing saddlebags and packs.

"The weather is growing worse," Mist said worriedly, taking firewood from a waxed skin and laying a fire at the center of the dome. "The water is still rising."

"What about the horses?" Shadow asked worriedly. "We've already lost two now."

"One of the domes is partly broken at one side," Mist said. "Donya and Farryn are enlarging the break and putting the horses inside. It is on higher ground, as this one is."

"Put some water to boil as soon as you can," Argent said as he pulled dry clothes out of Shadow's pack. "I want to brew some herbs for Shadow—while I'm doing it, for all of us."

"At least we will have herbs to brew," Mist said sourly. "There is little chance of having anything else to cook in such weather."

"You're right about that," Donya said brusquely as she entered the shelter, sluicing water off her armor. "Gods, that water's foul stuff! Oh, I've seen animals—a couple of squirrels, fish, even a deer—but they were all dead, bloated carcasses. Drowned, or the foul water, most likely. And that cursed lake! Gives me chills just looking at it, what I can see in this downpour."

"Well, then, don't look at it," Shadow suggested. "Better if you don't. You didn't leave Farryn out there by himself, did you?"

"I am here," Farryn said, drawing off his cloak. "I was investigating the other houses for traces left by the Stone Brothers."

"What kind of traces would still be here after two thousand years?" Mist asked doubtfully.

"These traces." Farryn ran his fingers over the ornate designs that covered the inner walls. "These are stories of our people, memories of great deeds. I had hoped for histories, perhaps, telling of the times after the Wind Dancers took their own road. But that is the task of the Enlightened Ones, to keep the records of our people. These are but small tales, tales of successful hunts, retelling of legends and the like."

"When I first saw those designs," Shadow said, "I thought they couldn't possibly be words. They look too much like decoration."

"They are decorative, of course. And they are not words, they are—reminders, perhaps. Our stories are told in song. And my song will one day make fine singing." Farryn shook his head. "But these are unfinished, as if the folk here left suddenly."

"Unfinished?" Donya said, looking around. "What do you mean?"

"Tales unfinished, small spots left without designs," Farryn said. "All the houses are the same. I do not know what to make of it. I pray we can find records with the answers."

"So do I," Donya said shortly. "Shady, are you getting warm?"

"I'm fine, Doe," Shadow said firmly. "Don't fuss."

"I can't help it; that's the second swim you've taken," Donya said worriedly. "If you sicken you'll slow us down. And you were drenched in that foul stuff."

"It's diluted with rainwater and plenty of it," Shadow assured her. "And I let the rain wash me clean before I got under Argent's cloak."

"I appreciate that," Argent joked. "You merely froze my back instead of smearing it with poisoned water."

"But what of the horses?" Mist asked. "If they had cuts or scratches on their legs—"

"I took clean water and earth from inside the broken shelter," Farryn said, "made mud, and with it plastered their legs well. As the mud dries and breaks away it will draw out the poisoned water from their coats."

Shadow laid Donya's cloak out to dry and moved to stand in front of the fire.

"How about those brewed herbs?" she suggested. "And a few rations for supper? And then, Doe, no matter what, I'm having a sip of Dragon's Blood."

"I don't care what you have, as long as you go to bed after you have it," Donya said firmly.

"Some liquor to warm your blood might be a good

thought," Argent agreed. "But we should all have a hot supper and an early bed after such a drenching. It's not summer yet."

"If we combine our pallets," Mist suggested, glancing at Shadow, "we could share bodily warmth."

"Now, that sounds better than Dragon's Blood," Shadow grinned. She moved over to sit against him, and Mist wrapped a blanket securely around them both.

"Spirit Lake," Farryn said suddenly.

"What about it?" Shadow asked.

"Our records showed a lake here," he said. "But nothing ill was said of it. Nor would my people have built their place on the bank of a poisoned lake. What happened here?"

Shadow shrugged. "Who knows?" she said. "Nobody in Allanmere has ever bothered about the Dim Reaches except to avoid them; the forest elves have done the same. When I was here before my companion guessed that the water washed up poisons from the soil, but how the poison got there—and why the flooding every year hasn't cleansed the soil—she didn't say. I also heard the theory that it was old magic, strange magic, gone bad. I could believe that; Fortune knows I've seen magic do some strange things. Remember Baloran's creatures, Doe?"

Donya nodded, shivering.

"I can tell you this much," Shadow said slowly. "Today wasn't the first time that that lake almost claimed me. And when I say there's nothing in Allanmere—*nothing*—more full of poison and evil than that lake, you can believe me, bet on it. And that means that if you value your life, maybe your soul, you don't stir a toe outside this shelter until morning, no matter what you hear—or think you hear."

"What did happen here, Shady?" Donya asked. "You never really told me."

Shadow shook her head.

"Just illusions, funny gases and dreams," she said. "I'd rather not talk about it, Doe, if you don't mind."

"All right, then," Donya said, surprised.

"Five houses hardly makes a village," Argent said after a moment.

"This is but a—a family group, you would say," Farryn said. "Those of close kin often live close together. The other houses are likely under the lake now. Some may have fallen."

"What about the temple?" Donya asked. "What do you know about this temple?"

"Nothing." Farryn shook his head. "By tradition, only the Enlightened Ones enter the temple, and none of them came with the Wind Dancers when our people divided themselves. The few Enlightened Ones we have now have never known a temple, nor have any of our folk now alive."

"What, a temple the worshippers can't enter?" Shadow asked. "What good's a temple that only the priests can enter?"

"Priestesses," Donya corrected. "Farryn said most of their, well, Enlightened Ones were women."

"Locked away in a temple with no men?" Shadow chuckled. "Now *that's* a sad fate."

"You know nothing." Farryn gave Shadow a condescending glance. "Our Enlightened Ones are also called 'instructors of young men.'"

"Well, that's better," Shadow agreed. "But who instructs the young women?"

"Whomever they—" Farryn stopped, his face intent. "Did you hear?"

"Hear what?" Donya demanded. "One of Shadow's lake spirits? Who could hear anything inside a foot of rock, especially with that storm going on outside?"

"I heard," Farryn said through gritted teeth, "the horses."

"There's no chance in the world—" Donya began.

"Hush, Doe," Shadow said, straining her keen ears. "I think he's right." She started to get up.

"Uh-uh, you're not even dressed," Donya said firmly. "Farryn and I will go." Before Shadow could say a word in protest, she had darted out the door, Farryn close behind her.

"Oh, no," Shadow said, scrambling for her clothes and weapons. "I am *not* letting them go out there alone with Spirit Lake! Mist, grab whatever weapons you have and come on! Argent, maybe you'd better stay here—"

"Don't even think that," Argent said firmly. "Not even for a moment."

The rain was an icy curtain of darkness penetrated only by the frequent lightning. The wind tangled Shadow's cloak around her arms and she threw it off impatiently, then dropped it on the ground. Where in this Fortune-be-damned swamp *was* Donya?

A growling roar, huge in its loudness, blended with the thunder, followed by a hideous scream—the death-scream of an utterly terrified horse. The sounds seemed to echo off the swamp, surrounding Shadow, but her keen ears had already picked out the direction of the sounds and her feet moved toward them without conscious thought.

Once she descended the small hill on which the shelter had been built, Shadow found herself in swirling water up to her waist, and loose mud that closed over her feet. She pushed onward as quickly as she could. Mist was somewhere behind her, cursing steadily as he went, and Argent, taller and less hindered by the water, was catching up.

There was another booming roar, and Shadow pushed herself faster. There was something ahead—the broken dome, shapes moving fast in the darkness; a horse thundered by, mouth foaming, its eyes rolling with terror.

"Catch that horse, Argent!" Shadow shouted back even as she stumbled on. Abruptly she bumped into something large and warm and she stopped. A brilliant flash of lightning illuminated a dead horse. It had been torn nearly in two.

Another flash lit the hill, and Shadow saw Donya silhouetted against the sky, her huge sword gleaming like a bolt of lightning itself; then from the top of the dome the darkness reared up its head and roared again, and Shadow was scrabbling madly up the hill toward them as quickly as her arms and legs would take her.

Surely what she'd seen *couldn't* have been a dragon?

It wasn't, Shadow realized as another flash of lightning gave her a better look at the behemoth straddling the crumbling dome like a wood-grouse over her eggs: it was a daggertooth, easily the most gigantic specimen of that creature Shadow had ever seen. Fortune favor her, a horse would be no more than a snack for such a beast!

A human—or an elf, for that matter—wouldn't make more than a bite.

Another resounding roar, and a cry from Donya—anger, Shadow was delighted to hear, not pain. Then Farryn was at Donya's side, his sword stained with daggertooth blood and his bright armor liberally bespattered.

The daggertooth had crawled forward on the dome so that its immense head leaned out over the crumbled opening, one foreclaw reaching down to swat idly at its prey. Several terrified horses milled, trumpeting shrilly, inside the broken dome, imprisoned by the behemoth above them.

The foreclaw reached again, and Donya swung her sword at the gigantic limb, but the tempered steel skipped uselessly over the hard scales. Shadow groaned to herself—out of habit, Donya had drawn her old sword, although the Kresh sword still hung at her hip.

Shadow briefly contemplated throwing a dagger, then quickly discarded the idea. If Donya's sword, with her strength behind it, couldn't penetrate that armor, then certainly Shadow's little dagger would be no good at all, and she'd only grabbed two: the odd one left of her matched pair, and Farryn's gift. If the bloody state of Farryn's sword was any indication, the dagger he had given her might well be sharp and hard enough to test the daggertooth's scales, but not with only the force of a throw behind it.

Mist was charging past her, a sword and the spear in his hands, and Shadow grabbed his arm.

"Wait," she said. "You're going to have to push that spear down the thing's throat to do any good. Donya can't cut through with her sword, and if that thing won't do it, neither will yours."

Mist watched the battle for a moment, then nodded.

"I will need a clear shot," he said. "Can the rest of you draw its attention?"

"Bet on it," Shadow said grimly.

Donya and Farryn were no more than keeping the daggertooth at bay, and Shadow realized why: if they moved back long enough to position for a decisive strike, the daggertooth could quickly slither down from the top of the dome, and in the water it could move like lightning. On top of the dome, at least, the daggertooth was limited in its movements and relatively slow.

Mist had joined Donya and Farryn, shaking his spear and shouting his plan over the storm. Shadow started to climb the hill again, only to be stopped by Argent.

"I brought your bow," he said, holding it out.

"Can you shoot?" Shadow asked. "I don't have any hands free."

"Yes."

"Then do that, and stay back," Shadow suggested. She was almost at Donya's feet.

"Stay back, Shady," Donya snapped. "This damned thing's plated in steel."

"Use the Kresh sword," Shadow said, ducking under Donya's sword arm to move to the side.

The daggertooth roared again and swiped with its foreclaw right over Shadow's head. Shadow ducked, swore, and instinctively cut upward with Farryn's dagger. The daggertooth roared again and blood sprayed Shadow's face: cold daggertooth blood. Donya dropped her sword—Shadow nearly fainted with the shock—and drew the Kresh blade, plunging in to distract the daggertooth away from Shadow, turning and slashing, overreaching a little with the unaccustomedly light blade. The pale metal opened a gash along the daggertooth's jaw.

Mist was struggling for a clear shot, but the daggertooth was thrashing its head now, enraged at the wounds inflicted upon it, and leaning forward over the edge of the broken dome to make short lunges at Donya and Farryn, who were fighting desperately to keep the daggertooth from simply sliding forward onto them. The edge of the dome was crumbling ominously under the weight.

An arrow whistled through the rain and thunked solidly into the daggertooth's neck just behind the head, where the skin was

softer. A second arrow plunged solidly into the side of the
daggertooth's head behind the ear. The daggertooth roared its
anger and pawed at the arrows, breaking the shafts off
jaggedly. Farryn took advantage of this distraction to dart in
and slash at the other foreleg, nearly severing it at the joint. The
daggertooth roared again as the leg collapsed under it, infuri-
ated with the pain; but the loss of the supporting leg slid the
daggertooth forward several feet more; now it teetered precariously over Shadow, a third of its body hanging over. Another
arrow bit into the space between leg and body.

"Mist!" Shadow yelled. "Throw me the spear!"

Mist was dancing here and there, trying for a clear throw, but
Donya and Farryn were too close, moving quickly themselves
to keep the daggertooth at bay. At last Mist ducked, rolled, and
pulled the spear after him, coming up at Shadow's side.

"From underneath?" he confirmed, planting the spear
firmly.

"Bet on it," Shadow panted. "The damn thing's going over
no matter what they do now. Better soon, before the whole roof
crumbles over."

"Then get out from under!"

"Right." Shadow ducked out quickly, slashing up as she
dodged between Farryn and Donya. Farryn's sword missed her
arm by only a fraction of an inch and another shower of cold
blood fell on her. Shadow grunted as Donya's elbow crashed
into her ribs, but then she was free. The daggertooth lunged at
the sudden movement, but Donya turned in a lightninglike
maneuver the like of which Shadow could only marvel at,
slashing across the daggertooth's eyes and blinding it.

"Let it go!" Shadow shouted. "Spear's planted!"

Donya and Farryn had little choice; the crumbling edge was
giving way, and the daggertooth slid forward, its bulk gaining
momentum as it fell off the edge. Mist dodged desperately
away as the daggertooth fell squarely onto the spear; the elf
disappeared in a sudden rain of falling stones and flailing
daggertooth. The daggertooth rolled over, its tail smashing
stones from the dome, the spear transfixing it but not piercing
the heart. Farryn and Donya darted in as one, two swords

striking unerringly. The daggertooth gave one final shudder and was still.

"We did it!" Donya panted amazedly. "We killed a daggertooth bigger than a house!"

"Let's hope we haven't killed Mist with it," Argent said, following Shadow forward. "I didn't see him get free before the thing came down."

"I am well enough," Mist wheezed. "But in the Mother Forest's name, will someone *please* get this monster's tail off me?"

Two horses were dead and another was lamed; Donya was relieved to see that Ambaleis was uninjured. Mist was badly bruised over much of his legs and torso; Farryn was badly gashed in one thigh, and Donya had an ugly torn cut on her shoulder.

"We'll have to carry Farryn back," Donya said slowly, retrieving her sword from where she'd flung it aside. "We can't let that water get into his wound."

"Doe, you can't lift anything with that shoulder," Shadow said patiently. "And Mist can't help either, and Argent and I together aren't strong enough to carry Farryn. See if you can get Ambaleis calmed down enough and he can carry both of you back. You may have scratches you don't know about yet. Then Mist and I will walk Ambaleis back here."

"What should we do with the creature?" Farryn asked, using the longer half of the broken spear as a cane to lean on. "Its presence frightens the horses."

"So does the thunder and lightning," Donya sighed. "No, leave it where it is. It's blocking the entryway; the horses won't pass it. We can deal with it in the morning."

"What about the dead horses?" Shadow asked.

"Forget the one that's in the water," Donya said slowly. "When you bring Ambaleis back, he can drag the others down the hill a little, but make sure they're well above the waterline. Cut off a good-sized piece and we'll put it on to roast. If we don't eat it tonight, we will tomorrow." She turned toward the horses.

"Wait." Farryn grasped Donya's arm with his alien hand, his strange bronze eyes gazing into hers levelly.

"What is it, Farryn?" Donya asked, and her voice had a strange tone.

"You fought nobly," Farryn said deliberately. "You honor Idoro Deathbringer's sword."

Donya barely smiled. "Thank you," she said. "You didn't do badly yourself."

"I am honored," he said, "to fight at your side."

"The honor's all mine," Donya said, flushing.

"Oh, for Fortune's sake," Shadow cried, "will you please kiss before we all drown out here?"

Donya and Farryn turned to gape at her in utter amazement, then looked back at each other. He leaned a little, she leaned a little, and they kissed while the rain poured down their blood-spattered faces.

"Good," Shadow said matter-of-factly. "Now are you two coming back to let me take care of your wounds, or are you going to throw down your cloaks and have at it here and now?"

Donya laughed to cover her flush of embarrassment, but she turned to fetch Ambaleis, the only horse accustomed enough to noise and battle to be of any use.

Argent stepped to Shadow's side and quietly handed her the bow and quiver.

"I'm sorry," he said. "I've wet it thoroughly, I'm afraid."

"No matter," Shadow grinned. "What's it for if not to shoot? And that was a pretty piece of shooting, too, Argent. If it hadn't been for your arrows, I don't know if Donya and Farryn could've made an opening for Mist to reach me with the spear."

Argent smiled rather sadly and looked over Shadow's shoulder.

"I'm no warrior," he said softly.

Shadow turned to see where he was looking. Donya had brought out Ambaleis and was helping Farryn to mount. There was a lingering quality to their touch that made Shadow grin; battle lust was a powerful thing, and if it hadn't been for her comment, likely they *would* have spread their cloaks then and there, rain and all!

She looked back at Argent, surprised at his wistful expres-

sion. Was it a warrior's skill he envied, or . . . Shadow
grinned quietly to herself and stored Argent's expression away
for later review.

"Better lead the horse back," she told Argent. "Mist's all
but staggering, he'll have a bad enough time on foot. I'll get a
piece of meat, if you'll bring Ambaleis back when they're
safely under shelter."

"That at least I can do," Argent sighed. "But take care of
yourself. It was your own orders that no one come out alone."

"Don't worry," Shadow assured him. "I won't be chasing
any lake spirits to my death tonight. Not that I'd get far in that
water, tired as I am."

She watched the four of them go, Mist leaning on the horse
for support while Donya and Farryn rode, Argent's silver hair
trailing into the muddy water. She turned to the fallen horses
and grimaced; horse wasn't much to her taste, but given a
choice of horse or trail rations, horse seemed a delicacy. Her
Kresh dagger sliced through the skin and meat like a hot knife
through butter. By the time Argent returned with the horse,
Shadow had cut off the choicest pieces.

Shadow slogged back through the water with Argent, letting
him carry the meat, and like the others before them they left
their wet clothes outside for the rain to wash out any foul water.

The herbs Argent had set to brewing perfumed the shelter
with their fragrance, and everyone was glad for a cup of the hot
tea. While Argent mixed a healing paste, and ground together
the fat and herbs, Shadow pulled her mirror from her pack
and tried the short spell, waiting for Aubry's face to appear.

The mirror remained blank.

"Doe, there's something wrong with this," Shadow said
slowly. "Nobody's answering."

"Don't panic, Shady," Donya said, clasping Shadow's
shoulder reassuringly. "Aubry may not be there right now to
answer. Try back later, and in the meantime, see what you can
do with this wound, will you?"

Shadow reluctantly put away the mirror, took a needle and
brandy-soaked thread, and carefully stitched the slash on
Donya's shoulder, then dressed and padded the wound tightly. .

"That shouldn't hinder you too much," Shadow told her friend. "But you're going to have to give your left arm a rest for a few days, or you'll pull the stitches loose."

Donya tried the arm gingerly, then smiled.

"You haven't lost your touch, Shady," she said affectionately. "The cuts you stitch hardly even scar. Why don't you take care of Farryn's leg?"

"I'll be happy to," Shadow shrugged, "if Farryn can stand a dishonorable thief tending his wounds."

"Is there no other?" Farryn scowled.

Mist shook his head, and Argent shrugged apologetically.

"I am an herbalist, not a healer," he said. "I have no experience at sewing battle wounds."

"Really, Farryn," Donya said disappointedly. "Shady fought bravely tonight. I don't know if I would've gone within dagger's reach of that thing. And her profession's got nothing to do with her ability to dress wounds."

"Very well, then," Farryn said uncomfortably.

"You're lucky," Shadow said, dabbing the wound with a water-and-brandy-soaked cloth to clean it. "That gash is with the muscle, not across it, or you might be lamed. Sorry," she added as Farryn gasped. "We don't know how fouled the daggertooth's claws might be. Want some Dragon's Blood before I go on?"

"I am well enough," Farryn said stoically.

Shadow shrugged and cleaned the gash thoroughly, stitching first the muscle and then the skin, applying plenty of salve. She bound the dressing as firmly as she could.

"Better watch that," Shadow advised. "You aren't going to be running anywhere for a few days at least."

Farryn glanced down at the wound.

"This is nothing," he said negligently.

"It won't be nothing if you split the stitches and cripple yourself, or get an infection in it and have to have the leg cut off," Shadow shrugged. "But it's not my affair."

Farryn looked inclined to retort, but Argent raised a weary hand.

"We're all cold and tired," he said. "Let's get what rest we can. Tomorrow will be no easier."

"That's a safe wager," Shadow said sourly. She turned to Mist. "Want to warm a very cold, tired elf?"

"If sleep and a warm body beside you is all you want," Mist said fondly. "I feel like I have been walked on by a dragon."

"Not a bad guess," Shadow chuckled. "I once heard that daggertooths and dragons were distant kin."

"Daggertooth? Is that what that was?" Argent asked, surprised. "Isn't that a southern beast? And I never heard of them growing so large. Why, that thing was over six man-heights long with the tail."

"At least," Mist groaned, feeling his ribs. "Really, my friend, I would prefer not to think about how many horses' weights worth of thrashing lizard fell upon me. Come, Shady, and share my pallet, chastely but warmly—and if you kick me tonight you will find yourself on the cold floor."

"No kicking, I promise." Shadow placed the meat where it would cook slowly, and banked the fire. A second trial of the mirror gave no more result than had the first attempt, and Shadow quietly put it away. She curled up beside Mist.

Although the light of the banked fire was dim, there was plenty of light for Shadow to see Argent glance from Donya to Farryn, then mutely retire to his pallet and lie down.

Farryn and Donya sat at the fire a little longer, stealing glances at each other. Then Shadow chuckled quietly to herself as they got up. They vanished from Shadow's field of view, but a moment later she heard Farryn's unmistakable steps as he dragged his pallet over beside Donya's.

"Fortune-be-damned good thing," Shadow whispered almost inaudibly to Mist. "I thought I'd have to use the vine-rotting potion on them before they'd get around to it."

"Potion?" Mist whispered back just as softly.

"Chyrie slipped a little vial into my saddlebag," Shadow told him. "A love potion, from what Aliendra told me. Chyrie never does *anything* without a reason."

"Shadow!" Mist's soft whisper was indignant. "Such a thing is an insult to nature! No true elf would do such a thing!"

"I guess I'm no true elf, then, because it was looking

tempting, but I didn't need to," Shadow whispered back. "A fight with a daggertooth worked even better."

"Well for your conscience that it did," Mist scolded. "Now go to sleep and do not think such things again."

Shadow chuckled again, very quietly, and cuddled closer to Mist's warmth, pulling the blankets over their heads.

NINE ═══════

"That's it," Shadow said quietly. "If you've got a miracle up your sleeve, Doe, now's the time to pull it out."

The storm had finally stopped; in fact, the sun was out, although it could be seen only intermittently through brief gaps in the dense, foul-smelling mists around Spirit Lake.

What sun there was, however, shone on a dismal scene. As the flooded Brightwater and its tributaries had pumped their waters into the swamp, as the springs that fed the Dim Reaches had been supplemented by rain and overflow, the swamp had risen rapidly. Now the muddy water reached more than halfway up the hills on which the shelters had been built, most of a man-height above the road. On the hill with the crumbled dome, Shadow could see that the water had almost reached the bodies of the daggertooth and the dead horses.

"That's it," Shadow repeated. "No way to find the trail or stay on it, either, for that matter. There's nothing we can do but wait here for the water to go down."

"That'll take days," Donya said, shaking her head. "Maybe a week. Allanmere doesn't have that much time, let alone Farryn's people."

"I don't see that there's any choice," Shadow shrugged. "I doubt if even Farryn can run over the water now, with his wound, and I *know* we can't."

"That," Donya said quietly, "is exactly what we're going to do."

"Are you fevered, Doe," Shadow said exasperatedly, "or have you just been at my Dragon's Blood? The horses can't swim through that stuff; one sip and they're dead, and then there we are."

"They're not going to swim, and neither are we," Donya said. She pointed to the dead daggertooth. "That's going to take us to the temple, right across Spirit Lake."

Shadow scowled at the daggertooth's body; then her scowl deepened.

"Donya, you can't possibly be thinking—oh, no!"

"The skin's so tough that nothing in the lake could rip through it, even submerged stumps or rocks," Donya said quietly. "It's plenty large enough once we skin it, clean the bones, and stretch the skin back over the ribs. All of us will fit, with room for at least part of our gear. I'd thought of a raft at first, but now there's no way to get to any trees to build one."

"And what about the horses?" Shadow demanded. "Are you prepared to just abandon Ambaleis, eh?"

"If necessary!" Donya whirled to face Shadow, her lips white with tension. "People are *dying,* Shadow, dying every day—every hour. If it means Ambaleis's life, if it means every one of our lives, we're going to get a cure back there! Enough rainwater's collected in the dome to last the horses a few days, and we'll leave them all the feed. Even if—if we can't come back for them, if it doesn't rain the water will go down and they'll wander back, probably to the forest where the elves will find them. If it does rain, they'll have more water. There's just nothing else to *do.*" She paused. "Did you try the mirror again this morning?"

Shadow nodded glumly. "Not a peep," she said.

"Then that's it," Donya said quietly. "We have to assume that things are—are very bad."

"All right! All right," Shadow said at last. "It's just—well, the idea of trying to boat across Spirit Lake is soil-your-trousers terrifying."

"Nothing's come out of the lake so far, unless you count the daggertooth," Donya argued.

"That daggertooth didn't come out of Spirit Lake, bet on it," Shadow said firmly. "The water's too poisonous, and there'd be nothing there for it to eat. No, this is just more twisted swamp-spawn. Worse things than daggertooths come out of Spirit Lake, and the only reason they haven't is that until this morning, the rain kept the mists from rising. Seems to be about the only good luck we've had."

"Then we're due for some more," Donya sighed. "Unless you've got a better suggestion."

Shadow looked over at the dead daggertooth and sighed, too.

"All right," she said. "Let's go tell everyone the good news."

"It seems shameful to waste all this meat," Mist said, peeling the last bit of hide neatly from the horse.

"We don't have time to dry it," Argent said with a shrug, "nor room to carry it. I wouldn't have even bothered with the daggertooth meat we *are* taking." He was irritated; scraping clean the daggertooth's hide was not to his liking any more than the near swim he'd had to make to the horses' hummock.

"It is not as tough as the horse," Farryn said, his knife moving more quickly and efficiently. "And it is tastier than trail rations, at least."

"Shady, what *are* you going to do with those?" Donya asked. She was cleaning the last flesh from the daggertooth's bones, with Mist's help.

Shadow worked the last tooth free.

"I don't know," she said. "Spearheads, maybe, something like that. Fortune knows they're sharp enough and hard enough. A souvenir, at least. Maybe they're worth something."

Donya laughed. "Well, set your greed aside for a moment and help us here, if you've got those paddles done."

"They're done, for what they're worth," Shadow shrugged. "There were only the two pieces of the spear, and those limbs Mist found have been dead so long they may break the first time we use them. I scraped clean a couple of long leg bones, just in case we might need them. I don't know how well those flat bony plates from the horses are going to do as blades, either."

"We'll find out," Donya said grimly. "Have you gathered up all the empty water and wineskins, and gotten the bladders ready?"

"Sewn and sealed," Shadow said, tucking the cleaned tooth into her pouch. "And I've checked them all. They all hold the air."

"Good. I'm counting on those to hold the boat level," Donya said. "The bottom's more curved than most boats I'm used to."

"There is no need to worry," Mist assured her. "The hide boats we use in the forest for fishing are similar to this. They are light and easy to handle, and they move quickly through the water. Taking the direct route across the lake, half a day should suffice."

"Not half a day," Donya said grimly. "Half a night."

Farryn looked up sharply. "What?"

"As soon as we're done here," Donya said steadily, "we're leaving."

"Doe, we won't get this done until evening," Shadow said, flabbergasted. "You can't possibly mean for us to cross Spirit Lake, of all places, in the dark when we're all tired!"

"I can mean it," Donya said, looking into Shadow's eyes, "and I do. Right now we've got clear skies to navigate by, when there's a break in the mists. Tomorrow it might be cloudy, or worse, it might be storming again."

"She is right," Farryn said, nodding. "Best not to waste the time. We can rest in the boat, in turns; there are only four paddles, in any event."

"All the large pieces of hide I could save are ready," Mist said. "I do not know how well they will serve, being fresh."

"The horsehide will go inside the bones, flesh side down," Donya said. "It'll help keep the water out and give us something besides bones to sit on. For the short time we're going to be using the boat, I don't think it'll matter that the hides are uncured. At least they're easy enough to work. Shady, can you make the stitching slits in the daggertooth hide?"

Shadow grinned and held up her Kresh dagger.

"Already done," she said. "They finished the edges first so I could do that. And yes, I cut up the tent hide into lacing to sew it with. As soon as Argent and Farryn are done, we're ready to fit it."

"Then we are ready," Farryn said, giving the hide one last inspection.

Despite their best efforts, the sky was darkening by the time the remaining preparations were made and Donya had given the boat its last inspection by using it to return to their camp and retrieve the remainder of their supplies. They were all tired and sore from the unusual labor, but Donya's urgency had infected them all and no one suggested they wait until morning. Shadow was bone-weary herself, but she was more worried about Donya; the warrior had become increasingly drawn and pale, and she would not allow Shadow to inspect her wound. All Shadow could do was insist that Donya rest first while the others paddled.

The boat slipped through the murky waters of Spirit Lake with gratifying ease, and the mists broke frequently enough that they could get glimpses of the moon and stars by which to navigate. The paddling was not too difficult, and by unspoken agreement, no one suggested waking Donya to take her turn.

"Listen to that," Mist murmured. "Do I hear whispers?"

"If you do," Shadow said grimly, "ignore them. Don't look at anything, don't listen to anything, and above all"—she gasped as a dark form seemed to dart just in front of the boat—"don't pay attention to anything," she finished. "And if anybody starts acting strange, knock them silly if you have to."

"What danger are illusions?" Farryn asked curiously. "They cannot touch you, can they, or tip over the boat?"

"No, but they can persuade you to do it," Shadow answered. "My traveling companion nearly killed herself, and I tried to take a swim in Spirit Lake. I'm not sure anything will happen, though, with all of us here together. I hope not."

"Shadow," Argent said quietly. "Look at Donya."

Shadow looked. Donya was curled up in the bow asleep in front of Shadow, but she had begun to twitch and toss, and she was mumbling something in her sleep.

"Do you think that Spirit Lake is affecting her dreams?" Mist suggested.

"I hope that's it," Shadow muttered, laying her paddle

carefully across the boat behind her. "Keep going as best you can, everyone, while I check her wound. I hope she hasn't gotten some Fortune-be-damned swamp-water infection."

To Shadow's dismay, Donya only half roused when Shadow crept over. The weary warrior muttered something irritable and stirred a little before closing her eyes again. Shadow carefully unlaced the top of Donya's shirt and peeled it back to look at the dressing. It looked and smelled clean, and Shadow was reluctant to expose the wound to the swamp mists when the healing herbs to make a new dressing were out of reach, but Donya felt fevered and Shadow had started to reach for the edge of the pad when Mist gasped.

"Shadow," he said faintly. "Her arm."

Shadow looked down at Donya's arm where it had fallen and bit her lip, her stomach knotting. Donya's change of position had pushed her sleeve up slightly, exposing her forearm.

It was covered with a red rash.

"How can she have the plague?" Argent whispered. "It's been days since we left Allanmere. Everyone who's caught the plague has sickened quickly."

"Donya has elvan blood," Shadow said distractedly. "That may have slowed the plague. Let's hope it'll continue to slow it, or help her fight it off, maybe. Argent, do you think just giving Donya some moonwort would help?"

"I don't think it will hurt her," Argent said dubiously. "It is, after all, a general healing and stimulating herb. Farryn, you've seen the box I was putting the moonwort in. Would you please find it for me?"

It took Farryn a moment to locate Argent's bag and find the moonwort box. Argent had packed it away deeply because any moonwort was now long drowned in the flood.

Argent extracted a leaf and handed it forward to Mist, who handed it to Shadow.

"See if you can get her to chew it," Argent said.

Shadow shook Donya slightly, then harder. At last Donya opened her eyes tiredly.

"What is it, Shady?" she murmured, rubbing at her eyes.

"You've got the plague, Doe," Shadow said gently. "Chew on this moonwort leaf and see if it helps."

Donya took the leaf and chewed it, making a face.

"Gods, that's terrible," she muttered. "Don't fuss, Shady, I'm just tired. Is it my turn to row?"

"No," Shadow lied. "You only just dozed off, but you looked flushed, and I was worried. Go back to sleep, and I'll wake you when it's your turn."

"Uh-huh." Donya sighed sleepily, then closed her eyes again.

"How much farther?" Shadow asked quietly when she was certain Donya was asleep.

"By the map, and how the stars have moved since we started, an hour or two at most," Farryn said equally softly. "But it is only a guess."

"Does anyone know," Mist asked, "how long infected humans can withstand the Crimson Plague?"

"The plague seems to run its course in two days or less," Argent said quietly. "We don't know, of course, when Donya first experienced symptoms. She would have kept it from us as long as she could."

"She hasn't looked well since before we left the city," Shadow remembered. "But there wasn't any rash when I tended her shoulder last night; I saw her change her shirt."

"The rash is not the first symptom," Argent said thoughtfully. "If she's been fighting the plague off, the exhaustion, the wound, and possibly exposure to the swamp and its unhealthy waters might have lowered her resistance. Perhaps, with rest and care, her elvan blood will give her enough resistance to fight it off."

The remainder of their journey, however, did not seem to be an encouraging omen. There were voices in the swamp, fragments of music, sudden outcries—some voices that one or another of the group recognized. Whenever the voices came, whoever heard it would start violently, looking at the others to see if anyone else heard, then shiver and return to paddling. They had to stop three times: once to rest and fortify themselves with some rations and wine; once when Farryn nearly jumped out of the boat, insisting he saw his people marching away from him; and once when Donya woke nauseated and vomited over the side of the boat until her raw throat bled.

After the last stop, Donya did not have the strength to even argue about taking her turn, but she was alert enough to keep watch while the others paddled.

"There," Donya said at last, pointing slightly to their right. "I can see the edge of the lake, and there's the hill that was marked."

"Praise to the gods it is not underwater," Farryn said thankfully.

"Don't get too grateful yet," Shadow warned. "The door probably isn't at the *top* of the hill."

"It is the hope of all our peoples," Farryn said adamantly. "I will find a way inside."

The hill was larger than they had thought, and farther away. At last, however, the boat scraped against the hill. Shadow helped Donya out of the boat, giving Farryn a stern look when he tried to take her place. Argent stepped carefully out, scrambling to avoid wetting his feet in the swamp water; then he gasped with delight and waded unconcernedly through the mud to reach the large patch of moonwort growing there.

Mist and Farryn pulled the boat up as far as they could, although there was nothing to tie it to. There was no guarantee, however, that the water would not rise farther; Shadow helped Donya to a relatively dry spot to sit and then returned to help Mist and Farryn unload the gear from the boat, just in case.

"You can wait here with Argent and help him pack the moonwort away," Shadow told Donya. "We'll leave the bags here with you. Mist, Farryn, and I will try to find this Black Door."

Donya shook her head.

"I think we should stay together," she said. "We're still practically sitting in Spirit Lake, and the mists haven't cleared any."

"We won't go out of earshot," Shadow said firmly. "But we need the moonwort, and Mist, Farryn, and I can look faster without having to help you along or carry the bags."

"All right, then," Donya said tiredly, and Shadow saw that she was shivering again, her arms clutched tightly at her middle as if she had a pain there. "I'll wait here. But don't go far."

"There's nowhere far to go," Shadow chuckled. She untied

one of the bedrolls and wrapped the blanket around Donya's shoulders. "Get Argent to give you another leaf. We'll hurry, Doe, I promise."

Farryn had already started eagerly up the hill; Mist was waiting anxiously, looking from Shadow to Farryn's retreating figure, and they had to hurry to keep the Kresh warrior in sight.

"Wait!" Mist shouted. "Where are you going?"

"I can feel it!" Farryn called back. "The temple! My soul hears it calling!"

"Well, it's waited two thousand years already!" Shadow yelled back. "It can wait long enough for us to catch up!"

Farryn shouted something incoherent back but did not slow; they had run far enough that Shadow could see what he was running toward—a huge black shape that loomed up suddenly ahead of them, a gigantic black mouth in the mists.

"Fortune's tits," Shadow breathed. The Black Door wasn't a door; it was a *door*—almost three man-heights tall and two wide, of a smooth, glossy black stone unmarred by time or weather or water, covered with the same type of graven reliefs that had adorned the domed houses.

Shadow stopped where she was. Even from a distance, something intangible seemed to reach out from the Black Door as if grasping at Shadow. It was something cold and aloof and powerful—not evil so much as *alien,* strange beyond any possibility of understanding and repelling because of its very alienness. This was a place, Shadow knew beyond any doubt, where she was not welcome—where none of them, perhaps excepting Farryn, would ever be welcome.

"I will get Donya and Farryn," Mist said, laying a hand on Shadow's shoulder. "We will bring the bags. You must watch Farryn. Honor or not, this is where his interests and ours part."

"You're right about that," Shadow murmured, squeezing Mist's hand absently before he left. Farryn was already at the door, running his hands over its surface as Shadow might caress a lover.

"How does it open?" Shadow said, hurrying to his side.

"Here." Farryn had found what he was looking for: an indentation in the stone in the shape of a six-fingered hand, fingers splayed. He reached for it.

"Wait." Shadow grasped his wrist quickly. "I want us all together before you open that thing. Who knows what's happened in two thousand years? It might surprise even you."

Farryn stared into her eyes coldly, pulling his wrist from her hand, but he waited there until the others came stumbling up the hill, Mist and Argent sharing the weight of Donya and the bags between them. Donya seemed no weaker than before, but Shadow could see that the rash had spread; now it peeked over the neckline of her tunic, and her hands were spotted.

"All right," Shadow said to Farryn. "Go ahead, then."

Farryn reached out eagerly but with a certain reverence, fitting his hand into the indentation in the door. He stood there for a long moment, then quietly removed his hand.

"I do not understand," he said at last.

"Maybe you didn't push hard enough," Donya suggested.

"It is not a matter of pressure," he said. "It is a matter of recognition. I am one of Adraon's children. Although I am no Enlightened One, still the temple should admit me." He shook his head. "That it does not means that the temple was sealed, that the Stone Brothers' Enlightened Ones sealed it against entry. Why they would do this I cannot understand, for no one could enter in any event but one of the people."

"Well, how do you open it if it's sealed?" Donya asked tiredly.

"I cannot open it," Farryn said simply.

"All right," Shadow said exasperatedly. "What is it? A lock? A sealing mechanism?"

"I do not know," Farryn said with a shrug. "What I know of the temples is what was told me by my elders. I know they can be sealed, but not why or how."

"Probably some strange kind of lock I've never seen before," Shadow grumbled, reluctant to touch the thing. Gingerly she reached out one hand to lay a fingertip against the black stone.

Immediately she snatched her hand away as if burned. The strange electrical tingling that had raced through her hand and arm had felt, indeed, momentarily like a burn, but the sensation was cold rather than hot.

"Come on, Shady," Donya said softly. "If anybody can open it, you can."

Shadow drew a deep breath and nodded. She set her teeth and touched the door again. This time she was not surprised by the sensation and found it not unbearable, but it made it difficult to examine the door; running her fingertips over the slab and around the edges, she knew she would miss any fine detail because her sense of touch was confused by the tingling.

"Sorry," she said at last. "I'm can't find a Fortune-bedamned thing. No keyhole, no lock, no latch, no pressure plate, no switch. I can't even find a crack where the door ends." She shrugged. "Well, I suppose there's no help for it."

"Shadow, are you sure that's wise?" Argent asked quietly. "That thing is steeped in magic. I can feel it from here. Is it wise to cross the magics of two different races?"

"It's not wise to stand around here arguing," Shadow said finally, "when we both know we have to get inside."

Shadow fitted her hand into the depression—she didn't have enough fingers, but that hardly mattered—and said, "Aufrhyr."

The tingling in her fingertips became a flame that raced up her arm to her shoulder and through her body like lightning. An answering heat flowed down from the bracelet on her left arm, through her hand and out her fingertips. Shadow opened her mouth to scream, but her throat was locked tight. She tried to pull her hand away, but it was as if the stone were glued to her flesh.

The others started forward—Shadow could see them out of the corner of her eye—but it was as if they were moving through thick syrup, slow as turtles. Then a flash of light darted from her bracelet down her hand, down her fingers, and sank into the black stone. Abruptly Shadow's hand was free—not only released, but thrown free, so that Shadow stumbled backward, rubbing the offended digits.

There was a low, deep grinding sound from somewhere deep in the earth, and the door began to move. It slid backward into the stone frame—Shadow had been unable to detect any line of separation—and slowly began to turn, rotating soundlessly on the center. Shadow gaped as she realized that the stone of the door was as thick as her arm was long. Finally the door stopped, dividing the opening of a stairway that curved down into darkness.

"Well," Shadow said dubiously, "it's open."

"That it is," Argent said, awed, "without a doubt."

"Mist, will you get the lanterns?" Donya said. "They're in that bag."

"Yes, I see them." There were three of them, hammered from the best brass, and extra oil and wicks.

"Fortune favor us, Doe, we're only looking through one poor temple," Shadow laughed uneasily, "not Zorodan's deepest hell."

"For all we know," Donya said wearily, "they might be the same place."

"Please," Farryn said, looking pained. "You speak of my people's temple."

"Sorry, Farryn." Donya mustered a tired smile. "I didn't mean it. Can you carry a lantern and give me an arm down those stairs, too?"

"I'll help you," Argent said quickly. "Farryn should walk in front, and he may need his hands free."

"That's a good idea," Shadow said immediately, "but I'm going in the front. I heard something click on those stairs, and nobody's setting toe-tip on one inch of stone I haven't checked first. No, Farryn," she said, holding up one hand, "don't bother arguing; you're going to wait right here while I check those stairs if I have to take this dagger you gave me and cut your feet out from under you."

Farryn frowned darkly, but Donya cleverly shifted until she was leaning on him.

"She's right, Farryn," the warrior agreed. "I'd trust Shady's ears and instincts with my life—with all our lives. It won't take her long to check the stairs."

"If *you* wish it," Farryn said pointedly, putting an arm around Donya's waist—and not, Shadow suspected, solely for purposes of support.

Shadow noted with some embarrassment that only Mist had had the presence of mind to take a large stone and wedge the door, although she suspected that a door that large would crush anything but a solid steel brace into so much swamp dust.

She squatted in the opening, carefully out of range if the door should swing shut. The air from the temple was cool. It was old air, but it smelled stale and dusty, not damp or fetid. There was no odor of mold or rot. Shadow thought of the wonderful construction of the domes, of the door, and shook her head in awe. Whatever else could be said of the Kresh, they were wondrous at stonework. Stone Brothers, she thought, people who molded stone and metal with their will. What kind of safeguards would they leave to "seal" a temple?

"Get me one of those spare horse bones, will you?" Shadow said to Mist. "The long leg bone. It's lashed to my pack."

Shadow hooked the lantern over the end of the bone and extended it carefully over the stairs.

If she had expected the entire temple to be constructed of the same strange black stone as the door, she was disappointed. The steps, walls, and ceiling were as marvelously wrought as the door or the domes, but they were of plain gray stone, albeit ground to the smoothness of glazed pottery. Sconces had been placed on the wall at regular intervals, but the torches in them had long since crumbled to dust.

She turned her attention to the top step. It was as unworn as if it had never been used; of course, if what Farryn had said was true, the Kresh had not lived in the swamp long enough to make much mark on stone. The top of the step was solid, no seam showing where it joined the wall, doorsill, or the step below it, and the dust on top of the step was undisturbed. The walls and ceiling above it were likewise featureless, with no slits, seams, or holes to indicate mechanisms. Shadow drew the lantern back and used the bone to carefully tap the step, first lightly, then with more firmness. When nothing happened, she dared a tentative foot, moving slowly until her entire weight rested on the step.

Shadow repeated this process on each step patiently, checking each stone carefully for tripwires or weight triggers. It was not until the eighth step that she saw something unusual: a little more dust on top of the step, a barely noticeable seam at each edge of the step, and a row of thin slits halfway up the wall.

"Got it," Shadow called back up. "Eighth stair. It's a step plate."

"Are you going to spring it?" Donya called down.

Shadow shook her head regretfully.

"I don't dare," Shadow said unhappily. "I'd rather know what I have to deal with, but for all I know, springing this one might set off any others, too, or shut the door behind me—and then who's going to get me out? No, we'll just have to step over and pray I haven't missed anything. Who's coming, and who's staying?"

"We must all go," Mist shrugged. "Argent to help Donya; Farryn, of course; you to find such defenses as you have found here. I am not much use," he said rather bitterly, "but I can carry a lantern and a sack, and given what we have seen of Spirit Lake, I would do little good remaining outside by myself."

"Well, then, come on," Shadow said impatiently. "Donya's only getting sicker while we're waiting. Don't bother bringing anything but the moonwort, an empty bag, and my small sack there. Watch that eighth step, and take it slow while I check the others."

Shadow found three more triggers as the stairway spiraled downward, as well as an odd-looking recessed patch on the wall that she avoided on general principle. She thought they had descended at least eight or ten man-heights when the stairwell finally opened into a long, wide hallway. Her lantern could only begin to light its vastness, and Shadow stopped in surprise.

Like the Black Door, this hallway was far taller than necessary and arched, looming at least four man-heights at the tallest point, and probably three man-heights wide. The left side of the hallway was broken at regular intervals by normal-sized doorways—piles of dust marking where wooden doors must have once hung—but the right side was a solid, unbroken wall, thickly covered with reliefs.

"Here is why I knew the Stone Brothers would not take their records away with them," Farryn said triumphantly. "They are here, here in the Hall of Records."

"What, this?" Argent asked, helping Donya to sit down on the last step. "I thought there would be books, scrolls."

"There are those as well, although if they were left here they would long have fallen to dust," Farryn said. "The Stone Brothers, wherever they have gone, would not go without their records. But the Enlightened Ones kept the permanent records, those written in stone, in the temple."

"But spells," Donya insisted. "Spells, potions—where would the records of those be kept?"

"They are not kept," Farryn said absently. Then he saw Donya's horrified look and said, "I will go to the inner temple and ask Adraon for what we require."

"Do you mean to say," Shadow said slowly, "that you've dragged us for days through this filthy, slimy hole of a swamp just so you could *pray*?"

"Not to pray," Farryn protested. "I could pray anywhere."

"Calm down, Shady," Donya said calmly. "Farryn would hardly have come all these leagues for something he could do at home. What's so special about this temple, Farryn?"

Farryn smiled at her gratefully.

"Like your folk, I suppose," he said, "we pray to our gods and hope they hear. In the temples, however, we speak to our gods and in return they speak to us. My people have no temple, for although when we settled there were still a few Stone Brothers to create one, there were no Enlightened Ones to open the way to the gods' realm. So none was built. Later, when at last some Enlightened Ones were born to us, there were no Stone Brothers left; nor were our Enlightened Ones trained in the temple secrets, for there was none to train them. So I came from my people here, and I will ask Adraon for help for my people, and if I am worthy, He will answer."

"*If* you are worthy," Mist said with an edge to his voice that surprised Shadow. "In the city you spoke as if what you wanted was here for the taking. Now it is *if* you are worthy, and *if* your god takes it into his head to grant what you wish."

"If I had told you all," Farryn said gently, "would you have come, or let me go?"

"Wait a minute," Shadow said mildly, raising a hand as Argent stepped forward hotly and even Donya looked ready to protest. "Never mind. Never mind. He told us what he told us, and now we're here. Whatever else, we're a couple of boxes of moonwort richer than we were before. Now that we're here, I don't see that the odds are much worse betting on a god than on Celene's mages, eh? That being said, we can stand here and argue, which doesn't stand to win us much; or we can all satisfy our sense of outrage by ganging up and slaughtering Farryn, which won't win us a thing; or we can go along with him and maybe, just maybe, win it all. I'm not afraid to put my trust in luck. What about the rest of you?"

Mist looked at Shadow and grinned faintly.

"I cannot argue," he said gamely, "with *your* luck, at the least."

Donya nodded and mustered a smile of agreement. "I agree," she said. "In Farryn's place, I suppose I'd have done the same—or worse."

Argent helped Donya to her feet, then left her leaning against the wall. He stepped up in front of Farryn, his eyes as cold as Shadow had ever seen.

"I'm no warrior," he said, his voice icy. "No doubt you could easily kill me where I stand. But you, who have spoken so often of honor, who cared enough for the Heir of Allanmere to share her bed—remember this: It has been days since we have spoken with Allanmere. Celene and her mages may have found a cure, or at least a treatment, for the plague already, and Lady Donya is here in this foul and dangerous swamp, far from any such help, by your doing. If she dies for lack of that care, I hope you and your precious honor can live with that knowledge."

Shadow stared at Argent, amazed to see the normally mild-tempered elf so enraged; then she saw Donya, no less flabbergasted than herself. Shadow grinned quietly to herself and raised one eyebrow thoughtfully.

Farryn laid one hand on the hilt of his sword, but made no move to draw it; his voice, when he spoke to Argent, was calm.

"I swore an oath that I would never raise my hand to any of you," he said quietly. "I will keep that oath if it means my death. I have lived with honor all my life, such as it is, and my god will answer me or I will die seeking such an answer. And when I have faced Adraon's judgment, I will gladly submit to yours." He turned quietly and walked to the reliefs on the wall, holding the lantern up so he could see more clearly.

"Farryn—" Shadow scrambled after the Kresh warrior, pulling him back way from the wall. "Look, if your god wants to kill you, that's fine. And if Argent wants to kill you, that's fine, too. But by all the gods here, there or everywhere, will you *please* let me check the hall first so some trap doesn't kill you?"

Farryn had to laugh at that, but he stood back while Shadow carefully inspected the carved wall and the floor, peering into the doorways on the other side, the light of her lantern fading as she disappeared down the long hall.

"They're empty," Shadow said after her inspection. "Just dust and a few metal spikes where the furniture must've been. Not so much as a hanging or a bowl. You must be right, Farryn; they packed up everything from chandeliers to chamber pots."

"The hall?" Mist prompted.

"Nothing but dust," Shadow reported. "Of course, it's hard to be sure with that wall covered with those designs; they could hide a lot, but I doubt if there're any more traps here, at least, otherwise your priest, ah, Enlightened Ones couldn't walk down the hall. There's nothing to mark a spot to avoid here, like counting steps, and the floor's as smooth as glass. There's a large room that might've been a study of some sort, some kind of kitchen or some such, and that's all except for a big stone door down at the end. I presume that's what you're looking for, Farryn."

"Yes." Farryn turned toward Donya, but Argent had already helped her up. Farryn turned and strode quickly down the hall, leaving the rest of them behind.

"Damn him!" Shadow muttered, snatching up the sacks. "Mist, help Argent with Donya, will you, while I catch up with our oh-so-honorable companion? Fortune favor me, I'd love to send *him* up against a dragon!"

"I'm not crippled," Donya said irritably, but she put her other arm around Mist's shoulders. "Next you'll have them building my funeral pyre."

Shadow whirled, dropping both bags.

"Don't you *ever* say that!" she hissed into Donya's startled face—or as close as she could get, lacking nearly two feet in height. "Do you hear me? Don't you ever even *think* about *anything* like that!"

Mist gaped, and Argent looked absolutely horrified, but Donya smiled affectionately and freed a hand to clasp her friend's shoulder.

"Don't worry, Shady," she said warmly. "I'm holding out fine."

Shadow mustered a weak grin in return and hurriedly picked up the bags, trotting after Farryn and sliding a little on the dust and the highly polished floor. The circle of light from her lantern bobbed along with her, and after one particularly wild skid an irreverent image of herself sprawling headlong and setting herself aflame slowed her steps somewhat. Strange how the hall hadn't seemed so long when she was inspecting every fingerlength of the floor and walls; strange how knowing that Donya was at one end of the hall made it so much longer.

Suddenly there was Farryn, standing so close to the large door at the end that his nose nearly touched the stone. He stood enrapt, eyes half-closed, as if he listened to something, but Shadow's keen ears heard nothing but their breath, and the slow footsteps of Mist, Argent, and Donya far behind them.

"What is it, Farryn?" Shadow asked. "What's the matter?"

Farryn turned, and for a moment his bronze eyes were more alien than ever because of the strange fire that filled them. Then he turned, and without a word walked *through* the stone of the door, and was gone.

Shadow yelped in amazement, putting out her hand to the stone before she thought. It was every bit as solid as it looked, but a sudden fire shot up through her hand as if she had suddenly thrust it into a forge. Hurriedly Shadow pulled her hand back and examined it; the skin was unharmed.

"What is it?" Donya gasped, and Shadow turned. To her dismay, Shadow saw that her friend had pulled free of Mist and Argent and finished the rest of the hall at a dead run, sword in hand. Donya teetered unsteadily on her feet, and the sword in her hands trembled, but the determination of her eyes was solid as the stone on which she stood.

"He just walked right through the Fortune-be-damned door!" Shadow said, still awed by the feat. "Right through it!"

Donya stumbled over and thumped the door with a gauntleted fist.

"Walked *through* it?" she mumbled. "It didn't open?"

"It doesn't open, best I can see," Shadow said, taking Donya's sword so the tall warrior could sit. Unlike Donya's old sword, the Kresh blade was light enough that Shadow could lay it down gently on the stone.

"Now what?" Argent said crossly. He helped Donya settle herself more comfortably and handed her a skin of wine. "Open this door magically as you did the other?"

"No." Donya's answer was immediate. "Shady, you're not to touch that thing. I saw what happened outside at that door, and I don't want you meddling again with this—this foreign magic. Farryn will come out; he has to."

"I suppose he does have to," Shadow acknowledged unwillingly. "But for Fortune's sake, he'd better not take too long about it."

"Oh, please." Donya accepted another moonwort leaf from Argent and followed it with a little wine. Shadow was troubled to see that the red rash had crept down her hands and was beginning to tinge her face. "I'm not much worse. Shady, see if you can find a more conventional way to get through that door in case we need it. Mist, take a look at those reliefs and see if you can make anything of them. Argent—"

"Argent is not moving," Argent said firmly. He was crushing several leaves together with a mortar and pestle. "I'm making a potion that I hope will at least bring your fever down. And if you don't lie down and rest until Farryn returns, I'm going to add something to make you sleep; and you'll drink it if I have to pour it down your throat by force."

It took Shadow only a short time to realize that there was no way to open the "door," if such it could be called. Even though she dared only the briefest of touches, it became readily apparent that the "door" was of one piece with the stone of the wall without so much as a hairbreadth crack. Shadow told Argent as much—Donya, despite Argent's protests that he had given her no sleeping draught, had fallen into an uneasy sleep.

Shadow joined Mist, who was nearly at the other end of the hall poring over reliefs by lantern light. They squatted down together, inspecting an odd spiral design carefully.

"Find out anything?" she asked quietly, so as not to awaken Donya.

"This seems to be a sort of history, beginning at the other end," Mist said thoughtfully. "These most recent reliefs are more pictorial than those we have seen before."

"Why?" Shadow asked curiously. "I can see what you mean, but why should their style have changed? If the quality of the reliefs had deteriorated, I'd have thought maybe some hasty record keeping because of some emergency, but these last reliefs are just as perfect as the others. Any thoughts?"

"Mmmm." Mist reached over to caress her thigh briefly. "Yes. I believe they are using more pictorial designs because they are attempting to portray something for which they had no words, perhaps, no regular signs. Look at this." He tapped a relief at the very end of the sequence, a rectangle with wavy lines filling its borders.

Shadow raised her eyebrows. "A Gate!"

"I think so." Mist traced the relief with his fingertips. "I believe that every person living in this place simply stepped through—to where, there is no way to know. But why now, why so late? If Farryn's story is true, and there is no reason to believe it false, why did they wait until their folk were weak and dying to create this Gate?"

Shadow shrugged.

"Fortune knows," she said. "Or maybe more appropriately Adraon knows."

"Exactly." Mist tapped the relief again. "The only possible conclusion is that until they created this particular Gate, they had no way of creating a Gate at all."

"A gift from their god," Shadow mused. "It makes sense—mages for priestesses, the temple sealed by magic when they left. You know, I'd lay money down that that inner sanctuary itself is a sort of Gate, a doorway into some place where a petitioner can speak directly to their god. A Gate, maybe, that only recognizes Kresh?"

"That seems to be the next reasonable conclusion," Mist agreed.

"So he's in there speaking with a *god*," Shadow murmured. "Do you know, I'm beginning to believe this may actually work out."

"I hope so." Mist barely smiled. "Shadow—there have been few occasions for us to speak privately—"

"And even fewer to do anything else privately," Shadow said wryly.

"Shadow." Mist laid a gentle finger over her lips, silencing her. "Be still for a moment."

"All right," she said, surprised. "All right."

"When this is over," Mist said, his large, pale eyes looking into hers, "when Donya is safe, when you have done what Allanmere needs of you, come back to the forest. Be my mate. We will live in Inner Heart, if you like, where you have many friends and there are more comforts."

Stunned, Shadow bit down hard to keep from making an automatic joke. She clasped Mist's hand warmly, turning it over to kiss the palm.

"I'm flattered, Mist," she said. "But I wouldn't make much of a mate. I—I'm barren." The admission was harder to make then she'd thought; somehow it had never really mattered to her before.

Mist touched her cheek softly.

"It does not matter," he said.

Shadow swallowed hard, deeply touched. For an elf of Mist's status and popularity to knowingly take a barren mate was tantamount to Donya dancing a High Circle in the middle of the city market—not strictly forbidden, but almost unthinkable.

"Mist," Shadow said gently, "what would I do in the forest? The only thing in the world I'm really good at is stealing, and I can't do that in the forest. I'd be totally worthless."

"You are a Matriarch," Mist said, shocked. "You are entitled to the honor and support of your people."

"Oh, so I'm to sit back and expect my kinfolk—or you—to feed and keep me?" Shadow asked archly. "Come on, Mist.

I'd be miserable, and sooner or later I'd make you as miserable as myself. Beside, Aubry's not ready to handle the Guild yet.''

Mist sighed disappointedly, but he said, ''I understand.''

Shadow was silent for a moment. Then at last she spoke, not meeting his eyes.

''I don't suppose,'' she said slowly, ''you'd consider joining me in the city? My room at the Guild's large enough for two, and the food's good.'' She grinned feebly.

This time it was Mist's turn to look uncomfortable.

''What could I do in Allanmere?'' he asked at last. ''Perform in some tavern as a dancer by day, and warm your bed at night? No.'' He sighed again. ''To live only for each other—the kind of love humans write songs about. A pleasant dream, but I fear you and I have seen too many years to long be satisfied with such an illusion.''

Shadow squeezed his hand.

''I'm afraid so,'' she said. ''I wish it could be otherwise.''

''As do I.'' Mist gave her hand a last kiss and rose, pulling Shadow up with him. ''Well—at least we are still some days from parting. Perhaps in that time we will think of some answer.''

''Maybe,'' Shadow sighed. ''Come on, Mist. I don't like to leave Donya alone so long.''

Donya was precisely as they had left her, and Argent was sorting through his bags, a worried frown on his face.

''I don't know what else to try,'' he said quietly. ''I don't have many herbs with me, nor Celene's mages.''

''She's fought it off for days,'' Shadow said, shaking her head. ''Why is she getting worse so fast now?''

Argent shook his head wearily.

''I am no healer,'' he said. ''I wish I were. I imagine that her elvan blood gave her some resistance, but as she favors Lord Sharl and not Lady Celene, I think her elvan blood is too weak to protect her completely.'' He sighed. ''I'm afraid the additional demands of this journey on her health, what with her wound and the unhealthy atmosphere of the swamp, have made her vulnerable.''

''Argent—'' Mist hesitated, glancing at Shadow. ''She has

been slow to fall ill. If Lady Celene has found a cure back in
the city, can Lady Donya survive long enough to return?''

Argent's haggard look was answer enough, before he slowly
shook his head.

Suddenly Donya herself sat up, rubbing her forehead.

''What was that?'' she asked. ''I felt the floor shake.''

''Oh, gods,'' Shadow moaned. ''Not a Fortune-be-damned
earthquake, too!''

''It's not that,'' Argent said suddenly. ''Look at the door!''

The door seemed to shimmer slightly. Slowly a foot
emerged, then a knee, and then slowly, as if stepping through
a gauze curtain, the rest of Farryn followed. He stepped
out—his eyes glazed—stumbled, and nearly fell. Mist hurriedly steadied him.

''By the mercy of Adraon!'' Farryn whispered. ''What I
have seen!''

''Never mind what you've seen,'' Shadow said urgently.
''I'm more interested in what you've brought away.''

''Shady,'' Donya chided. ''Give him a moment. Farryn, can
you tell us what happened?''

''I stood before my god,'' Farryn said slowly. ''I was
weighed—gods, how I was weighed! But I am one of Adraon's
children, and He was merciful to my unworthiness—''

''I don't care how worthy or unworthy you are!'' Shadow
shouted. ''Did you get the swamp-rotting cure?''

Farryn started, as if suddenly awakening out of sleep. He
looked around at them slowly; then his gaze came to rest on
Donya. He took a deep breath and sat beside her on the step,
taking her hand.

''I must ask your forgiveness,'' he said softly. ''Adraon
offered me a potion to cure the plague, and a wreaking that
would drive the invaders back to their own land and close the
way behind them forever—and bid me choose. There was no
other decision I could make.''

There was a moment of utter silence.

''Do you mean to say,'' Mist said slowly, ''that you were
offered a cure and *you didn't take it*?''

Farryn never looked away from Donya.

''The plague weakens us but does not kill,'' he said

unhappily. "But these invaders will wipe our people from the land forever. There was no other choice I could honorably make. At least you will know that your city is safe from invasion."

"Yes," Donya said steadily, although her hand was shaking. "That *is* more important. There's nothing to forgive. I would've made the same decision myself, Farryn."

"Well, *I* wouldn't have!" Shadow shouted. "Damn you both! And damn me if I can stand another swamp-rotting *second* of you two and your idiotic honor and duty and self-sacrifice!" She whirled and slapped her left palm against the door.

"Shadow, don't!" Donya screamed, half rising.

"AUFRYHR!" Shadow roared.

And stone swallowed her.

For a moment there was nothing—no sense of her body, no breath, no heartbeat, no awareness of her surroundings. Was this death? Then stone spat her forth like a fruit seed.

Gradually Shadow became aware that she was standing in what might be loosely termed a room simply due to the fact that she was standing on a floor. In front of her was what appeared to be an altar—a plain stone table, massive and unornamented but for the now-familiar reliefs. The top was empty.

Silence.

Shadow turned to look around her. Grayness stretched in all directions, and the grayness was silence—a silence that seemed to whisper softly.

"Well, kill me or not!" Shadow called out. "What's it going to be?"

"My, aren't we bold?" a voice asked behind her, and Shadow whirled to face—

—herself.

The figure sitting casually on the edge of the altar, one leg curled comfortably under her, was Shadow from the coiled ebony braid to the tips of her leather boots—but this Shadow wasn't swamp-muddied, sweaty, and badly in need of a long bath; this Shadow was spotlessly clean and neat down to the last hair. Shadow wondered irrelevantly if she'd ever looked that good.

"Well?" the other Shadow demanded. "You wanted to be here, here you are. You wanted a god's attention—you've got it. What have you to say for yourself?"

"I'm not—you're not a god," Shadow said dubiously.

"How do you expect to face a god if you can't face yourself?" the other returned. "At any rate, I'm the one you get to deal with. So go on—deal."

"If you're a god, or—or from a god," Shadow said bravely, "then you already know what I want. A cure for the Crimson Plague."

The other Shadow held up a flask in one hand, a scroll in the other.

"A simple potion," she said. "It can be mixed by any herbalist from plants which grow both near Allanmere and near Wind Dancing. What will you give for it?"

"Anything I have," Shadow said quietly. "Anything I am."

"And who are you," her twin mocked, "that Adraon should answer your plea?"

"I'm Shadow, Guildmistress of the Guild of Thieves," Shadow said proudly, "elvan Matriarch and daughter of Songwater, emissary of the High Lord and Lady of Allanmere and heart-sister of its Heir."

The other Shadow threw back her head and laughed.

"Are you indeed?" she said. "Guildmistress? At the slightest excuse you abandon your post. Nothing would delight you more than to be rid of it forever.

"Matriarch, daughter of Songwater? A sad jest. You wear your elfhood like an extra blade, good to have when it's of use, easy to set aside when it's inconvenient. You abandoned your people and left them to their fate when it suited your whims, abandoned their god, abandoned even the name they gave you. You keep what customs suit you and cast the rest aside like a sour apple, along with any responsibilities you might have to your people.

"Royal emissary? You had to be bundled off like a shy maiden to an arranged marriage. It took all but a royal command to pry you away from your wine and your soft bed.

"And heart-sister to Lady Donya. How pitiful," the other Shadow said scornfully. "After three years of enjoying her companionship, her protection, her loyalty, you abandoned her like you've abandoned every responsibility you've ever had. Your excuse? Ah, poor tenderhearted Shady couldn't bear to watch her friend grow old and die. What you meant was that she'd become a drag on you, a poor mortal human whose burdensome human morality and pitiful human mortality would one day become an inconvenience.''

Shadow's twin laughed again, tucking the flask and scroll into her sleeves.

''Your soul's as barren as your womb,'' she mocked. ''You're nothing but a leech, sucking everyone and everything you touch dry and giving nothing back. Adraon has nothing but contempt for you.''

Shadow clenched her fists and choked back a sob. It was true, every bitter word. From the darkness around her she heard her own words, so innocently arrogant—''I know this Fortune-be-damned Guild would be more trouble than it's worth.'' ''My spirit grew until the forest wasn't big enough to hold it.'' ''Personally I find it easier to let a lot of big, overmuscled, armored humans get hacked at instead of me.'' ''In time, Allanmere will get too small for me again and I'll move on to see what the rest of the world has been doing.'' ''It's hard to watch them grow old and feeble and finally die.''

''Your gold, your Guild, fancy weapons and contacts and Matriarch status, they are only masks,'' the other Shadow taunted, ''masks behind which you hide your own inadequacy, crutches to get you what skill or guile cannot. What are you without them?''

Shadow stood for a moment, swallowing the lump of tears in her throat, breathing hard and gazing dispassionately at her twin. Then she walked silently to the altar and laid her daggers on it, one at a time. Next were her lovely handcrafted tools. She spoke only to say the word to unlock her bracelet, and it joined her Guild sigil on the altar, and her pouch of gold, and her earrings. She pulled the jeweled pins from her braid, letting the long braid uncoil, and dropped the pins; they jingled musically against the smooth stone.

Shadow picked up the Kresh dagger from the altar and drew it from its sheath, gazing at the bright metal. Then the dagger flashed, and the ebony length of Shadow's braid joined the dagger on the altar.

Shadow stepped away, looking stonily at her opponent.

"If those things are all that's gotten me through over five hundred years," she said quietly, "then they're worth more than you say. Surely they should be worth a simple potion and a scroll, shouldn't they?"

The other Shadow raised an eyebrow. "Are they?" she asked.

"No." Shadow raised her head. "They're not. And I'll tell you why: they're nothing. They're not masks, they're not crutches, they're nothing. Take them away, Adraon or whoever you think you are, and I'm still here. I'm still here, and I'm still me, still Shadow: elf, thief, woman. I can lose everything and I'll still have that. No one gave me those things and no one can take them away from me. And that's who I am that the gods should answer my plea—no, my *demand*. I'm Shadow, damn you, and I'll take what I want if I have to go through every god above, below, and in between to get it!" With that she launched herself at her opponent.

Her twin dodged, but not quite quickly enough; she overbalanced as Shadow hit her and they fell to the floor together, legs tangling.

The other Shadow was as quick and skilled as Shadow herself, not wearied by days of rough travel, and armed besides; Shadow could hardly manage to keep her opponent from drawing a dagger as they grappled. Suddenly she rolled free and crouched, breathing in gasps, as her twin leaped to her feet, dagger poised to throw.

"Who are *you*," Shadow panted, "who can't defend yourself against a pitiful leech, tired and unarmed, without all the advantages? I'll tell you who you are: you're a pitiful excuse for a god who needs magic and weapons and tricks, who tries to make others seem small so that he looks big. And no matter what you do to me I'm still the winner, because I'm *Shadow*"—she reached into her sleeve and drew out the potion and the scroll and held them up triumphantly—"the *best* Fortune-be-damned thief that ever was!"

The other Shadow slowly straightened, her mouth twitching

into the slightest of smiles; she raised the dagger to touch its tip to her forehead in salute.

"You are that, at least," she said. Then she was gone. Shadow thought for a moment she heard a deep chuckle, but then it, too, was gone.

Shadow stood slowly, panting. She tucked the vial and scroll securely into the front of her tunic, then stepped back to the altar. She slipped the bracelet onto her wrist first, then collected her belongings until only the long black braid remained on the altar. She touched it once, smiling, then turned away, slipping the jeweled pins into her pouch.

To her surprise, where the door had been before was now only a clear portal, a rectangle in the grayness through which she could see them all on the steps: Argent, worried and talking to Mist; Donya, only semiconscious, her head pillowed on Argent's leg; and Farryn, pacing back and forth impatiently. Shadow looked at them, took a deep breath, and stepped through.

This time there was no feeling of transition; she stepped out of grayness into the dim light of the temple. Mist yelped in surprise and half rose; Farryn stepped forward amazedly. Argent simply turned to her, his eyes anxious.

"Shadow!" Mist said suddenly. "Your hair!"

"I know," Shadow said ruefully. She sat down on the step next to Donya and pulled the vial from her sleeve.

"Is that—" Argent said fearfully.

"Bet on it," Shadow said firmly. "It'd better be, or I have a god to throttle."

Farryn made some incoherent sound, which Shadow ignored. She handed the scroll to Argent, pulled the stopper out of the vial, and dipped a fingertip into the liquid, then gently moistened Donya's lips with the herb-scented potion. Donya reflexively licked the liquid away, then opened her eyes a little.

"Shadow!" Donya croaked. "Are you—your hair!"

"It'll grow back," Shadow said tenderly. "Hold her up more, Argent. Doe, can you swallow this?"

"Bet on it," Donya whispered.

"I'm more inclined to kill him than free him," Argent said grimly.

"Argent!" Donya said, shocked. "He's prevented Allanmere from a second Black War! How can you say that?"

"If it weren't for the fact that if we kill him, we'll get that
invasion, I'd agree with Argent," Shadow said wryly. "But
that would hurt Donya. At any rate, it's Mist's decision, not
ours. He's Aspen's representative."

Mist turned to Farryn.

"I can never understand you," the elf said slowly. "If you
had chosen as you did because you thought the humans' plague
was no affair of yours, that at least I could understand; once my
folk felt the same, and many still do. But this 'honor' you speak
of, that let you draw us on this quest and then choose not to
cure this plague that you yourself brought among us, that I
cannot understand. But it matters little. As Shadow says, if you
are not freed we will have a second Black War, and that I can
understand. So you will go free to return to your people, but
there is something you must do first."

"If I can do it, I will," Farryn said calmly.

"You will take the formula for the potion back to Allanmere
first," Mist said. "You know where Allanmere is, and we will
give you the map. And you will give the formula to Lady
Celene and her mages."

"I will," Farryn promised. "I will use the secret door into
the gardens by which we left, and I will place the formula in
Lady Celene's own hand. Also I will tell her where the horses
were left, and give her the tidings that Donya is well and will
be home soon."

"Thank you," Donya said softly. "Mother can send someone through the Gate to the elves. That campsite isn't far from
the forest; somebody could be sent to fetch the horses before
their food and water runs out."

"The horses," Shadow laughed. "Allanmere dying of the
plague, and she's worried about her warhorse."

"I *like* that warhorse," Donya said mildly, and Shadow was
so relieved to see her friend sitting up and talking that she
laughed even louder.

Farryn stepped to face Shadow and handed her his other
dagger.

"Whatever you think of me," he said, "I will sing your song

to the Wind Dancers.'' He smiled a little. ''Whatever courage
it takes to face a god, surely it takes ten times as much to rob
one.''

Shadow had to grin. ''I suppose I can't argue with you on
that,'' she admitted.

Donya held out her hand and Farryn took it, pressing it in
both his own alien hands.

''You,'' he said, ''I will never forget.'' He raised her hand
until her fingers touched the amulet hanging at his throat;
deliberately, he closed her fingers around it.

''You honor Idoro Deathbringer's sword,'' he said gently,
''as you have honored me.''

Donya smiled, and Shadow was surprised to see her lips
quiver a little.

''I won't forget you, either,'' she said. ''I wish—'' Then she
was silent, and Farryn smiled his understanding.

''As do I,'' he said gently. He touched the torc around his
neck. ''May I keep this as a remembrance?''

''Please do,'' Donya said, smiling. ''Besides, if you don't,
how will Mother understand you?''

''You have the mind of an Enlightened One,'' Farryn
smiled. ''Good-bye, Donya Daggertooth-Slayer.''

''Good-bye, Farryn the Fearless,'' Donya returned, her smile
as wide as his.

Farryn gave her a last look, touched the amulet and his lips
in what might have been a salute, and was gone. Not even a
ripple on the surface of Spirit Lake marked his passing.

Donya sighed only once.

''Let's go,'' she said quietly. ''It's a long way home.''

''This,'' Argent said, his voice strained, ''is a crazy idea.''

''Probably,'' Shadow agreed tiredly.

They had been paddling for several hours and still hadn't
reached the Brightwater. Shadow had insisted they camp at the
temple rather than start immediately, given Donya's weakness
and everyone's exhaustion. Donya, eager to be home, had
argued, but Shadow had made a counterproposal to regain the
time.

''The water's high enough that we can simply paddle west

and join the Brightwater," she said. "Then the current will do the rest, and we'll be back to Allanmere in a few hours instead of days."

"If it's that simple," Argent said gently, "why didn't we come up the river in the first place?"

"I considered it," Donya said. She ticked off points on her fingers. "First, it would've required a large boat and crew to go upriver when the river was so swollen, and there aren't any elvan boat crews; we couldn't let possibly infected humans out of the city in a boat. Besides that, it would've ruined any chance of keeping this a secret. Second, it would've meant that I would've *had* to bring a troop of guards, transport them, feed them, and get them through the swamp. More delay. Third, just the setup for the boat trip would've added more delay. And fourth, but most important, it would've meant trying to travel through a part of the Dim Reaches where there're no roads or trails at all, something Shadow says—and after what I've seen, I agree—is impossible."

"But with the swamp flooded," Shadow added, "it doesn't matter where the roads are. We're going to have to do most of it by boat anyway, and it's only a short trip to the Brightwater by water. Going with the current will be fast in our little boat; a little risky, yes, but no more so than boating back across Spirit Lake. We can leave the river just northwest of the palace, walk around on foot, and back in through the same way we came out."

It sounded simple enough in theory, but in practice the trip was not so easy. Shadow had no landmarks to navigate by west of the temple, and the sun was hidden behind heavy clouds that could mean another storm. Shadow fervently prayed not; in their little makeshift boat and with no shelter, another sudden flood could mean their death in the swirling waters where the Brightwater emptied into the Dim Reaches, and the river would be twice as treacherous.

No one even considered letting Donya paddle, although she was already much improved, and even without Farryn's weight the three of them were hard-pressed to make any speed at all. Shadow and Argent were equally unaccustomed to heavy work, and unless they took frequent rest stops, Mist's more powerful strokes caused the boat to steer somewhat erratically.

"There," Mist said finally. "I hear the river, I believe."

Shadow strained her keen ears, but she smelled the river before she heard it: the miasma of the swamp was replaced by a cleaner set of odors, a fresh, wet, spring smell carried on a gentle breeze. Then she heard the river, and the sound of it put fresh strength in her arms.

Merging with the river was more difficult than controlling the boat once they were on it. The muddy river moved quickly enough, but other than dodging the uprooted trees and occasional animal carcasses floating on the water, it was simply a matter of keeping their daggertooth boat stable and holding on. It seemed like no time at all before the wall of Allanmere appeared.

"Best work our way to the bank now," Mist advised.

"All right," Shadow agreed, lending her paddle to the effort. "Not that it wouldn't make fine telling in the marketplace, pulling up to the docks in a boat made of a hollowed-out daggertooth."

"If there's anyone in the marketplace to hear it," Donya said grimly.

That quieted them all, and they silently bent to their work. Leaving the river was harder than joining it, but at last they drew their strange boat onto the bank rather closer to the palace than they had meant to land.

"We've got to save this thing," Shadow said apologetically when Donya suggested simply letting the boat go. "*Somebody's* got to see it."

Shadow was surprised to see no patrols walking the top of the wall, especially around the palace; then she shook her head. Of course, with the plague they were more needed to control riots in the city than on the wall, especially if Farryn had told Celene that there would be no invasion. But the grounds also were quiet, when they entered through the concealed door on the north wall. Shadow couldn't even hear any citizens at the palace gates.

"I don't like this," Argent said. "Where are the guards?"

"There is one," Mist said, pointing.

Shadow breathed a sigh of relief when the Palace Guard

came into view. For a moment she had had the horrible notion that every human in the city was dead.

Then, as the guard saw them, stared incredulously, and shouted, an equally horrible notion occurred to her, for a black armband was tied to the sleeve of the guard's uniform. Looking up, she saw what she had missed before: that the windows of the palace were hung with black curtains.

"Donya—" she said cautiously, but the tall warrior had already followed her gaze up to the windows.

"My parents—" Donya whispered. Then she dropped her packs and was running toward the palace; all the elves could do was try to keep up. Donya, however, had the advantage of a head start and longer legs; she was already out of sight when they entered the palace. Only the rapid thudding of Donya's boots and the ragged wheezes of her breath let them track her through the stone corridors, pushing black-banded servants aside recklessly as they went.

They found her in the High Lord and Lady's quarters, slumped on the floor and weeping quietly, her head in Celene's lap. Celene looked up at them, and although her eyes were red and full, her face was calm.

"He died two days after you left," she said quietly. "We tried everything—every potion, every spell we could think of, but we could only give him a little time. So little time. He made me promise I'd say nothing. He knew Donya would only insist on coming back and he—we wanted her well away from the city. Besides, she was the only hope we had."

Celene smiled tremulously.

"And you succeeded, all of you. The formula you sent back—the potion works almost miraculously. Even now mages and healers are distributing it in the city. And then to learn there will be no war—"

"If Farryn reaches his people in time," Mist warned.

"He seemed certain he would," Celene said softly. "Even if some of the barbarians win through, they will likely be defeated in cities far to the north of Allanmere."

"Spreading the plague as they go," Argent said grimly.

"No. Farryn promised that he would give copies of the formula to traders who circulate among the northern cities,"

Celene said. "I have likewise given it to the merchants who will leave our city."

"But won't they just spread the plague to other cities when they do leave?" Shadow asked worriedly.

"I would advise maintaining the quarantine for another moon," Celene said. "The trade goods are not a danger; my mages have determined that the disease is only carried in a living host. Every exposed person must be treated with a cleansing spell we've created. We're still trying to see if a large area can be so cleansed by pooling the mages' power. But that's only a suggestion."

"Suggestion?" Donya said, knuckling tears from her eyes.

Celene lifted the chain holding the Seal of Allanmere over her head and placed it around Donya's neck.

"It is your decision now, daughter," she said quietly.

There was only one sound in the room: a quiet *thump* as Donya, who had stood firm against dragons, demons, and a giant daggertooth, slumped unconscious to the floor.

"It's only shock, exhaustion, and residual weakness from the plague," Healer Sweyn reassured Shadow and Celene, patting Donya's hand. "Some hearty, fresh food and a good night's rest will finish the cure with no help from me. Incidentally, who treated that wound on her shoulder?"

"Guilty," Shadow said apologetically.

"An excellent piece of work for a field treatment," Sweyn congratulated her. "However, here in the city I'll thank you if you have a little more respect for my clientele than you have for the merchants' purses."

"Don't worry, I don't have a healer's permit," Shadow laughed. "I'd be just as happy if I never had to stitch another wound in my life!"

"If you don't mind," Donya interrupted wearily, "I'd like to be alone with Shadow for a little while."

"All right," Healer Sweyn said. "But not too long. I want her to sleep."

Celene squeezed her daughter's hand.

"If you need me," she said gently, "I'll be in the next room.

I want to get the details of your journey from Mist and Argent.''

When the others were gone, Shadow thought Donya would speak, but she simply lay there, staring at the ceiling, fingering the heavy medallion around her neck.

Shadow thought of a thousand things to say, then discarded all of them as callous, inane, or useless. She sighed, pulled a flask of Dragon's Blood out of the pack at her feet, and took a sip directly from the flask.

"Give me some of that," Donya said suddenly.

Shadow raised an eyebrow and handed Donya the flask, reaching for her pack to find the cups; before she got one out, however, Donya had already put the flask to her lips and taken a large swallow. She would have taken a second if Shadow hadn't snatched the crystal flask back, wincing a little as some of the potent liquor splashed on the front of Donya's nightgown.

"That's enough," Shadow said firmly.

"I want to get drunk," Donya said remotely. "I want to get really, really drunk."

"Don't worry," Shadow chuckled. "On that much Dragon's Blood, you will. At least you're already in bed, so you won't hurt yourself when you fall on your face." She squeezed Donya's hand gently. "Want me to get you a sleeping potion?"

"Only if you can find one I won't wake up from," Donya mumbled.

"Oh, come on, now," Shadow chided. "This isn't the Donya who helped kill the biggest daggertooth in the world."

"No," Donya whispered. "This is the Donya who couldn't save her father."

Shadow took another ginger sip of Dragon's Blood and sat silently for a moment.

"When I left the forest," she said at last, "I thought it was a grand adventure—the world was my grape, just waiting for me to get there and suck all the juice out of it and spit out the seeds. It wasn't what I thought it was. I made a good friend and he died, and I didn't like the hurt I felt. And then later, when I learned that all my kinfolk were gone, killed in the Black

Wars while I was dancing from city to city, I—well, for a while I hurt till I didn't want to live. I told myself I'd never go back, never know for *sure* that they were gone. That way they were still alive, in a way, at least to me. I didn't have to feel that hurt while I could still hope they were alive.

"Sometimes I made human friends here and there," Shadow continued. "Not as good a friend as you've been, but friends here and there —allies, lovers. And I'd travel with them a little while, and then I'd leave. Just like I'd planned to leave you, Doe, when we parted ways. I didn't want to see them—to see you—grow old and feeble and die, so I ran from the hurt, telling myself that as long as I didn't *know,* all those friends were still alive, in a way, and I didn't have to lose them."

Donya nodded, still staring at the ceiling. A slow tear trickled down her cheek.

"It took a god to show me what I'd been hiding from myself," Shadow said gently. "That I wasn't running from pain—I was running from all the good things that made the hurt worthwhile, and still losing all the people I loved. And maybe losing them all the sooner because I wasn't there to help them sometime when they might need me. And losing the joy, too, of being there when they *did* need me. It's good to be needed, Doe, and to need people. And maybe it's good to hurt, too; I don't know. But I know it's no good to throw away all the good times just to run from the hurting. I may never be through traveling, Doe, but I'm through running away. Mourn your father, and remember him, and then wipe your eyes and go back to enjoying the good times and the people you love. And who love you."

Donya turned to look at Shadow, and her lips were trembling.

"I didn't get to say good-bye," Donya whispered, and then they were in each other's arms, weeping in silence for all the good-byes that had never been said.

At last Donya sat up, wiping her eyes on her sleeve. Shadow handed her a kerchief, then took another and blew her nose resoundingly. Donya gaped at her friend, then chuckled weakly and blew her own nose even louder. Shadow grinned and

honked again; Donya was lifting her own kerchief when
Shadow seized her wrist.

"Don't, don't," she said, laughing helplessly. "You'll
knock down the walls."

Donya gaped at her, then howled.

"What is it?" Shadow gasped, laughing herself, although
she didn't know why.

"So I'll knock down the walls," Donya choked. "Why not?
It's my palace now!"

Shadow collapsed on the bed, shrieking with laughter until
they both ran out of air. Gradually their laughter faded to
gasping chuckles, and they both reached for the bottle of wine
at the same time. This set them off again.

"Now I guess I really will have to get married," Donya
gasped when she could manage to swallow a little wine.

"Well, that's one problem I *can* help you with," Shadow
grinned. "Guess what? You'll never guess. I've found you a
husband."

Donya took a prodigious swig of wine and chuckled again.

"Is this another joke?" she asked. "Don't do it, Shady, I'm
so drunk I might just laugh myself to death. I nearly did it a
minute ago."

"No, I'm serious," Shadow said. "I really did figure out
who you should marry. He's perfect."

Donya glanced across the room to the table where the Kresh
sword rested, and a fleeting expression of pain crossed her face.
No longer laughing, she swallowed the rest of her wine.

"All right," she said slowly. "Who?"

"Argent."

"Argent?" Donya looked at Shadow blankly. "Why Argent?"

"He's perfect." Shadow shrugged. "He's an elf, and he's
about as serious and responsible as elves get. He's a *town* elf,
so he's knowledgeable about the laws and the economics of
Allanmere. He's even been a good friend of your parents for
years, so he's familiar with what goes on at the palace. And as
a bonus, he's been trading so long with the forest elves that
he's well known and popular with them, too. And he cares for
you a lot more than you know."

Donya was silent a long moment, eyeing Shadow thoughtfully.

"But how do I know he's fertile?" she asked slowly.

"You don't." Shadow grinned. "How do you know *you're* fertile? Take a chance. I'll tell you this, though: I don't know about his fertility, but I can vouch for his talent between the furs."

"And what if he's not?" Donya asked. "Going to turn more of your lovers over to me?"

Shadow shrugged again.

"If he's not, then so help me I'll arrange your very own Fortune-be-damned High Circle right here in the privacy of your own palace," she grinned. "We'll kill that dragon when it lands."

Donya was silent again. Then she reached for Shadow's flask of Dragon's Blood and, before Shadow could stop her, took another swallow. She glanced across the room at the Kresh sword lying on the table.

"Do you think," Donya said very, very quietly, "that he got back in time to save his people?"

"I'm sure of it," Shadow said firmly. "His god wouldn't have bothered to answer him and then send him back to fail. He'll save his people, and he'll have a song to sing that'll make a hero of him. I wish I'd found out, though, what happened to the rest of them. The Stone Brothers, I mean."

Donya turned her head away to stare at the wall.

"He told us that," she said. "While you were—in there. He said they'd built a Gate and returned to their home in the west. He thought someday his folk would try to seek them out again."

Shadow had to shake her head at the image.

"Can you imagine them all," she said slowly, "the whole lot of them, just flickers in the wind, flitting west like glasswings over the water?"

Donya was silent for a long moment.

"All right," she said at last. "Send Argent in."

"What, now?" Shadow asked, surprised.

"Now, while I'm drunk enough to do it," Donya sighed. "Mother said she'd stay a moon to advise me, then she wants to go back to the forest and mourn my father.'' Her lips compressed; then she shook her head briskly. "Send him in, please."

"All right, but can I stay?" Shadow begged. "I wouldn't miss this for all the moondrop wine in the Heartwood."

Donya shrugged listlessly. Shadow patted her friend's shoulder comfortingly, then hurried out and all but dragged Argent back in from Celene's room after convincing Celene, with some difficulty, that Donya wanted to talk to Argent *now*.

Argent sat down on the bed beside Donya, clasping her hand. "I grieve with you," he said gently. "He was a dear friend."

"Thank you." Donya's hands shook a little, but Shadow thought that was probably from the liquor; the grieving daughter was gone now, and the Heir—no—the High Lady of Allanmere was sitting in her place.

"If there is any way that I can help you," Argent said, "you have only to ask."

"Then I will." Donya looked at him squarely. "Marry me."

Shadow, standing unobtrusively near the door, groaned silently. Argent simply stared blankly for a moment.

"Marry—" he said helplessly.

"I need a husband," Donya said quietly. "And Allanmere needs a High Lord. I ask you, for my sake and the sake of Allanmere, will you marry me?"

Argent was silent for a long moment, his eyes searching Donya's. At last he sighed.

"I would be honored," he said. "If you'll make the arrangements, it will take me only a short time to turn my half of the business over to my sister."

"We'll say half a moon," Donya said remotely. "The announcements have to be posted and arrangements for a festival made. A little celebration is just what the city needs, once the sick are cured."

Argent bowed over her hand and left quietly. Shadow took his place at Donya's side.

"Fortune favor me, Doe," Shadow sighed, "I've *robbed* people more romantically."

"What's romance got to do with it?" Donya said bitterly. "My romance has gone north to become a hero."

"Well, have a little mercy on Argent," Shadow chided. "If he's not in love with you, he's well on his way. Don't punish him for the Compact and its traditions. Who knows, he may turn out to be the great love of your life. You didn't like Farryn at all for a while, remember?"

"He insulted you," Donya said sullenly.

"If that's what it takes," Shadow teased, "I'll let Argent beat me black and blue." She took Donya's hand, and her friend's empty eyes wrenched at her heart. "You know, Mist asked me to be his mate."

"He did?" Donya looked up, astonished. "What did you say?"

Shadow shrugged. "Ah, you can't move a city mouse to the forest," she said uncomfortably, "no more than you can grow a tree in the middle of the marketplace. We'd have made each other miserable."

"Oh, Shady," Donya sighed. "What a mess we've made of our lives, haven't we?"

"Oh, I don't know," Shadow grinned. "All I ask is this: If I have to arrange that High Circle, I'd better get an invitation!"

"Of course," Donya chuckled gamely. "And all the wine you can drink."

"Oho!" Shadow chortled. "Don't tempt me to pray that Argent *doesn't* get you pregnant."

"All right, all right," Donya smiled. "But you'll sit at my side for the wedding feast, won't you?"

"Bet on it," Shadow said, shaking her hand.

Mist checked the saddlebag for the last time, his fingers lingering on the buckles as if to postpone mounting. He turned back to Shadow and took her hand, pressing a kiss into her palm.

"I've got something for you," Shadow said awkwardly. She pulled out of her pouch the acorn she'd taken at the festival and folded it into his hand.

"You plant it," she said.

Mist smiled a little.

"Next to mine?"

Shadow grinned ruefully and shook her head.

"Plant two trees together and one always grows taller, until the shorter one withers and dies in its shade," she said.

Mist touched her cheek gently, and she saw the understanding in his eyes. "Where, then?" he said.

"Find a sunny place where the roots can dig deep," Shadow told him. "And plant them close enough that sometimes, maybe, when the wind is right, their branches will touch. Will you do that?"

Mist smiled, took her hand, and placed a kiss in the palm, folding her fingers around it.

"Bet on it," he said.

TEN ═══

The mourning black had been replaced with festive colors for the wedding. A feast had been laid in the largest hall, its walls lined with polished silver shields, and the mood was gay. Few were still sick with the plague, and those who were still bedbound were recovering. There were fewer to celebrate a royal wedding, but they were more eager to celebrate for all that.

In fact, Shadow thought wryly, the only unenthusiastic celebrants were the bride and groom. Donya was stunning in a dark red gown that emphasized her tanned skin and dark hair, and Argent was equally handsome in a pale green that set off his light skin and silver hair, but their smiles were somewhat stiff and their laughter had a hollow ring. Shadow sighed to herself, replete with rich food and fine wine. If this was the best they could do for the wedding festival, what in the *world* was their wedding night going to be like?

Thoughtfully she pulled the small bone vial Chyrie had given her from her pouch. Midnight Dew.

Spitting in the face of nature, Shadow thought ruefully. No proper elf would do it.

She looked at Donya's determined smile.

She looked at the vial.

"May the Mother Forest forgive me," she sighed. "Just this once."

"No, really," Shadow said sincerely. "It was a beautiful ceremony. And Aspen was just perfect. I hadn't seen a full elvan mating ritual for the longest time. It was a nice touch."

"I'm glad," Donya smiled. "You don't think it was too much, having the investment at the same time?"

"No, no," Aubry assured her. "Most of the city's busy, you know, trying to get things working again. It's just as well to get it all done in one day. It wasn't traditional, but why not? Tradition's what you two make it, now."

"Well, here's one tradition I hope you'll keep," Shadow said. She handed Donya a cut-crystal bottle of wine and held up two glasses. "The very, very best moondrop wine for you two to toast each other. It'd better be good, after what I paid for it."

"You mean after what *I* paid for it," Aubry said wryly.

"Well, you deserved it," Shadow grinned. "I spent several very worried days when you broke that mirror."

"I'm sorry," Aubry said humbly. "I didn't expect another break-in at the Guild. At least they didn't get as far as the treasury."

"Thank Fortune for that," Shadow sighed. "Well, Doe, go on!"

"But aren't you and Aubry having any?" Donya asked, surprised.

"Not your wedding toast," Aubry scolded. "Go on!"

Donya poured the two glasses full, taking one while Shadow handed the other to Argent.

"Go on, Argent," Shadow urged. "You know how it's done."

Argent smiled a little wistfully and raised his glass.

"Warm rain," he said, gazing into Donya's eyes, "rich soil, and ripe seed; the blessings of the Mother Forest on our mating."

"May our children be many as the leaves of the tree," Donya said softly, surprising all three elves. "May the sun shine bright upon them."

They touched glasses and drank, and Shadow smiled quietly to herself.

"What now?" Donya asked when she had finished her glass.

"Now," Aubry said patiently, "you finish the bottle in your room, in bed, while we warn the servants to leave your meals outside the door for the next three days."

Donya glanced at Argent and flushed a little.

"Maybe that's not such a bad idea," she said, a smile tugging at the corner of her mouth. "If you and Shadow will cover our escape."

"If you swear faithfully to finish the bottle," Shadow said sternly, "it's a deal."

Grinning mischievously, Donya spit into her hand in a most un-High-Lady-like fashion and held it out. Shadow laughed, spit into her own palm, and sealed the bargain with a hearty shake, then grabbed Donya's pendant and pulled her friend's head down to whisper conspiratorially in her ear.

"Plant your acorn from the festival outside your window," Shadow murmured. "When you get a chance."

"You know," Donya said, hugging her friend, "I do believe I will."

Shadow watched them walk away, and grinned quietly to herself. She accepted a goblet of wine from a passing servant and glanced at the nearest polished shield. Her reflection gazed back, strange with its short, curling hair and, perhaps, something new in the sparkling black eyes.

"To roads, and friends, and dragons conquered," she said softly. She raised her glass, and her reflection toasted back. "To Shadow, here and now."